AGED FOR MALICE

(A Tuscan Vineyard Cozy Mystery—Book Seven)

FIONA GRACE

Fiona Grace

Fiona Grace is author of the LACEY DOYLE COZY MYSTERY series, comprising nine books; of the TUSCAN VINEYARD COZY MYSTERY series, comprising seven books; of the DUBIOUS WITCH COZY MYSTERY series, comprising three books; of the BEACHFRONT BAKERY COZY MYSTERY series, comprising six books; and of the CATS AND DOGS COZY MYSTERY series, comprising nine books.

Fiona would love to hear from you, so please visit www.fionagraceauthor.com to receive free ebooks, hear the latest news, and stay in touch.

ISBN: 978-1-0943-9106-9

BOOKS BY FIONA GRACE

LACEY DOYLE COZY MYSTERY
MURDER IN THE MANOR (Book#1)
DEATH AND A DOG (Book #2)
CRIME IN THE CAFE (Book #3)
VEXED ON A VISIT (Book #4)
KILLED WITH A KISS (Book #5)
PERISHED BY A PAINTING (Book #6)
SILENCED BY A SPELL (Book #7)
FRAMED BY A FORGERY (Book #8)
CATASTROPHE IN A CLOISTER (Book #9)

TUSCAN VINEYARD COZY MYSTERY
AGED FOR MURDER (Book #1)
AGED FOR DEATH (Book #2)
AGED FOR MAYHEM (Book #3)
AGED FOR SEDUCTION (Book #4)
AGED FOR VENGEANCE (Book #5)
AGED FOR ACRIMONY (Book #6)
AGED FOR MALICE (Book #7)

DUBIOUS WITCH COZY MYSTERY
SKEPTIC IN SALEM: AN EPISODE OF MURDER (Book #1)
SKEPTIC IN SALEM: AN EPISODE OF CRIME (Book #2)
SKEPTIC IN SALEM: AN EPISODE OF DEATH (Book #3)

BEACHFRONT BAKERY COZY MYSTERY
BEACHFRONT BAKERY: A KILLER CUPCAKE (Book #1)
BEACHFRONT BAKERY: A MURDEROUS MACARON (Book #2)
BEACHFRONT BAKERY: A PERILOUS CAKE POP (Book #3)
BEACHFRONT BAKERY: A DEADLY DANISH (Book #4)
BEACHFRONT BAKERY: A TREACHEROUS TART (Book #5)
BEACHFRONT BAKERY: A CALAMITOUS COOKIE (Book #6)

CATS AND DOGS COZY MYSTERY
A VILLA IN SICILY: OLIVE OIL AND MURDER (Book #1)

A VILLA IN SICILY: FIGS AND A CADAVER (Book #2)
A VILLA IN SICILY: VINO AND DEATH (Book #3)
A VILLA IN SICILY: CAPERS AND CALAMITY (Book #4)
A VILLA IN SICILY: ORANGE GROVES AND VENGEANCE (Book #5)
A VILLA IN SICILY: CANNOLI AND A CASUALTY (Book #6)
A VILLA IN SICILY: SPAGHETTI AND SUSPICION (Book #7)
A VILLA IN SICILY: LEMONS AND A PREDICAMENT (Book #8)
A VILLA IN SICILY: GELATO AND A VENDETTA (Book #9)

CHAPTER ONE

The kitchen table in Olivia Glass's farmhouse was covered in papers. Area plans of various shapes and sizes were crowded over the polished wooden boards. Olivia stared down at the maps, her brain abuzz with excitement. She felt desperate to uncover the clues hidden in the labyrinths of squiggles and lines.

Thanks to the finds that she'd made since buying the derelict property, Olivia was certain that a collection of old wines was stashed away in a secret place. Would the collection be small or large? Would it be worthless, or contain prized treasures of great historic value? She had no idea which would be the truth, until she found it.

Peering at the papers, she couldn't even make out where the farmhouse was. Her talents were in the creative, intuitive fields, and she was a hopeless map reader. She never knew where north was, and at critical moments – like when arriving at a busy intersection – she had a terrible habit of confusing left and right.

Luckily Danilo, her boyfriend, was a brilliant map reader. He'd first picked up the clues drawn into the label of the old wine bottle Olivia had found in her barn. He'd realized that these seemingly random lines were in fact the missing part of the map they'd found in the store room high in the hills.

Now he was leaning over her shoulder, absorbed by the challenge, the streak of pink in his dark hair tickling her cheek. The pink wasn't his choice. His niece was a hairdresser. Two weeks ago, she'd created the stunning blond color that Olivia now sported. She was thrilled with the multi-faceted tones of honey, platinum, and sand that shimmered in her hair.

"This is the road going past your farm. Here it is on the big area plan. And here it is on your wine label." Danilo pointed from one to the other and Olivia nodded wisely despite the fact she couldn't see where the lines overlapped at all.

"So now." Danilo drummed his fingers on the table thoughtfully. "Now we need to find a more detailed plan. This one is still too general. I need to work out where this contour line goes."

A contour line? That sounded like a very vague guideline, Olivia worried. What if it wasn't going to be possible to pinpoint the exact spot? She worried that this entire project might end up being nothing more than a disappointing waste of time.

From the lounge, her friend Charlotte's voice rang out. Olivia looked up, beaming as she heard it.

"Who's a good kitty? You, Bagheera. You're a good kitty! I can see how happy you are there, on your blanket by the radiator. You must be patient. Mom will be back soon."

A moment later, Charlotte sauntered into the kitchen, grinning in delight as she shook back her long, red-streaked hair.

"How amazing is it to have a video call with my own cat? The house sitter I hired after extending my stay here adores him. Bagheera's doing great with her. Although I could tell he was missing me."

"Well, you've been in Italy nearly three weeks longer than planned. You'll have some apologizing to do," Olivia joked.

Charlotte gave an expressive shrug.

"Circumstances out of my control, I'm afraid."

"Exactly," Olivia sympathized. "A whirlwind holiday romance, and a whole new set of local work projects, could never have been predicted."

She was thrilled that her bestie was still in Tuscany after extending her air travel visit. Imagine if she moved here? Charlotte had already realized she was going to have to spend a lot more time here for work. She was the content and site manager for an online supplier of international goods, gifts, and luxury hampers to the States. Thanks to demand, the company had started to specialize in the Mediterranean region and needed to source more products and information from the area.

"What's going on with the map?"

Charlotte leaned over Olivia's other shoulder. Danilo had folded two of the maps so that the relevant sections were next to each other, and placed the wine label beside them. He was carefully marking off points on the biggest map using a finely sharpened pencil.

Glancing at Danilo's eyes, dark and intense in his handsome face, Olivia saw he was completely focused on his task. A carpenter and woodworker by trade, Danilo knew all about the importance of perfection in his craft. Now he was applying the same skills to solving the puzzling clues.

But it seemed that they'd reached a stumbling block. Danilo gave a disappointed sigh.

"We need a larger scale map. This one is just not detailed enough to pinpoint the location."

Olivia nodded, feeling devastated that the answers were so near, but yet so far. What could be done, she wondered. She couldn't dig up her whole farm in the search. It was a vineyard, not a mine!

In fact, a week ago, she'd gotten in a team of contractors and plowed and planted several acres within the hilly terrain. She'd spent all her available money on this project, which included installing expensive irrigation pipes, even though she was uneasily aware that it stretched her to her limits. She'd become used to living in the red, with no cash reserves at all. Those precious grapevine seeds in the ground were her hopes and dreams for the future. She'd chosen the sites with care, using the experience she'd gained to decide in which area the local Sangiovese grapes would grow best and on which slopes the vermentino grapes, that preferred cooler conditions, would thrive.

She couldn't afford to tear up a planted area in the vague hope that some bottles were buried underneath. Not when these seeds would take two years to become viable, wine-producing vines.

Suddenly, she remembered, with a leap of her heart.

"I have a more detailed map! They gave me a large scale site map and house plan when I bought the farm. I stowed it away upstairs and forgot all about it."

Olivia hurtled up the staircase to the second floor, which consisted of two pretty bedrooms with gorgeous views over the rolling Tuscan countryside, and a shared bathroom.

She stormed into her bedroom. Her black-and-white cat, Pirate, curled up on the yellow duvet, raised her head and stared at Olivia. Pirate was clearly annoyed by this untimely interruption, Olivia thought, as she grabbed the folded map from the bottom of the wardrobe drawer where she'd put it away months ago.

After rubbing Pirate's head in apology, she ran downstairs again.

"Here you go," she announced, placing the detailed map on the table.

"This is exactly what we needed. Let us see if we can find answers now." Danilo squeezed her arm affectionately before turning his focus back to the pages.

"Is that a river?" Charlotte asked curiously, pointing to a wavy mark on the map.

“It is a contour line,” Danilo explained, and Olivia suppressed a snort of laughter that her bestie’s map reading skills were clearly on par with her own.

“Follow the contour,” Danilo murmured to himself, and now she could hear excitement in his voice. His pencil stabbed decisively into a blank area of the property map.

“It’s there? You’re sure?” Olivia asked, her voice squeaky with excitement. Was it really possible that Danilo had managed to interpret the sketchy information on the wine label and pinpoint the exact place?

He nodded. “The three points are a triangle. It covers a very small area, nestled behind a hill in the north of your farm. My feeling is that the central point of the triangle will be the place to start. If we don’t find anything, we can examine each outer point as well.”

“Shall we go?” Charlotte asked. “We don’t need a flashlight, do we? It should stay light for a while. The afternoons are getting longer now, and so much warmer!”

“Spring is here,” Olivia agreed, as Danilo opened the kitchen door, which led out to a paved courtyard surrounded by herbs. Olivia had painstakingly tiled and planted the area herself. At the far end of the courtyard was the Wendy house where her goat, Erba, lived. And beyond that was a pathway winding through the grasses and shrubs into the wild, rolling terrain of her farm.

No wonder it had been so expensive to plow up, fertilize, irrigate, and plant such rugged land, Olivia thought, as she powered out of the door, hot on Danilo’s heels.

“I’m getting my sandals!” Charlotte shouted. “You go ahead and I’ll catch up!”

As Olivia jogged over the rocky and uneven path, she was overtaken by a determined orange and white goat. Erba must have been nosing around the fragrant oregano bushes near the closest vine plantation. Now, Olivia was impressed by her goat’s turn of speed. She was clearly delighted that her family had decided to go for an impromptu run.

“I’m on my way!” she heard Charlotte yell breathlessly behind her as she crested the hill. Pausing for a moment, Olivia admired the dramatic view of her farm, feeling satisfied that it had achieved a new character with some of its rolling wildness tamed and planted.

Danilo charged down the hill, neck and neck with Erba. Veering away from the path, he headed to one of the most rugged areas within her farm.

“It’s here! Just over this ridge!” he shouted. Scrambling over the hill, he disappeared from sight.

Olivia followed, feeling breathless with excitement.

Just a few more steps and she would reach the place where she was sure the wine collection was hidden. In another moment, her hopes and dreams would become reality and she would uncover the secrets her farm had kept hidden for so long.

With her heart pounding, she scrambled up the slope.

CHAPTER TWO

When Olivia reached the top, she stopped. Breathing hard, she stared – first in disbelief, and then in dismay.

There was a reason why this part of her farm was so remote and unexplored, and why she'd never considered planting vines there.

A huge, big, immovable reason.

Gazing at the massive boulders that filled her view, Olivia felt her hopes crumble around her. The map must have been a red herring. All their work, all their excitement, had been for nothing.

Her farm would keep its secrets forever. Nothing of any value could possibly be buried in this crowded, rock-strewn area.

"Well? Can you see a building or anything?" Charlotte puffed out the words as she climbed up to join her. Olivia turned, and on seeing the disappointment in her face, Charlotte's shoulders slumped.

"There's no way anything can be buried here," Olivia said sadly.

She gestured to the piles of boulders that littered the small valley.

They literally covered every yard of ground. In some places, they were piled so high that Danilo, who was scrambling over the unforgiving terrain, was completely hidden from view.

"Oh, no," Charlotte said, and now she sounded just as devastated as Olivia felt.

From behind the large pile, a cheeky orange and white face appeared. A moment later, Erba sprang adventurously onto the biggest heap. Olivia stared in wonderment as her sure-footed goat picked her way to the top of the mini mountain, and stood there, peering down at them with a quizzical expression on her face.

Olivia couldn't help but laugh, glad to find some comic relief in this frustrating situation. Charlotte rolled her eyes.

"Your goat's such a character," she observed. "But you're right. Nobody would bury a stash of old wines under all those boulders. It seems like the whole map is just a practical joke, leading you to the most inhospitable area of the farm. Perhaps the original owners drank all the wine and didn't have any left to put away."

She sighed sadly.

Olivia caught sight of Danilo once more. He was moving around the giant boulders, holding the map, his face intent. Clearly, he was doing his best to triangulate the exact spot, despite the massive barriers in his way.

The freshening wind tugged at Olivia's hair, blowing the multicolored blond strands over her face, and she smoothed it back with her hand. The sun was starting to set, sinking into the faraway forested hills. She glanced back at her farmhouse. Perched on a ridge a few hundred yards away, the modest stone building was bathed in golden light. The olive and ash trees overlooking the jewel-green growth of her first vine plantation looked stately and majestic.

The beauty of the scenery comforted Olivia. Her farm was the most gorgeous place in the entire world. Never mind the frustrating mystery of the old treasures. That wasn't why she'd bought the land. She'd bought it so that she could live in the quaint, comfortable farmhouse that now felt like home, and do her best to nurture the land into a productive wine farm.

Step by step she was getting there, even if her progress was frustratingly slow. In two more years, she could have several small commercial batches of Sangiovese, vermentino, and blended red wine ready for market. If there was another fall frost, which was likely in her high-lying farm, she could harvest the wild vines and make another ice wine, hoping to replicate the surprising success of the first one she'd made.

"It's ironic that such a big rock fall occurred right here," Charlotte sighed, clearly less willing to let go of the idea than Olivia was.

Olivia stared at the boulders again. They loomed dark as the sun began to set beyond them. A sudden suspicion had occurred to her.

She scrambled down the slope and did exactly what Danilo had done. She prowled around the strewn boulders, looking at their size and shape, touching the cold, rough rock.

Behind the biggest pile, she met Danilo. He, too, was placing his hand on a large boulder, looking puzzled.

"Olivia, I am wondering where these rocks came from," he said, echoing the thoughts she'd just had.

Excitement surged inside Olivia all over again. In a rush, her determination returned.

"It's not like they could have fallen from anywhere. There's no mountain nearby to cause a landslide. And although my farm's terrain is rocky, they're scattered around. Not all stacked together in one place. There's no reason for them to be here," she agreed.

"Someone went to a lot of trouble to pile them up. The biggest pile is on the exact place where the map triangulates."

Danilo pointed to Erba, standing proudly atop the rocky mound, and his face warmed as he stared at Olivia's naughty goat.

"At first, I thought that nothing could have been buried here because of the rocks. But if they'd been brought in afterwards, then it makes things different." Olivia felt goosebumps prickle her arms, and not just because of the freshening wind.

"Exactly. These rocks could have been laid down on purpose, to hide what was below and make it impossible to dig up," Danilo said, sounding excited.

"How easily could they be moved?" Olivia glanced doubtfully at the pile. The boulders must weigh tons.

"You would need specialized machinery," Danilo agreed.

Olivia knew what that meant. Money!

The farm swallowed money, there was no doubt about it. The vines planted now would take two years to start yielding. Olivia was trying not to think about the financial viability of the project and how she, as a single person on a sommelier's salary, was going to take it where she wanted.

"We'll have to wait a while then," she decided, frustrated that this captivating treasure hunt would have to be shelved until her savings had recovered.

In any case, there was no guarantee of finding anything underneath. It could simply be that while clearing the land, the original owners had decided to place all the rocks in one location. Perhaps they'd wanted to build a wall or a special feature, and never gotten around to it.

In despondent silence, they trailed to where Charlotte was waiting.

"Well, now that we've all finished looking at big rocks, it's time to think about what's for dinner," her ever-practical friend said, trying to lighten the atmosphere. "I was wondering if we should try making that baked pasta dish tonight, with artichokes and spinach."

"Good idea," Olivia said, feeling cheered by the promise of a tasty dinner.

As they strolled back to the farmhouse, Danilo took Olivia's hand.

"Ever since I was young, I have heard the rumors about a valuable wine collection hidden away in the local area. We have all heard them," he said thoughtfully.

Shivers chased down Olivia's spine and she was grateful for the warmth of Danilo's hand in hers. It was spooky and mysterious to imagine that such an ancient stash, a local legend, might be hidden here!

"At least, if they are here, they're safely guarded," she said, trying to see the positives in the situation.

"The pasta dish requires cream. Do we have enough cream?" Charlotte asked, sounding suddenly anxious. "I can always take a trip to the village and buy some. It doesn't sound as if you can skimp on the cream. The recipe was very strict about the quantities. And the butter, also," she added cheerfully.

"There should be enough. I had this dish in mind when I shopped yesterday," Olivia reassured her.

"Are we expecting anybody to join us for dinner?" Danilo asked curiously as they rounded the corner of the farmhouse.

"No, why?" Olivia asked, confused.

"Oh," she said a moment later as she noticed what he'd seen. Headlights, bright in the now-dusky evening, were swinging into her driveway.

Olivia's first thought was that someone had gotten lost. People occasionally used her drive to turn around after realizing they'd taken the wrong road. But this time, the car headed briskly through her ramshackle gateway, and up the gravel-lined drive.

"Is it one of the Vescovis?" Danilo asked.

That had been Olivia's first thought also. The Vescovis, who owned La Leggenda where she worked as sommelier, would occasionally pop in if they were passing by. Marcello and Antonio would usually call first, but Nadia would often arrive unannounced, laden down with tasty treats from the local bakeries. But this small Fiat didn't belong to any of them.

"Perhaps someone needs directions," Olivia said, letting go Danilo's hand and waving at the car, which had stopped behind Danilo's pickup.

The driver got out and, to Olivia's confusion, he opened the trunk. From it, he lifted a large, new-looking travel bag and a smaller, matching valise.

"I think you may have taken a wrong turn," Olivia called as she hurried over, hoping that her warning would prevent him from needlessly unloading any more luggage. Hopefully, Danilo could help with the map reading to set this poor man onto the right path.

But, to her confusion, the driver marched around to the passenger side and opened the door with a flourish.

"Signora," he invited.

Olivia skidded to a stop and stared in astonishment at the tall, slim, well-coiffed woman climbing confidently out of the small car. She blinked rapidly, wondering if she was perhaps hallucinating. This couldn't be happening. It simply couldn't! Could it?

"Hello angel! Surprise! My goodness, I never dreamed you had bought a place so far away from civilization!"

Olivia felt as if her entire reality had warped as her mother, wearing a smart pant suit and a pair of stylish, new-looking boots, paced triumphantly toward her.

CHAPTER THREE

Staring quizzically at Olivia, Mrs. Glass let out a bell-like laugh as she approached.

"Your face is a picture. I wish I could send a photo back to your father. He's holding the fort back home in New York."

"I had no idea you were coming," Olivia whispered as her mother embraced her, enveloping her in a cloud of ChanelN°5. Like the new boots, Olivia suspected this was an airport purchase. Her hair was exactly the same as always, immaculately groomed in its neat blond bob, and her blue eyes looked very bright behind gold-framed spectacles.

"I did mention to you that I would book a ticket as soon as my passport was issued," Mrs. Glass chided her. "It was ready much faster than I expected, and Andrew found an excellent special offer, so lo and behold, I was on a plane the very next day. I thought it would be fun to surprise you."

She smiled at Olivia, who noted the expression had a hint of steel.

As her shocked brain tried to process the sudden arrival of her mother, Olivia began to suspect that it hadn't just been a need for surprise that had prompted this unannounced visit. She wondered if her mother had wanted to catch her off guard.

If so, there was a bigger motive for the trip than an impulse vacation and Olivia was sure she knew what it was. Mrs. Glass had made an in-person visit to persuade her only daughter to move back home to the States.

Mrs. Glass turned to see Charlotte and Danilo approaching.

"Charlotte, how wonderful to see you," Mrs. Glass enthused. "Are you also visiting Olivia? And who's this young man?"

Removing her spectacles, Mrs. Glass eyeballed Danilo.

Watching her mother's face, Olivia knew with absolute certainty that she was here on a mission. This was not a friendly visit but more like a carefully planned military operation. That meant if she introduced Danilo as her boyfriend, she'd be landing her poor beau in a world of trouble.

Finding a serious boyfriend in her daughter's life wouldn't be well-received. She would take against Danilo, seeing him as a threat, and Olivia didn't want their relationship getting off to a rocky start from which it might never recover. She'd mentioned Danilo in previous emails but Olivia knew only too well how her mother could read selectively and only take in what she wanted to hear.

As the thoughts flashed through her mind, Olivia decided, instinctively, to protect herself and her relationship for the time being.

"This is my friend Danilo, who lives nearby," she said.

"Hello, Daniel," Mrs. Glass said, extending a regal hand.

Olivia cringed, feeling mortified as she saw the shocked hurt appear on Danilo's face. She wished she could whisper in his ear why she'd done what she did. She was realizing now it had been a terrible decision. Her efforts to keep him below her mother's radar had deeply wounded him. Feeling suddenly sick, Olivia feared that he might be rethinking their entire relationship based on her dismissive introduction.

And her mother had gotten his name wrong. That wasn't intentional. Olivia knew her mother was terrible with names, and suspected her hearing wasn't as good as it used to be. Hence the reason she, herself, spoke in such piercing tones. She should have corrected it immediately but in the stress of the moment, she'd missed her chance.

Her mother had been on Tuscan soil only a couple of minutes, and already Olivia felt as if her life was crumbling around her.

With his face set and grim, Danilo picked up the larger valise and marched toward the farmhouse. Grabbing the smaller case, Olivia hurried after him.

As she reached the front door, Charlotte whispered, "I'll make up the spare bedroom quick with fresh linen, and move my things into the downstairs study."

That was an additional complication, Olivia realized with another unpleasant jolt. Her farmhouse only had two proper bedrooms and Charlotte had been occupying one! Thank goodness she'd purchased a sleeper couch when she furnished the small study. At least Charlotte would have a comfortable place to rest her head.

"We'll take the luggage upstairs in a minute," Olivia said to her mother, buying time for the bed making to be done. "In the meantime, would you like to see the closest vine plantation? And I can show you the barn that I've renovated into a winemaking room."

"Let's do that," Mrs. Glass replied graciously.

Feeling a sense of unreality, Olivia headed out of the house and into the deepening twilight, leading the way up the curved path to her barn. She was proud of the large doors she'd painted and installed, and the rows of lanterns along the wall which she thought added a medieval charm to the spacious interior.

Opening the doors, Olivia snapped on the lights and felt a thrill of excitement as the warm light flooded her barn. She'd made one successful batch of ice wine in this place so far. She could do more!

Mrs. Glass, however, seemed less impressed.

"You don't need specialized equipment?" she asked curiously. "This building seems rather empty."

Olivia bit her lip. Her mother was absolutely right. She did need specialized equipment! She needed more fermentation vats and more barrels, just for a start. They were expensive, and if she saved up, she hoped she might be able to afford them before her new vines produced their first grapes.

"It's still in the planning stages," she stated bravely.

Turning, her mother spied Erba, standing in the doorway. Even though her goat knew there was no wine currently fermenting in the barn, she was still remaining quietly hopeful about the possibility.

"What a pretty goat," her mother said, and Olivia smiled with relief. Erba, with her customary flair, had managed to redeem the situation.

As her mother approached Erba, she scrutinized her closely.

"She's pregnant, is she?" Mrs. Glass asked, as Erba pushed her orange and white head against her thigh in a friendly way. "I don't know much about goats, but she looks to be quite far along. When is she due to have her kid?" Her mother gave a tinkling laugh. "Kid! Isn't that funny? Or do they usually have more than one?"

Olivia goggled in horror, her gaze swiveling from her goat to her mother and back again.

She'd never considered this possibility! Surely Erba was still too young? But maybe she wasn't. Time had flown since she had adopted her, Olivia realized, panic surging inside her at the thought of this unwanted event. Of course kids were in Erba's future; she was part of a dairy herd! But if she was pregnant, she'd soon have to stay with her herd. Milking happened very early in the mornings. That meant she would have to stop being Olivia's adopted goat. She would no longer have Erba's cute, playful presence in her life.

Olivia hadn't even wanted to think about this happening in the future. But now, already? Her mother was right. Erba's belly did look rather round.

"Let's take a walk to my closest vine plantation," she said in a strangled voice, desperate to change the subject. Her probably-pregnant goat was an extra stress she simply couldn't deal with right now. "I'm sure you're keen to see the first grapevines I personally planted on this land? They'll hopefully be mature enough to produce grapes at the end of this coming summer season. I'll also pick grapes from all the wild vines that grow around this property. That's how I made my first batch last season. I made an ice wine," Olivia said proudly.

She followed the paved pathway down the hill, with her mother's heels clip-clopping along the cobbles behind her.

Pregnant? Erba?

Olivia couldn't get the thought out of her mind.

Determinedly trying to banish it, she gestured to the rectangular plantation of vines that she'd planted last fall, feeling proud of how tall and healthy the young plants looked. They were going into summer as ready as they could be.

"It's rather small, isn't it? Compared to the vineyards in California," Mrs. Glass said, sounding confused as she gazed at the modest plantation.

"This was my very first one, and I didn't have many seeds," Olivia explained apologetically. "The land's so hilly that most of the new plantations are fairly small too, but at least there are more of them now. They're dotted around all over the place," she explained.

Except where the boulders were, Olivia thought.

"The plantations in California are enormous. I mean, they use golf carts or actual tractors to get from one side to the other. Perhaps now that you have some experience, one of those California farms might consider taking you on. On the marketing side, of course," her mother mused thoughtfully.

"Shall we go inside? It's getting chilly," Olivia suggested.

She needed a glass of wine. Badly. She felt deflated by how unimpressed her mother was over her new venture. And, come to that, over Italy! But she had known deep down this would happen. Her mother was not yet convinced and perhaps never would be, of Olivia's commitment to her new life. Until she was, she would be unable to see anything good in any of it.

Her mother was very strong minded. Or stubborn, as others preferred to phrase it.

Hopefully, over a good dinner, her stance would thaw and she would be able to start appreciating the glorious country where her first-ever international visit had landed her. Then Olivia could explain that Danilo was in fact her serious boyfriend.

She pushed open the front door and gave a last, anxious look back at Erba, who was trotting around the side of the farmhouse, heading for her dinner.

Was she pregnant?

Her flanks did look round!

Had it taken her mother's fresh eyes to notice this catastrophe in the making?

Olivia closed the door and followed her to the kitchen, feeling completely discombobulated.

"Red or white wine, Mrs. G.?" Charlotte asked, taking a glass from out of the kitchen cupboard.

"White, please. Oh, that reminds me, Olivia, I brought you a gift," her mother said. She rummaged in her purse and handed over a small parcel.

"Wineglass charms! Thank you, Mom." Olivia tried her best to drum up genuine enthusiasm for the silver, beaded, New-York-themed charms in the small box. She couldn't help feeling they were yet another hint that she didn't belong here.

"White wine coming up. Shall we decorate the glasses with these cute charms now?" Charlotte said, clearly hell-bent on keeping things cheerful.

As Charlotte handed Olivia her glass, she hissed in her ear, "Bed's made!"

Danilo was making a start on dinner. His back was turned as he focused on the pans, where the delicious fragrance of garlic was starting to permeate the kitchen. Olivia knew from his silence that he was badly upset. If only she could explain why she'd done what she did. But in this small kitchen, with all of them crowded so close, there was going to be no chance to have a private chat.

Without giving Danilo some background, those wounding words would continue to fester. Olivia was starting to panic that by the time she did explain, it would already be too late. When, and how, would she get a chance to repair the damage she'd done?

CHAPTER FOUR

To Olivia's relief, dinner was ready in record time. The baked pasta dish smelled divine. She wished she felt hungrier, but somewhere in between her mother climbing out of the car and introducing Danilo as her friend, her appetite had vanished completely.

"I'm sure you must be looking forward to seeing lots of local sights while you're here," Charlotte said, valiantly attempting to keep the conversation flowing.

"If Olivia's not too busy, I am sure we'll be able to do some sightseeing," Mrs. Glass replied.

Seething inwardly, Olivia had to bite back the comment that if her mother had given her a day or two's warning, she would have had more of a chance of booking time off work. Marcello was away this week, and Olivia had no idea if it would be possible for her to take leave. She'd have to find out tomorrow.

She dished up the food, wishing that this delicious creation could have been eaten under less tense circumstances.

"I cannot stay long," Danilo said as he dug his fork into the steaming, cheesy layers.

"What a shame. Are you heading out elsewhere, Daniel?" Mrs. Glass asked. To Olivia's bemusement, she seemed to have taken a liking to him. Olivia knew she wouldn't have done that if he'd been introduced as her boyfriend.

Given this development, it might be better not to blurt out that they were in a relationship, she wondered, agonizing over the difficulty of the decision.

"His name's Danilo," she muttered, in an attempt to fix some of the mess, but her mother wasn't looking at her. She was waiting expectantly for him to reply.

"I'm heading home. I have to finish off polishing a set of wooden tables," Danilo explained with a tight, apologetic smile before wolfing down another mouthful of food.

That was also not true. He'd been planning to stay the night at Olivia's. He'd even brought along his gym bag. He could have varnished the tables in the morning, but she couldn't blame him for wanting to leave as fast as possible.

"How lovely. So you work with wood?"

"I do," Danilo tried for a polite, joyless smile.

"That must be very artistic and creative," her mother enthused.

"It is," Danilo answered, sounding less-than-enthusiastic himself.

"Olivia's also creative. How long have you two known each other?" Mrs. Glass asked curiously.

This was her chance. As Olivia was drawing breath to spill the truth about their relationship, Danilo replied again.

"Not long," he said. "Only a couple of weeks."

She stared at him in consternation. Clearly in the worst mood she'd ever seen him in, he was now agreeing with her fake story and that meant she could move no further with her confession.

"I'm going to head into town," Charlotte said, brightening as she glanced at her phone. "Artoro just messaged me to say he'll be free in half an hour. The criminals of Siena have been holding back, he says. His case load is under control. So we're going to meet up for coffee and cake."

Charlotte grinned merrily and, despite her own worries, Olivia couldn't help feeling a flash of excitement that her bestie's romance was clearly going well.

While Olivia was struggling with her last mouthfuls, wishing she had more enthusiasm for her meal, both Danilo and Charlotte were already stacking their plates in the sink.

"Ciao," Danilo said formally.

"Let me walk you out," Olivia jumped to her feet, her serviette fluttering to the ground. But it was too late. Danilo had already marched outside.

"Go and say goodbye to Daniel. He seems a very charming young man," her mother urged her, as Olivia sprinted out of the kitchen and broke land-speed records catching up with her angry 'friend' just before he climbed into his car.

"Danilo, Danilo, I'm sorry!"

She grabbed his arm as he turned to face her. He looked every bit as hurt and distressed as she'd feared.

Knowing she had only moments to make things right, Olivia did her best.

"I'm sorry. It was a spur of the moment decision."

"To say I was just a friend?" Danilo's eyebrows rose together with his voice.

"No, no. To stop my mother from giving you a hard time all night. Danilo, I know she has an ulterior motive for being here, and when she gets that way, she's impossible. I didn't want her to focus negatively on you. I – I –" Olivia found herself almost sobbing with the need to speak her next words. "I want you and her to be friends, and not to get off on the wrong foot. Now that she thinks you're not a threat, she likes you. Otherwise, she'd have had problems with you from the start, and I know she could have said hurtful things. I didn't want that to happen, because – because you're a part of my life. An important part."

Danilo stared at her and she couldn't read his face.

"I must go," he said curtly, and climbed into his car without a kiss or a hug or a proper goodbye.

Feeling sick with stress, Olivia ran back to the farmhouse. Her mother had already cleared the dishes with her customary efficiency, put the leftover food in the fridge, and had turned the coffee maker on.

Olivia would rather have had another glass of wine at this tense time, but it looked like coffee was the only polite choice.

Her mother turned to her, and her next words threw Olivia all the way onto the back foot.

"My angel, I decided to book this visit to confirm something, which I now see very clearly," Mrs. Glass explained.

"What is that?" Olivia asked, feeling nervous.

"Your home is in a beautiful, friendly, and safe country where there are so many opportunities. You have so many directions to apply your talents."

Olivia blinked. Had she been wrong? Was her mother actually complimenting her humble farmhouse and her brave attempts at starting a vineyard? It sure sounded like it!

"You think?" she asked incredulously.

"I see so much potential in your future," her mother continued with a sweeping movement of her arm.

"Thank you," Olivia said, feeling emotion surge up. Prematurely, as it happened.

"Given all of that," Mrs. Glass continued in brisk tones, "it's absolutely beyond me why you felt the need to move to Tuscany."

Olivia gaped at her mother. She'd never expected that conversational bombshell to land.

"But – but Italy is my home now!" she protested.

"It's not your home and never will be. Do you seriously think you will ever be accepted by the local community? Sweetheart, I don't want you living your life as an outsider, far from the support of your family and friends."

"Charlotte might move here," Olivia argued in a small voice.

"Might? Because of a vacation romance that's lasting a few days longer than she expected?"

"Her work wants her to relocate," Olivia mumbled, but she could tell her mother wasn't convinced.

Perhaps the worst part of all of this was that there was a grain of truth in these warning words. It felt as if Mrs. Glass was tapping into her deepest fears, the ones she'd never thought about. Wondering if she *could* ever be accepted into the community, and if Danilo's family *would* ever take her seriously.

"I thought we could look at some opportunities back home, as a comparison point. I've brought along a folder of simply gorgeous apartments that you could easily afford if you sold this farm, particularly now that you've fixed it up a bit and done some planting and landscaping. And as for jobs, well, New York is truly the land of promise for advertising creatives at this time. Wait until you see what's out there, and the salaries. From what I understand, your wage now is only just making ends meet. Your farm clearly needs a great deal more capital investment for it to be successful. You can't build it up when you're barely scraping by."

Olivia thought uncomfortably of her to-do list that seemed to multiply exponentially week by week, and the sleepless nights she'd been having when she thought about how she would juggle her day job with the increasing demands of all her new plantations. She needed to hire full-time help, but that wasn't even a possibility at this stage.

Inexorably, her mother continued. "Never mind years, it will take decades to grow a business like this when you can't afford what you need."

Olivia felt herself waver. Perhaps she should just have a look. It would be wrong not to sensibly weigh up her options. What if Danilo never forgave her, she thought with a thrill of fear.

"You need to start taking responsibility for your life," her mother urged.

That comment jerked Olivia out of her indecision, and a wave of anger washed over her. She was thirty-four years old. In just over a week, she'd be thirty-five. She didn't need her mother treating her like a child, which was exactly what she always did when Olivia acted in a way she didn't approve of.

"I'm perfectly capable of making my own choices," she shot back. Even if they were bad ones, she added silently to herself. "Hundreds, in fact thousands of Americans move to Italy and fit in just fine. I have a life, and a future, and a job. If it takes decades to make my wine farm a success, then so be it. As long as I'm happy, it doesn't matter."

Her mother's face hardened in the way that it did when Olivia spoke against her.

"You're being very foolish," she warned in threatening tones. "Choices have consequences."

"If you traveled all the way to tell me that, you've just wasted your trip," Olivia flashed back, finally losing it. "You said you came here for a vacation, and to visit me. You can either enjoy Italy and have fun with your only daughter, or spend the entire time arguing. It's your choice." She turned and headed for the kitchen door, needing some air. At the door, she thought of something else and turned back.

"All choices have consequences, including yours. Perhaps you should think about that." she delivered her parting shot, in tones just as threatening as her mother's had been.

She stomped up to her room, seething with angst over how badly the day had turned out and worrying that, with her mother on a mission, tomorrow would be even worse in ways she hadn't yet imagined.

CHAPTER FIVE

The next morning, as she strode out of the farmhouse heading to work, Olivia was still fuming over the events of last night. Frustration boiled inside her as she remembered her mother's words. Mrs. Glass had an ability to get inside Olivia's head and plant doubts, even when she'd done her best to ignore the fearmongering. As a result, she felt rattled and out of sorts.

In contrast, her mother had been all calmness and charm this morning, drinking coffee with Charlotte and planning a walk to the village as if their confrontation last night had never happened. That made it even worse. Was Olivia the only one who felt scarred by the conflict?

Glaring suspiciously at her goat's chunky belly, Olivia had to acknowledge, not for the first time, that she and her mother really did rub each other up the wrong way. She loved her mother, but right now, her interference was souring their relationship, which had never been as close as Olivia thought it should have been.

Was it like this because Olivia was an only child?

Or were their personalities too different for them ever to get on without conflict?

Olivia hoped that she could forget her worries by immersing herself in work. It was going to be a busy day, especially if she was going to get enough done to take time off the following day. Marcello wasn't yet back at the winery. He was traveling to France today on the next stage of his mentorship in the world of organic winemaking. That meant Olivia was in charge. Her angst over her mother mustn't cause her to lose focus on her job, she warned herself.

As she headed down her favorite road, lined with tall cedar trees that looked majestic in the glow of the morning sun, Olivia started to feel better. And, when La Leggenda appeared in front of her and she saw its sun-kissed stone buildings cradled in the verdant hills, she felt her misgivings disappear and confidence in her future return. This was her workplace, filled with her colleagues and friends. She belonged here!

Olivia strode up the paved driveway to the winery's elegant main entrance, glancing appreciatively at the planters in the parking lot. They were filled with lavender and geraniums that were now blooming with color.

With a scrunch of wheels, Jean-Pierre, her assistant vintner, pulled up in the lot and climbed out of his tiny Renault.

"Buongiorno, Olivia," he greeted her.

"Buongiorno," she replied with a smile as she walked between the elegant stone pillars and through the wide entrance door. Inside the lobby, the resident statue had been decorated with a springtime-themed wreath around its neck, and La Leggenda's latest vintages were displayed on a table together with a vase of bright flowers, and a sumptuous bowl of seasonal fruits. It felt uplifting to walk in and breathe the summery aroma of melons and figs, Olivia thought. The table had been her idea, to add a personal and welcoming touch to the winery.

She felt grateful that her job was constantly expanding, allowing her to use her talent and experience in marketing, as well as learning every day about winemaking. Her mother was wrong. This was her dream career. Even if her own winery did take decades, there was opportunity for unlimited growth in this role.

"Olivia, I think we should update the tasting sheets, especially with Collina Wine Week kicking off soon," Jean-Pierre suggested as they headed into the large, airy tasting room. "Can we include the collaboration wine that we made with Collina Cellars? I tasted it yesterday and it is a wonderful blend of vermentino and sauvignon blanc. I found it to be fruity and very deliciously fragrant, with a hint of a sparkle."

"That's a great idea," Olivia praised her assistant sommelier. She was proud by how passionately the tall, lanky Frenchman was embracing his job. He was taking ownership of the tasting room and growing his skills with every day that passed.

She, too, was looking forward to Collina Wine Week. It was a promotional event where locals from the area were offered free tastings and a discount on their first bottle purchased.

Marcello had started it as an experiment last year, and it had been wildly successful. It had built La Leggenda's name in the area, together with an enormous amount of goodwill. Sales through the year had reflected this.

Olivia couldn't wait to experience it this year. It would be the first time she was involved. How exciting it would be to promote their wine to the wonderful locals of Collina, and reward them for their loyalty and support. She hoped that she and Jean-Pierre would make Marcello proud.

Jean-Pierre headed behind the wooden counter and made his way purposefully to the back office. Heading to Marcello's office, Olivia knew that in a few minutes the printer there would start humming as Jean-Pierre sent through the updated sheets.

Meanwhile, she had a host of orders to check. The La Leggenda reds had sold extremely well during the winter season, both in Europe and in the other international markets where they'd managed to get a foothold. As a result, there was a surge in demand for their white wines with the onset of summer.

Olivia didn't want to promise what she couldn't deliver, and clearly Nadia, Marcello's younger sister and the estate vintner, felt the same. Olivia had barely sat down on the leather chair in Marcello's office before Nadia came rushing in.

"Olivia! I have an idea!" Nadia exclaimed.

"What is it?" Olivia asked. She had a feeling it was going to be a good one. Nadia's dark eyes were blazing with excitement.

"I would like to make a new white wine blend this year. There are a few fields in our new winery near Pisa that are producing vermentino and sauvignon blanc grapes of exceptional quality. I want to blend them with the La Leggenda whites and create a new label. Not quite as high-end as our wines, not quite as mass-market as the other winery. Something in between the two that we can position as ultra-modern, top quality, and take internationally at an even more competitive price point. We will have enough stock to fulfill demand, and hopefully sell what we produce."

"I love that idea," Olivia enthused. "I will think of some catchy names and play with visuals today, as soon as I've dealt with all the suppliers. Have you spoken to Marcello about it?"

This was a major step for the winery to take. Even though she was in charge, Olivia knew she'd feel more comfortable if Marcello had given it his seal of approval. Most likely, he'd have some great ideas too.

Nadia shook her head. "I wanted to run it past you first. Now that you love it, I will present it to him. And in the meantime, I will experiment with some blending." She gave Olivia a conspiratorial wink before rushing away in a whirlwind of energy.

Olivia turned her attention to the orders and went through them, working with care and attention. She focused carefully on the details so that she didn't make a mistake with the numbers – her weakest point. Replying to every mail and message in an efficient, friendly way would strengthen the winery-supplier relationship.

As she completed the last order, her phone rang.

"Buongiorno," she answered.

"Olivia, it is Gabriella."

Olivia tensed as she recognized the shrill voice of the restaurateur who had been her rival since the day she'd started at La Leggenda.

"How can I help?" she said in extra friendly tones.

"The restaurant has received a wedding booking." Gabriella sighed in an expressive way that said, clearly, such an event was likely to bring trouble along with it. "A party of seventy guests. They are looking at the last Saturday in July. We will need to book out the whole winery for that day and night, as they will require a place to dance."

"No problem." Quickly, Olivia scribbled a note on the desk calendar. "I'll put a quote together. Do you have the details?"

"I wrote them down as I spoke to the mother of the bride."

"I'll get the page from you now," Olivia said.

She grabbed the bookings folder, and rushed through to the restaurant, where Gabriella was stationed at the reception desk. Her tawny hair was done up in an immaculate bun.

She hoped that this quick encounter would strengthen the bonds of – well, friendship was the wrong word. The bonds of tolerance, Olivia decided, that were slowly developing between them. But a wedding booking was dangerous ground.

After all, the last wedding at La Leggenda had resulted in a murder!

Luckily, Gabriella didn't seem to be thinking about that traumatic time as she stared at Olivia in a not-unfriendly way.

"This is our third wedding booking already for the year. Clearly, marriage is in the air," she declared, handing over the paper.

"It's great to see that we're becoming popular. Is this a local party?" Olivia asked.

"They are from Britain. Let's hope they are less difficult guests than Americans." She gave Olivia a sidelong glance.

Olivia knew she was remembering all too well what had happened last time.

It would be better to defuse the situation and agree. Becoming defensive about her home country was definitely the wrong move, when the wedding party had in fact been obnoxious, difficult guests, and when one of them had killed the groom-to-be.

"You're telling me," she said firmly, thinking suddenly of the other demanding American houseguest she was currently having to deal with in the form of her mother. "I think we should add a surcharge for any party from the United States."

Gabriella cackled in glee. "I will tell Marcello we've decided on it!" she exclaimed.

Pleased that she and her erstwhile rival had been able to share a humorous bonding moment, Olivia returned to the tasting room.

When she walked in, she blinked, unable to believe what she was seeing. She stared, her mouth falling open in shock. This couldn't be happening! Could it?

Marcello was standing inside the lobby doors.

Her boss was back? Unannounced and unexpected, and a week earlier than she'd hoped to see him. He was supposed to be in France! What was he doing here?

In the surge of delight that overtook her as she saw him, Olivia didn't even stop to think that something might have gone wrong.

CHAPTER SIX

Olivia hurtled across the tasting room at a run. She flung herself into the arms of her handsome boss and gave him an enormous hug.

Marcello's warm embrace wrapped around her and he hugged her back just as hard, clearly as delighted to see her as she was to see him. That was a relief, because as she stepped out of his arms, Olivia felt embarrassed about her impulsive actions, in front of a surprised-looking Jean-Pierre and a group of tourists who'd just sat down at the counter.

"It's so great to see you. Was your flight to France delayed?" Olivia asked.

Only then did the worry hit her. What if something terrible had happened? She stared up at him anxiously, hoping for an explanation that would set her mind at rest.

Smiling, his blue eyes bright and piercing in his tanned face, Marcello shook his head.

"The residency I was going to attend in the Loire Valley has been postponed by two weeks. So I am here for a while, although I will be traveling again soon."

"You must have learned so much," she said, feeling relieved that there was no crisis.

"Let us talk in the office," Marcello said.

Olivia hustled down the corridor, glad that she'd finished all the morning's tasks. It was a relief to sit down in the visitor's chair, while Marcello walked around the desk to his normal spot.

"I am extremely pleased with how things have been running and with your management," he praised her. "You have not only kept everything up to the minute, but have been creative and proactive in expanding our business and dealing with crises. For example, thanks to the recent arrival of a swarm, we now have a thriving beehive." His deep blue eyes sparkled as he spoke.

"It was Gabriella's idea to keep them," Olivia reminded him, feeling bowled over by the praise but firmly resolving to give credit where it was due.

Marcello nodded. "In addition, you have been a fair and kind manager. Your praise and encouragement, given generously, has created an environment where every person feels valued and tries to do better. This is exactly the vision that I have always had for my winery – that it must be a happy place where people, just like the plants, are nurtured and can flourish."

"Thank you, Marcello." Olivia's heart swelled with the praise as his proud smile warmed her.

"Now, onto what I have learned. I have acquired a wealth of information." Marcello shook his head as if he couldn't believe the scope of the knowledge.

"That's so exciting. When do we start putting it into practice?" She felt hopeful that thanks to the changes that Marcello would make, La Leggenda would soon be one of the most successful organic vineyards in Italy.

Marcello reached across the desk to turn his large screen so that both of them could see. As he swiveled the screen, his fingers brushed against hers. The touch was accidental, but even so, Olivia still couldn't stop the jolt of electricity that tingled through her every time their skin made contact. Quickly she moved her hand away, feeling guilty at her reaction, especially since her relationship with her beloved Danilo was currently so fraught with issues.

"I have created a checklist for us," Marcello explained. "On it, I have implemented a priority scale of ideas. I divided them into three categories. The ideas for now, that we can start immediately. The ideas for soon, that we can phase in over the coming weeks. And the ideas for long-term, that we can put into practice when the seasons change, or when infrastructure is created and it is timely to do so."

"That sounds wonderful," Olivia enthused, impressed by the elegance of the plan.

"Later today, I suggest that you, Nadia, and Antonio take a drive around the estate with me. We can all look at the plan and, field by field, we can discuss what needs to be done. They may want to adjust the plan as they have been working with the fields and plants."

Olivia loved the way her fair-minded boss immediately respected the input of others. She had learned from the best, she thought with gratitude.

"And you, Olivia? How are things going with you?"

What a question! From Marcello's tone, he was asking about her on a personal level. Olivia wished she could unload about the stress of having her mother arrive, but that was best left unsaid. Then she thought of something exciting she could tell Marcello.

"Remember I messaged you how we'd worked out the old map? Well, yesterday evening, we actually found where it points to. It's a small field and it's covered in boulders of various sizes. Mostly large," Olivia grimaced.

"Do you think there is something concealed under them?" Marcello sounded eager.

"I suspect there's something, because the boulders must have been transported there, and in one place they look to be deliberately piled up. Possibly, they're on top of a stash of old wine. I've got no idea how big it is, or whether it has value, but there's a possibility it does."

"Ever since I was young, I have heard the rumors about a large, hidden, and extremely valuable wine collection in this area. Can you move the rocks?" Marcello's eyes were blazing. Clearly, he was now as invested in this hunt as Olivia.

"Not without machinery. Most of them are too big to move manually, so it will have to wait a while." Olivia said. She didn't want to tell Marcello in so many words that she couldn't afford the machinery, but she guessed he understood.

"That is incredibly exciting."

He reached his hand out and covered hers with his warm palm. Again, Olivia couldn't suppress that tingle inside her, even though she knew the hand clasp was only a friendly gesture. There had always been chemistry between them. She had to accept that when he touched her, she would blush like a tomato and her pulse would pound audibly.

That was just how it was!

"Olivia, what I would like to do is –" Marcello began.

But Olivia never found out what he was planning to say.

At that moment, she became aware of a minor commotion from the tasting room and Jean-Pierre shouted, "Please, mademoiselle, wait!"

A moment later, a triumphant, bell-like voice rang out.

"Olivia! There you are!"

Snatching her hand away as she spun around in horror, Olivia was aghast to see her mother standing in the office doorway.

She jumped to her feet so hurriedly she almost tipped her chair over.

"Mom! I didn't know you were planning on visiting the winery today," she choked out. She hadn't thought her mother even knew where the winery was. She'd planned to come by with her tomorrow if she was able to get time off. Too late for that now – here Mrs. Glass was, dressed in a smart cream jacket, with an expectant smile on her face but a look in her eyes Olivia didn't like at all.

"This is my boss, Marcello Vescovi." Overcoming her shock for long enough to remember a polite introduction, Olivia turned back to the surprised-looking Marcello.

"This is my mom, Anthea Glass, although most people who know her, call her Mrs. G. She arrived yesterday for a surprise vacation."

And since then the surprises haven't stopped, Olivia thought bitterly.

"How wonderful to meet you. So you're the man who's lured Olivia away from her true calling in the advertising industry?" Mrs. Glass asked, raising her well-plucked eyebrows as Marcello stood hastily.

"A pleasure to meet you, Mrs. G. I hope you had a good flight? Are you feeling rested today and ready to enjoy your visit to our country?"

Nobody was immune to Marcello's charm, not even her mother on a mission, Olivia realized in relief. Marcello, beaming warmly, enfolded her mother's hands in his own before giving her the traditional Italian greeting of a kiss on each cheek.

"Would you like to see our winery? May I accompany you on a walk around the main buildings? And, of course, we will treat you to a wine tasting."

Marcello ushered Mrs. Glass out of the office with Olivia following, relieved that he was taking control of this potentially tricky situation.

"Let us leave the building by the side door. This cozy courtyard was originally an outdoor seating area for our restaurant, before we enlarged the restaurant and created a new area for it. I love to sit here on summer days, as it gives an exquisite view of three of our biggest vine plantations."

Marcello gestured to the hills beyond, where neat rows of vines curved across the slopes.

"Now, into the restaurant! What a privilege it is to have such a beautiful space for guests to enjoy top quality food both inside and on our balcony. We consulted with a local interior design firm to create the right ambiance here."

"It certainly looks charming," Mrs. Glass admitted as they walked through the high-roofed building, decorated with plants and vines. The white-clothed tables were immaculately laid with fine silverware and colorful flowers, ready for the day.

"And now, here is the hall where visitors enjoy our wines," Marcello said, ushering Olivia's mother into the tasting room. "This building is over a hundred years old, and was recently renovated into a magnificent space for guests to enjoy. I will leave you here, and must attend to a few urgent matters in my office. By the way, I assume that you will want to spend some time with your daughter? Olivia has worked extremely hard and must definitely take the day off tomorrow to show you some sights."

"Oh, thank you," Olivia said, filled with relief that she'd be able to get away.

"And now, I will hand you over to our capable assistant vintner, Jean-Pierre."

Mrs. Glass fluttered her eyelashes at Marcello as he gave her a final warm hand clasp.

"Jean-Pierre, this is my mother," Olivia said.

Poor Jean-Pierre had tried to stop Mrs. Glass from gate-crashing her meeting with Marcello, she realized, seeing her assistant vintner flush pink as he tidied the tasting sheets behind the counter.

Mrs. Glass was staring at the tasting counter, with its dramatic backdrop of wine barrels, with a considering expression.

"So this is what you do, Olivia? You're basically a glorified bartender?" she said in puzzled tones.

Looking at Jean-Pierre's appalled expression, Olivia wished the floor could swallow her up. She caught his gaze and knew that she was turning just as crimson as he was.

This wine tasting was turning into a bigger nightmare than she'd feared, and it hadn't even started yet.

CHAPTER SEVEN

"Perhaps you would like to introduce my mother to our wines," Olivia invited her assistant. She needed his help. There was no way she was going to be able to take her mother through the tasting menu.

"Of course," Jean-Pierre said nervously.

"Perhaps two white wines, and my rose?" Olivia asked. She didn't think her mother would enjoy the reds. Given that her current tipple was a wine and lemonade spritzer, Olivia doubted that any of the wines on the menu would hit the right spot.

"I'm going to step outside," she said, as Jean-Pierre produced the estate's latest vintage vermentino white. It was a prizewinning wine that had already won several awards. She knew that would not have the slightest effect on her mother's opinion of it.

Rushing through the lobby, Olivia headed to the refuge of the parking lot, where she made a panicked phone call to Charlotte.

"What's up?" her bestie answered.

"It's an emergency. My mother's arrived at the winery!"

"She has?" Charlotte sounded incredulous. "She told me she was going for a walk. Oh, dear, but I see some La Leggenda pamphlets on the kitchen table. She must have seen how close the winery was and decided to take a stroll there."

"I need rescuing." Olivia hissed. "I've got so much work to get through today if I'm going to be able to take time off tomorrow."

"I'm on it," her friend promised. "I'll be there in ten, and whisk her away for a lovely lunch in the village."

"Thank you," Olivia said in heartfelt tones.

She headed back into the tasting room where Mrs. Glass was struggling with the second wine on the list, while Jean-Pierre hovered helpfully.

"It's very sour. I'm not sure your winery has got the recipe right. Is it supposed to be so bitter? It tastes off."

Olivia burned with mortification as Jean-Pierre helpfully produced a can of lemonade from under the counter.

"Some of our guests prefer a mixer. Can I add a little of this to your glass?" he offered.

"Yes, thank you. The lemonade will save it, I hope. It strikes me that you Tuscan winemakers have a lot to learn. Our California industry is much more up to date with the needs of modern wine drinkers such as myself," her mother chided as Jean-Pierre added a tot of lemonade to the tasting portion.

"We are always learning," Jean-Pierre agreed humbly.

"This is much better. My advice would be to offer this mixer as your standard. It will make the experience much more pleasant for the majority of your guests. At least, until you've fixed your wines," Mrs. Glass advised.

Never mind the floor swallowing her up, Olivia was wishing the building would fall on her head. How on earth was she ever going to live this down? Jean-Pierre must feel mortally insulted.

But, as she glanced at him, she saw that he was, in fact, struggling to keep back a grin. He had that expression on his face where he was trying to hold a laugh in. Jean-Pierre thought this was uproariously funny.

Olivia couldn't see a trace of humor in it herself. But she was relieved that her assistant was taking this unprecedented situation in good spirits.

She headed to the lobby and peered anxiously out. Thank goodness, there was Charlotte, accelerating up the drive as if she were practicing for a drag race.

Her bestie skidded to a stop in the parking lot and scrambled out.

"I have some great ideas for activities," she confided to Olivia as they hustled inside. "I thought we could have lunch in the village and then introduce your mum to the two rival bakeries. You know how funny they can be. I bet they'll put on the performance of a lifetime, pretending to feud over her business."

"That sounds wonderful. Thank you so much. I owe you, seriously."

"Not at all," Charlotte said, giving Olivia a grateful grin. "After all, I've been staying with you for much longer than I planned. This is the very least I can do."

She marched into the tasting room and in loud tones filled with fake amazement, announced, "Well, what a surprise! Mrs. G? I didn't expect to bump into you here. I came to pick up a bottle of wine for dinner tonight. Would you like to come with me to the village when you're done? I'm starving and fancy a toasted provolone and Parma ham panini and a giant cappuccino."

“That sounds wonderful,” Mrs. Glass agreed, nodding regally as she tipped more lemonade into her tasting glass.

Olivia smiled gratefully. “I’m thrilled you can spend some time with Charlotte, Mom. Tomorrow, we can sightsee, but I’ve still got a lot to do here today, so I’ll see you later.”

She gave her mother a kiss on the cheek before rushing away, relieved to have escaped from the excruciating scene that was still playing out in the tasting room, with one wine left to go. Jean-Pierre might find her mother hilarious, but Olivia was all out of resources in the sense of humor department.

*

It was late in the afternoon by the time she’d finished her long and busy, but productive and rewarding day. She always felt energized after work although as she headed out, a burden of worries weighed down on her shoulders again.

Danilo would be here again tonight – if he wasn’t so offended that he never spoke to her again. Her ‘good friend’ Danilo! How would she solve the catastrophic situation she’d created? And what about her goat? Olivia cast a suspicious glance at Erba, gamboling alongside. She’d have to treasure every precious moment with her goat whose girth, to Olivia’s horrified eyes, seemed to be growing by the minute.

As Olivia strode along, she decided that the best solution for Danilo would be to pretend that their friendship was starting to blossom into something deeper. Rather fast, in fact. That would allow her mother to feel invested in their developing romance and that meant she might take it better.

But, as she reached the sand road leading to her farm, she frowned. Ahead of her was a large yellow excavator, trundling steadily up the steep hill.

Where was it going? Olivia wondered.

Her eyes widened when she saw it was turning through her farm gate. It was joining a front-end loader that was already parked there.

“What on earth?” Olivia said aloud. She broke into a run, powering her way up the steep hill and sprinting through her gateway.

Had her mother decided to re-landscape the farmhouse, she wondered, suddenly terrified by how far her crazy parent would have gone in her ‘Make Olivia Sell Up’ project.

Rushing into the farm, Olivia found her mother in conversation with the driver of the first vehicle. Or, rather, not in conversation, as the driver didn't seem to speak a word of English.

"Are you sure you have the right place?" Mrs. Glass was asking for what was clearly not the first time. She seemed to have decided that the reason the driver couldn't understand her was that she wasn't speaking loudly enough.

"ARE YOU SURE YOU HAVE THE RIGHT PLACE?" she yelled in polite but deafening tones. "PERHAPS YOU HAVE TAKEN A WRONG TURN, SIR, ARE YOU FAMILIAR WITH THE AREA?" She waved her arms looking, for a moment, rather Italian herself.

The driver shook his head in confusion, neither the volume nor the arm waving making any headway with their conversational impasse.

"Non capisco," he replied and then, deciding to take a leaf out of the Mrs. Glass communication handbook, said the same thing again, only louder.

"NON CAPISCO."

"Don't shout at me," Mrs. Glass complained, sounding irked.

Quickly, Olivia ran over.

"He's saying he doesn't understand you," she told her mother. Turning to the driver, she switched to Italian. "Can I help you signor?" she asked.

"Si, si," he replied, smiling in relief. "I am Giovanni. Marcello has sent us here. We have come to remove the boulders which you need moved."

"Marcello sent you?" Olivia repeated, feeling shocked. She'd mentioned it to her boss, but why had he ordered the machinery? Had he misunderstood her? Anxiety curdled inside her as she wondered what this would cost.

At that moment, her phone rang. It was Marcello himself on the line.

"Ah, salve, Olivia!' he said cheerfully. "I forgot to tell you, I asked my friend Giovanni to bring a team to help with moving the rocks on your farm."

"I – er – that's great," Olivia said faintly, wondering how much Giovanni would charge. Even a special rate would be outside of her budget, but then Marcello spoke again.

"I have told him I will pay. I am glad to contribute to this, as a thank-you for your work while I was away," he said.

"Oh, Marcello, that's amazing," Olivia said. She was filled with gratitude at her boss's generosity, but also hesitant to accept it. "Can't I pay you back? Over three months, perhaps? Or at least reimburse half?"

"No. It is my gift to you," Marcello said firmly.

"Thank you again," Olivia said in heartfelt tones. She turned back to the drivers. "It's all good. Let me show you where to work," she smiled.

"Are they supposed to be here?" Mrs. Glass asked as the men climbed out of the excavators. "What are they here to do?"

Olivia decided it would be better to keep things simple.

"They're moving some rocks to clear a piece of ground," she said.

Her mother raised her eyebrows. "So this isn't a mistake? Do you trust them to do a good job, since they don't speak a word of English?"

Tuning out her mother's infuriating comments, Olivia walked with the men past the farmhouse and through the rolling ground.

"Here is the field," Olivia pointed to the boulder-strewn area.

The two men both looked surprised.

"Who would have piled all those boulders up?" the other driver wondered aloud. "How did they get there? Some of them look like large building stones. I can see why you need them removed. Where would you like us to put them?"

That was a good question.

"Along the edge of the field, I think," Olivia decided. Hopefully there, the boulders would provide an attractive border to the rolling field.

"We will start tomorrow morning. It should not take more than a day," Giovanni said.

Thanking the men again, Olivia headed back with them, feeling glad that this important issue had been addressed. But, as she reached the farmhouse, her relief turned to concern.

Erba was perched on top of the excavator, looking triumphant as she surveyed her domain from this new platform. And Danilo had arrived. He was talking to her mother and looked both confused and annoyed.

Olivia hurried over, and her mother peeled away from the conversation and hurried over to her, speaking in a stage whisper.

"Daniel is here," she said unnecessarily. "I explained to him that you'd hired a crew. For some reason, he seems rather put out by it."

With her blood pressure spiking, Olivia hurried over to her beau.

"What's going on?" Danilo asked, frowning. "I thought you were going to wait before clearing the field."

"I was. But Marcello organized this as a surprise. He's paying for it, so I couldn't really say no," Olivia explained.

"Marcello?" Danilo snapped, glowering at the name.

Olivia felt her stomach tighten. After the bombshell of being introduced as 'a friend', he'd now discovered her handsome boss had subsidized the rock removal. She couldn't blame him for being mad all over again.

She wondered if Danilo thought his life was falling apart at the seams right now, because she felt hers was.

"I couldn't refuse, and it's sensible to get it done now," she justified.

Danilo spread his arms angrily.

"Olivia, I came here to discuss it with you. I was going to pay for the field to be cleared. I wanted to offer yesterday but your mother was here, and I couldn't stay the night as I was 'just a friend'!"

Olivia bit her lip, feeling mortified. The situation was worse than she'd imagined. Danilo was furious and the events of the past twenty-four hours had placed their relationship at risk.

"I'm so, so sorry," she muttered to him. "I didn't want my mother here. She just pitched up. And I didn't ask Marcello to bring the crew. He really did do it as a surprise and to thank me for managing the winery. I'm sorry everything has turned out so horribly. I wish I could rewind time and do things again, and try to get a better outcome."

Danilo sighed.

Even though Olivia could see he was still fed up, she was grateful that her boyfriend, despite being an emotional Italian, was very fair minded.

"Alright then. Tomorrow, I guess you will be touring with your mother?"

"Yes, I have the day off from work, and need to keep her entertained. I thought I'd take her to Lucca," Olivia said. "We had such a good time there. It was one of my favorite days ever, exploring that town with you. I need her to fall in love with Italy and if anywhere can do it, Lucca can."

Danilo's face didn't warm at the memory of the perfect, romantic outing they'd enjoyed. Instead he nodded, looking grimly resigned.

"Someone will need to be on site to supervise the crew. I'll do it."

Olivia stared at him in consternation. She hadn't even thought about that. And meanwhile, Danilo was being generous enough to put his annoyance aside and offer to help out.

"I can't thank you enough. I don't know what to say," she said, taking hold of his hand.

"It's the least I can do." He shrugged irritably.

"Are you staying for dinner?" Olivia asked.

Her mother overheard her words.

"Oh, Daniel, I hope you'll stay!"

Danilo shook his head. Despite all Olivia's apologizing, he was still miffed. "No. If I'm going to spend the day here tomorrow, I have work to do tonight."

"Oh, are you spending the day here? Then we must book you for dinner tomorrow night. Are you free then, Daniel?"

Olivia felt a sense of wonderment. Introducing Danilo as 'just a friend' had activated her mother's contrary instincts and now, she clearly couldn't wait to see romance bloom.

"Thank you for the invitation. I will be there," Danilo said formally. Then he drove away, not returning Olivia's anxious wave.

She trailed back to the house with a heavy heart. Every action she took was having unintended negative consequences and she feared that the knock-on effect would continue.

Her only hope was that Lucca, with all its beauty and charm, would succeed where she herself had failed, and change her mother's views on Italy.

CHAPTER EIGHT

"Are we ready to go?" Olivia called to her mother.

It was a beautiful spring morning, mild and sunny, the perfect day for exploring Lucca. Olivia wished she'd slept better instead of tossing and turning all night, unable to let go of her worries. She hated feeling this hovering sense of doom. Unfortunately, being around her mother always made her feel anxious.

For a moment, Olivia wondered if the feeling could possibly be mutual, but banished that thought immediately. Mrs. Glass never seemed to experience a moment's anxiety, despite being very good at causing it in other people.

There she was now, sweeping regally downstairs.

Olivia grabbed her purse and hustled out of the door. They climbed in the car and she drove carefully around the bulky excavators, and headed out of the farm gate.

"Lucca is one of the prettiest medieval cities in the area," she told her mother, as they joined the main road. "It's known for its amazing stone walls that encircle most of the city. And it has a lot of beautiful churches."

She smiled, remembering the fabulous outing she'd enjoyed there with Danilo a couple of months ago. What an adventure their day had been. Danilo was a wonderful travel guide, and his local knowledge combined with his mischievous sense of humor had kept her entertained from start to finish.

That was partly why she'd chosen Lucca today. She could be confident her mother would have an enjoyable time.

Although, looking at Mrs. Glass's face, Olivia wasn't sure. She had no idea if her mother was ready to relax and appreciate Tuscany, or whether she was still engaged in Project Bring Olivia Home.

Time would tell, Olivia thought, as she headed onto the highway.

"Is there anything you want to buy while you're here? Perhaps a gift for Dad?" Olivia hoped they could include shopping as part of the day's experience. Last time she'd visited Lucca, Danilo had treated her to a gorgeous pair of shoes. She'd bought him a stylish scarf, and a set of placemats showing Lucca's most famous tourist attractions.

"Oh, your father has everything he needs already," Mrs. Glass replied airily. "You know how difficult he is to shop for."

And, with that, Olivia knew that this day was not going to be the lighthearted outing she hoped for. Her mother was still on her original mission. Olivia was going to have to bust a gut to convince her to fall in love with Italy.

*

If any place in Tuscany could do the job, it was Lucca, Olivia thought, as the ancient walls of this historic town came into sight half an hour later. She'd chosen the back roads for an easy and relaxing drive, and because Danilo had explained that this approach gave the best view of the city.

"Look at those walls," Olivia breathed, easing the Fiat along the narrow strip of tarmac. At this hour there was always slow traffic heading into town. Olivia didn't mind as it gave her more time to admire the view. Unlike most Etruscan towns, Lucca was not a hilltop town, but nestled cozily into its surroundings, protected by those well-preserved stone walls.

"It's rather small," Mrs. Glass said disparagingly as they eased through the traffic. "Everything here seems cramped and narrow. I guess that's why you can't drive spacious cars." She sighed, shifting her legs for the umpteenth time.

Olivia bit back an angry comment. If only her mother would get off her high horse and simply appreciate the day. She could be insufferable when she chose, and she was clearly choosing now.

With his local knowledge, Danilo had driven straight to a parking lot where he said there were always a few empty bays, and Olivia did the same now, relieved to find an open space just where she'd hoped.

"Our morning tour will start with a visit to the Piazza di Mercato, which is the old site of the Anfiteatro Romano, or the Roman amphitheatre," she said in her best tour-guide voice. "It's the center of the town and there are some great bistros where we can energize ourselves with a coffee."

Olivia was starving for a coffee, and longing for a cornetto, or some other light breakfast treat. In between her morning chores she hadn't had time for any of that.

"Oh, I already had a coffee," Mrs. Glass said airily. "I couldn't possibly have another. Charlotte made me a huge cappuccino first thing this morning, and I ate several cookies that tasted very strongly of lemon zest. I hope they don't give me the runs! I don't want to risk having to go to the restroom while we're touring. I don't trust these Italian facilities. In a place like this, what if they're not clean?"

Olivia felt her plans crumble around her. The bistro on the historic square made excellent coffees. Better still, they could be enjoyed while taking in the ambiance of the square itself. The oval shaped, paved structure was surrounded by beautiful buildings made of ocher stone, with scenic wrought-iron balconies. These buildings had preserved the outline of the original amphitheater as they were constructed. Viewing it had been a memorable start to the day the last time she'd been here. But clearly caffeine was not on the menu.

"All right," she agreed, trying not to sound grumpy. "We can skip the square, and head straight to the cathedral."

"A cathedral sounds wonderful," her mother agreed. Olivia thought she sounded apologetic, as if she'd realized that she was being a killjoy.

Changing direction, she walked away from the road that led to the square. The Duomo di San Martino cathedral was close by – with Lucca being a small town, all attractions were an easy stroll from each other. She could already see its tower and felt a sense of excitement that, in a few more steps, the cathedral itself would come into view. She was sure her mother would be astonished by its beauty.

They neared the cathedral at the same time as another tour group. Walking alongside them, Olivia heard the gasps of amazement and appreciative comments from the tourists.

To her disappointment, her mother was silent as she took in the cathedral's stunning façade, with its numerous, delicately crafted arches in white marble. Since it was a fine day, this noble structure looked even more dramatic against the clear blue sky.

"This is a Romanesque cathedral," Olivia explained. "It was actually rebuilt in the thirteenth century over an earlier church. Isn't that incredible, to be in a place where historic buildings from so long ago are still intact?"

"It most definitely is," her mother agreed.

"How amazing is the level of detail. All those archways! Do you want to take a photo?" Olivia urged her. She hadn't been able to stop photographing the façade when she'd last been here. She'd joked to Danilo that she'd felt like a paparazzi.

"Oh, no, angel, I'm not taking my phone out of my purse. It's staying safely zipped up. I don't want it pickpocketed or snatched."

"But – but that won't happen here," Olivia said. The cathedral's entrance wasn't even crowded, and everyone else had their phones out. Everyone!

Giving up on the photography, she suggested, "Shall we head inside? There's so much to see. I think you'll love the stone carving of St. Martin and the beggar, and the pulpit is magnificent."

They joined the short line of visitors and Olivia paid at the entrance.

Stepping inside the cathedral's cool confines felt like entering another world. Olivia felt a sense of deep awe to be walking through a structure that was many centuries old.

"This is the most famous piece in the cathedral," she said, pointing to the effigy of Christ on the cross. "It's carved from cedar wood, and it's still used in celebrations today. They used to carry it through the streets in a procession every September."

"My goodness. That sounds rather barbaric," her mother offered.

"It isn't," Olivia protested, dismayed that the conversation was already dropping to this level.

"How do you know? Have you seen it?"

"No. Dan – er." Too late Olivia remembered she must be careful about mentioning past history with her 'friend.' "I came here in February. It was very cold, but beautiful. In any case, they don't take it out of the cathedral any more. They decorate it inside the cathedral."

She paused, looking at her favorite artwork – the statue of St. Martin, on horseback, leaning over to give a piece of his cloak to a beggar. She thought the statue, and the generosity it represented, was beauty personified. She could have looked at the horse all day. The proud steed looked both noble and kind.

"It's rather cold in here," Mrs. Glass complained.

"Well, we'll soon warm up," Olivia said, trying not to grit her teeth any more as her jaw was already rather sore. "After this cathedral, we will take a walk around the actual city walls of Lucca. It's the most amazing experience to walk along the walls themselves, and there's a special surprise that we'll see a short way ahead."

They exited the cathedral and Olivia was pleased to remember the quick way through the winding, cobbled streets that led to the city walls. She felt happy to be among other tourists following a similar route.

She breathed a sigh of relief as they stepped onto the immaculately paved walkway that topped the wall. Of course, it wasn't only a walkway. The paving was as wide as a small road, and flanked with trees and grass, just like a park. The entire city was encircled by this verdant band of greenery, which people used to walk, run, cycle, and even rollerblade. The views changed every step of the way, and Olivia loved the fact that there were always two vistas – one looking outward, over the rolling countryside and cultivated fields, and one looking inward, over the quaintly gorgeous, compact homes, with more trees dotted among them.

"The total distance of the city walls is about four kilometers, or two and a half miles, and the entire route is lined with trees. Don't you love the view?" she asked.

"We're not walking the whole way are we?" Mrs. Glass replied.

"Only as far as you like. There are many benches on the route, and even a few bistros that were originally military towers, but converted to a much better purpose," Olivia smiled. She'd done the entire circuit with Danilo. With frequent stops to admire the view, it had taken them around an hour.

"It certainly is beautiful up here."

As they strolled along, Olivia felt thrilled that the peaceful and scenic walkway had finally allowed her mother to take in the gloriousness of Tuscany. She and Danilo had raced each other along one well-kept stretch of paving. She'd cheated with a head-start and had narrowly won. She remembered being breathless with laughter as they collapsed on one of the pretty benches to rest their legs.

"There is the surprise." Hoping that this would add to her mother's enjoyment, Olivia pointed out the unique landmark. "It's the Guinigi Tower, which is Lucca's most important tower. It's positioned between two palaces, and what sets it apart is that it has a hanging garden! Those are real live oak trees growing on top of it."

"Full sized?" Olivia could hear the fascination in her mother's voice as she shielded her eyes and peered at the tall, ocher-colored tower.

"Yes. Isn't that amazing? One of the features I love most about Tuscany is how green it is. They never miss an opportunity to plant trees and shrubs. And I adore the flower pots on all the balconies."

When she and Danilo had visited Lucca, he'd booked to be part of one of the small groups to walk up the tower. Two hundred and thirty-two steps had passed in a flash, and she'd never forgotten the unique experience of standing in the shade of an oak tree while at the top of Lucca's mightiest tower.

She didn't think her mother would want to do the climb, but decided to ask anyway.

"We can walk up it if you like?"

"Definitely not. I believe a vacation should be relaxing, not a gym session! If you want to walk up, go ahead. I'll wait at the bottom."

Olivia began agonizing inwardly. Did her mother really think she'd do that? Walk up a tower for no reason, abandoning her on her own, when she lived in the area and could come back any time she liked?

Her patience was beginning to fray, and she suspected her mother was testing its limits deliberately.

"Why don't we end our trip in the Piazza di Mercato? We can have a light lunch there, and head home afterwards," she suggested.

She didn't know how much longer she could keep her cool without some sustenance to help her along.

Of course, her mother was ready with a comeback.

"There's so much food in the refrigerator at home. And I need a siesta. Is that what they call it here? At any rate, we ate rather late last night and I imagine that's the tradition in this part of the world."

Sighing, Olivia resigned herself to a hungry drive home.

Never mind blood pressure, her mother was also playing havoc with her blood sugar, she thought, taking refuge in humor.

Apart from a moment on the top of the walls, she didn't think her mother had enjoyed the outing at all. In fact, if she'd deliberately set out not to enjoy it, she had succeeded wildly in her task.

The only possible way that today could be redeemed was if the excavators uncovered the treasure she'd dreamed of finding. Heading out of the pretty, though unappreciated, town, Olivia set her sights and her hopes on what might be waiting back home.

CHAPTER NINE

Olivia had never been more relieved to see the rickety gates of her farmhouse come into view. That had been the most stressful outing ever. Who would have thought Lucca could be made un-enjoyable?

Was her mother going to make things as miserable as possible until Olivia capitulated and agreed to return to the States, she wondered, confused. To add to her stress, they'd been stuck in unexpected, heavy traffic on the way back and it was now already mid-afternoon. So much for a light lunch, she thought with hungry regret.

As she drove through the gateway and saw the flattened tracks that the heavy machines had left in the gravel, she forgot her growling stomach and remembered with a thrill of excitement that the crew had spent the day hard at work.

While she'd been enduring a tortuous, truncated tour of Lucca, Olivia thought, reveling in some alliteration to summarize the awful day, the crew had been tirelessly transporting boulders.

She hoped that all their efforts would produce results, and decided to go straight there to have a look.

"I need to check on the progress in the field. It's rather late for lunch but we could have a snack when I get back," she said as she parked the car, but to her surprise, her mother seemed to have forgotten her tiredness.

"I'll come with you and see what this crew has been working on all day," Mrs. Glass replied. "I see Daniel's car is here also."

Olivia wished she had the energy to correct her mother's pronunciation of his name, but in her starving state she decided rather to leave it. She climbed out and stood in the lengthening shade of the olive tree, the afternoon breeze cool and fresh on her skin.

Turning, she saw Charlotte's Fiat heading through the gates. Her bestie was home, too. Olivia hoped she'd had a good day.

Charlotte jumped out of the car.

"Hello, all. Did you enjoy Lucca, Mrs. G.?"

Olivia braced herself for the tirade of criticism that she knew would follow, but to her surprise, her mother replied enthusiastically.

"What a quaint and scenic town it is. We saw a few sights and walked along the medieval walls – so pleasant! I said no to lunch, though, as I've realized what lavish dinners people enjoy here."

"So glad you had a great time," Charlotte smiled.

Was her mother being serious? Was she deliberately presenting her best self to everyone except her daughter? Olivia felt flummoxed by her reply.

"Shall we go down to the field?" she asked.

"I've been thinking about that all day," Charlotte agreed.

They set off along the paved path, with Olivia striding ahead, remembering proudly how she'd set all the cobbles in place herself. A hundred yards from the farmhouse it petered out – Olivia had run out of energy and cobbles by that point – and they followed the faint track through the grass to where she could hear the growl of the excavators at work.

"Hey, Danilo!" she called eagerly, seeing him standing at the entrance to the field.

"Hey, Olivia!" He hurried over and gave her a big hug and kiss. Staring up at his handsome, smiling face Olivia felt relieved that he was back to his normal, good-tempered self. At least one thing was going right today.

Seeing her mother and Charlotte approach over the ridge, she hastily stepped away from her 'friend.' After what had happened, she still felt as if she had a lot of apologizing to do. But for now, there was no time. Now that they'd arrived, Danilo was excitedly updating them all on the progress.

"This is the biggest pile they are working on now. It's where the boulders have been clustered most densely. I have instructed them to work very carefully as they remove the last few. I am hopeful, Olivia. These boulders were heaped up here. There must be a reason for it."

"How extraordinary. Why would they do that?" Mrs. Glass wondered aloud.

Charlotte squeezed Olivia's' arm supportively. Olivia could feel she was taut with excitement.

Danilo looked at Olivia again, more closely this time.

"I have a flask of coffee with me. Would you like some?"

Olivia almost burst into tears with gratitude.

"I'd love some!"

"I also bought refreshments from the bakery for the crew. There are a few ciambelle left."

Her mouth watered at the prospect of digging into one of the donut shaped bread snacks, chewy to eat and fragrantly flavored with fennel seeds.

"You don't know what a lifesaver you are," she murmured, feeling thankful beyond words for his considerate kindness as she took one and passed the packet to her mother.

As she munched on the ciambelle, and drank the rich, creamy coffee, Olivia stared around the now-cleared field. The two machines she'd seen yesterday were driving back and forth, and a third, smaller excavator was working on the field's perimeter, where the boulders had been neatly placed to form an attractive border. Now, Giovanni was attacking the final few hold-outs.

Machinery throbbed and gears shifted as he skillfully teased one of the remaining three boulders loose. With a bang and a clang it settled into the scoop and he reversed quickly, chugging over to the field's perimeter.

Olivia held her breath as the vehicle returned, and started working on the biggest boulder, bulky and solid among the long, verdant grass. She was pleased to see that this terrain was reasonably flat and looked to be one of the more fertile areas on her farm. If nothing else, she had cleared a very promising vineyard-to-be.

But at that moment, Danilo caught his breath and grabbed her hand.

"What? What?" Olivia was jumping out of her skin with the tension of the moment.

"Look there!" he said, pointing at the flattened space where the boulder had been.

"I see something!" Olivia couldn't breathe. She nearly choked on her ciambelle. Quickly, she gulped the last of the coffee to wash it down.

"It looks like a stone frame," Danilo said.

"Perhaps it's demarcating the area where something was buried?" Olivia could hardly believe she was uttering the words.

"Buried treasure?" Mrs. Glass asked. She sounded as caught up in this enthralling moment as they were.

"I'm hoping so," Charlotte replied.

Danilo stepped forward and shouted out in rapid Italian as the excavator returned. Translating the words as he spoke, Olivia heard him asking Giovanni to work very carefully in this area and not disturb what was being uncovered.

"Si, si," he shouted back.

Handling the heavy machine with sensitive mastery, he nudged and rolled the final boulder a safe distance away before capturing it in the scoop.

As the excavator chugged off to the field's perimeter they all rushed forward.

Olivia's head was spinning as she stared down at the incredible, impossible sight. She gripped Danilo's hand.

"The stones are a frame," she said in a shaky, incredulous voice. "A door frame, set in the ground!"

"And there's the door," Danilo said, sounding equally flabbergasted.

Taking in the sight with disbelieving eyes, Olivia saw that the rectangular stone frame set into the ground measured about one by two yards – roughly the size of a squat doorway. The solid wooden door embedded in the ground was framed by the stone. It was dirtied with clods of earth and trailing grass, and as she watched, a beetle scuttled away.

She could see the crushed areas of stone where the biggest boulder had lain. It had been placed directly over the frame, covering it without damaging the wood, and then the others had been piled into place to hide it completely.

"Well! A door in the ground? I see there's a latch and handle set into it. What do you think is under it?" Mrs. Glass asked curiously.

"I guess a small cave. Or maybe something shallowly buried," Olivia said.

"Are we going to open it?" her mother pressed.

Danilo turned and shouted to Giovanni again.

He, in turn, shouted to the driver of the front-end loader, who jumped down and hurried over, carrying a flashlight.

A flashlight was a good idea, Olivia thought. If the cave was deep, then it might be dark under that door.

The driver of the small excavator rushed over, carrying a shovel. He scooped some of the earth away and then Danilo grasped the handle and pulled it open.

Loose earth strewed over the ground, and another beetle made a run for it as he hefted the old, heavy door upward. Hinges shrieked, and Olivia breathed in cool, stale air as the door was lifted wide.

It was so dark under it she couldn't see a thing. She grabbed the flashlight that the driver handed her. To her astonishment, the beam shone onto rugged wooden steps that descended steeply into the darkness. Someone had constructed a proper cellar.

"There's a massive staircase. This goes into an actual underground room!" she exclaimed.

"Well? Are you going in?" her mother asked excitedly.

Olivia hesitated. Fears surged inside her. She knew she should go first, but the dark, ancient tunnel below her felt creepy. What if there were spiders, or worse, lurking? Although what could be worse than a spider? Olivia was petrified of them.

"I'll be right behind you," Danilo reassured her, clearly picking up on her fear. Olivia knew that was a lie, because if Danilo saw a spider he was likely to outrun her. His phobia was even worse than hers.

She'd just have to hope that this underground chamber didn't contain any nasty surprises of the arachnid variety. At any rate, when Danilo placed his warm hand on her shoulder, his touch gave her the resolve she needed. This was her farm and her find. Of course she must lead the way.

Gripping the flashlight tightly, she stepped onto the first of the rough wooden stairs that led into the cool, musty darkness.

CHAPTER TEN

The flashlight beam danced over the rough wood and raw concrete ceiling as Olivia descended the stairs. The uneven planks creaked under her weight, and she hoped that one of the steps wouldn't suddenly collapse. This stairway was steep and long. The underground room was deeper than she'd expected, and she wondered if that meant it might also be larger.

Finally, she saw ground ahead. It was raw, bare earth that had been compacted into solid floor, goodness knows how long ago.

She lowered herself onto it gratefully and turned to shine the flashlight for Danilo as he eased his way down the final, steep step.

Then she shone the light around the room and they both drew in a gasp of astonishment.

This was no simple bunker. It was a large underground cellar. All the way around the room, rows of rough shelves had been built out of ancient looking planks.

Bottles and bottles of wine filled the shelves. Lying serenely on their sides, they were so thickly coated in dust that only the shapes clued her in that they held wine. And there were a lot of shapes and sizes! Some traditional, others less so, and a few bottle types she'd never seen before. How old was this wine? she wondered.

The collection was vast. Her brain boggled that such a huge consignment could have been carefully buried in this secret place.

It was not only wine, she saw, taking in the full extent of this discovery. To the left of the stairway were a few oaken barrels with tools of the trade stacked on their grimy tops. There were old-fashioned corking mechanisms that Olivia only recognized thanks to her historic reading. She saw wine openers, too, and even a few crystal glasses, dull with dust.

"This is incredible! Mamma mia!" Danilo breathed.

Olivia surveyed the room again, feeling disoriented as she took in the scale of this discovery. Was she dreaming? Ever since she'd allowed herself to hope there was wine hidden on her farm, she'd fantasized about uncovering something like this.

"There are so many bottles. Danilo, how old do you think they are? Could they possibly have any value?"

It was unreal that this cellar had been buried under her feet the whole time. When she'd gone for walks on her farm, and passed through this strange boulder-strewn field, she must have trodden right over it without even knowing.

"We must find out the value," Danilo said. "My friend Begni will be the right person to evaluate this collection. He's the expert in Florence, where you took the bottle shard."

"The bottle shard!" Something at the far side of the cellar, resting on the lowest shelf, caught Olivia's eye.

She shone the flashlight on it. It looked gray with dust, but she recognized the shape. This was exactly the same gourd-like bottle that the shard had come from. Never would Olivia forget the shape and curve of the glass, manufactured in a century so ancient that bottles were still stored on their bases and not on their sides, as winemaking had later evolved.

Danilo had seen it too. His voice was taut with excitement.

"Olivia, look! It is an intact shaft-and-globe bottle, the same as your fragment."

"It might not be the same glass. Perhaps it's a more mainstream model," Olivia theorized, not wanting to get too excited, because disappointment – which was all too likely – would be heartbreaking. It was better to manage her expectations upfront.

Danilo paced over to it. Following him, Olivia couldn't resist glancing at the dust-strewn bottles. As she walked, sand showered onto her. She glanced up. The raw concrete ceiling was patchy, and seemed to have been seriously impacted by the damp.

Danilo bent down and rubbed the gourd-shaped bottle with the edge of his shirt.

"It's the same unique glass. Remember that mottled, blackish green? And not only is it a perfectly intact bottle, it also looks to be sealed. It has the original wine inside!"

Olivia trained the beam on the bottle. She couldn't hold back the blaze of excitement that consumed her. This bottle was identical to the shard. The flashlight picked up the dull gleam of the weirdly beautiful, mottled glass.

"I wonder how much wine is left. It might have evaporated. This was centuries ago. They couldn't seal bottles the way they do now."

"But it has been well stored, and perhaps the seal was sufficient. At any rate, it looks intact. Olivia, this alone – remember, Begni said not a single bottle crafted from this glass is known to exist? He said it would be a priceless find. Who knows what a collector would pay? And this is just one – one of hundreds!"

He gazed around the rough shelves. Olivia shone the light, following his gaze. The bottles were so dirty she couldn't tell what they were. They could be worthless junk. But at least they knew one prized find was waiting here.

"We need to get it valued as soon as possible. I don't think we should move it until then. What do you think?" she suggested.

"Yes, I agree. There is too much risk of disturbing, or breaking, what lies here. It must be transported with care and expertise. Since it has been here for decades, perhaps longer, a day or two more won't hurt," Danilo agreed.

Another shower of gravel and concrete chunks spattered on them from above and a few small stones thudded onto the floor. Olivia shook sand out of her hair.

"This ceiling is very crumbly. Let's go up and tell the others," she said.

She couldn't wait to break the news about their find. What an exciting surprise. Even if the collection proved worthless, she'd never forget the thrill of seeing these rows of ancient bottles.

Carefully, she climbed the stairs. After the musty depths of the cellar, the afternoon light seemed very bright.

"Did you find anything? What's down there?" Charlotte asked, her voice taut with excitement as she grasped Olivia's arm to help her out.

"It's a fully stocked cellar. The shelves are packed with ancient, and I mean really old, bottles," Olivia announced proudly.

Charlotte's jaw dropped. "Serious? Like, how old?"

"There was so much dust we couldn't see, but we did pick out one extremely rare and ancient bottle which on its own is supposedly very valuable."

"That's amazing!" Charlotte breathed. Mrs. Glass looked captivated by the words.

"Thank you so much," Olivia said to Giovanni, handing him the flashlight. "I appreciate the great job you did today."

"A pleasure. Anything for my friend Marcello," he grinned.

Just in time, Erba leaped off the back of the excavator where she'd been perched, as with a clank and a growl, the three men started up their machines and headed out of the field.

"Let's go back to the house. We need to discuss what to do next," Danilo said.

Olivia was reeling with astonishment as they followed the pathway back to the farmhouse. She had no idea how she would go about selling the bottles, if any were sellable. Those big, beautiful barrels she was longing to keep. She could imagine them one day, in a place of pride in her tasting room, polished and restored to their full glowing glory.

They trooped inside the house. The kitchen felt warm and cozy after standing on the breezy hillside.

"I'm going to fetch a warm jacket. Can I bring a sweater down for you, angel?" Mrs. Glass asked, heading upstairs.

"Thank you," Olivia called.

Grabbing her arm, Charlotte did a happy dance around the kitchen.

"You worked so hard on this farm and it's as if it's personally rewarding you now," she said.

After the happy dance, Olivia sat down at the kitchen table, still weak at the knees with shock, and Charlotte made a fresh pot of coffee.

Mrs. Glass came downstairs carrying a sweater and a thick jacket. "I've got to message your father back. He's asking how I enjoyed my day," she said. Perching on the nearest chair, she bent her head over her phone, frowning.

"First and most importantly, do you have a padlock?" Danilo asked Olivia as he sat next to her.

"A padlock? I might have one somewhere. Why?" she asked.

"We need to lock that door," Danilo said firmly. "With a padlock and chain, I can lock it into the doorframe."

Olivia stared at him, perplexed. "But the door is hidden at ground level in the middle of a deserted field. You can't even see it unless you fall over it. Isn't that a waste of time?"

"We need to do it," Danilo insisted, his voice firm. "We have found a collection that could be extremely valuable. We have to secure it."

Olivia thought he was mad, but decided to humor him anyway.

"We can do it tomorrow. If you need a chain as well I'll pick one up from the hardware store after work."

"I will call Begni first thing in the morning," Danilo confirmed.

"Do you think we should tell the press? Surely this is a fascinating local story," Charlotte said, placing the steaming cups onto a tray. "This could add to the tourist appeal of this area!"

She sat down and passed the milk and sugar around.

Olivia thought a press conference sounded like a brilliant idea, but Danilo was shaking his head emphatically.

"No, no, no," he insisted, and Olivia could see his mind was back on security again. "Nobody must say anything to anyone. Not until the collection has been examined, and the bottles are in safekeeping."

"Do you really think someone might try to steal it?" Olivia asked.

Danilo sighed, sounding frustrated. "Of course. I am certain this collection is extremely valuable. I am guessing it's worth a fortune. Greed tempts people into crime – you know it, Olivia. And, in this small town, word travels like wildfire. It has to stay a secret," Danilo implored her, his face as serious as she'd ever seen it.

"I do not want it stolen from you. Or for you to be in danger as a result of this find," he said, grasping her hand in his.

Danger? Until that moment, Olivia hadn't considered the possibility, but as he spoke, she started to feel worried and nervous. This uncovered cellar might attract trouble to her doorstep, she realized somberly.

*

That night, Olivia couldn't sleep at all. She tossed and turned, causing Pirate to have to patiently climb over her again and again, resettling herself in a quieter part of the bed. Her thoughts were racing. What would this collection mean for her? What did 'valuable' equate to?

Olivia was sure that cold, hard reality would be different from her hopes and dreams. Most likely it would be worth a modest sum. The old bottle, although of rare value, might not be easy to sell. Who would want it anyway? A museum, perhaps? She didn't think museums would shell out thousands for historic wine bottles. Or were there collectors that would genuinely pay for ancient, undrinkable wine?

But now that she'd entertained some hope, Olivia had to acknowledge what it would mean if the collection was worthless. Despite fighting her mother's words every step of the way, those dire predictions had gotten inside her head. It *would* take her decades to develop her own winery, starting from her current point of 'totally broke.' Her salary was reasonable and in fact generous for one person to live comfortably on. However, unsurprisingly, it didn't stretch to starting a winery from scratch.

Did she want to spend the rest of her life on a shoestring as she plunged all her extra money and time into this bottomless pit of a project?

How would she capitalize her nonexistent business? How would she pay for the labor she would require to tend and harvest all her vines? It wasn't a one man job. Making the single batch of ice wine had pushed her to her limits. That wine had sold so well because of its rare value. Producing more traditional wines would place her in a very competitive market where it might not be so easy to make a quick profit.

Thinking of the struggle that lay ahead, Olivia realized that she hadn't considered the extent of it until this moment. With happy optimism, she had ignored the realities of her predicament, until her mother had so thoughtfully presented them to her.

Sighing, Olivia turned over yet again and checked the time.

To her relief, it was morning. She guessed that at some stage during the long, troubled night, she'd managed to doze. Feeling sleep deprived and full of indecision, she padded over to the window and pulled back the curtains to stare at the rosy sky.

What would the new day bring, she wondered with a shiver, remembering Danilo's warning the previous night.

CHAPTER ELEVEN

Arriving at work ten minutes earlier than usual, Olivia decided to find Marcello straight away. She needed to thank him personally for sending the crew and update him on the exciting discovery.

To her surprise, as soon as she walked into La Leggenda's lobby, Marcello rushed out of his office.

"Olivia. I saw your goat from my office window."

"I've got such amazing news to tell you!" Olivia shared.

"Isn't it incredible? A wooden door set into the ground, and an underground cellar, filled with wine!"

Olivia stared at Marcello in astonishment.

Was her boss psychic? She'd never before suspected he had such abilities. How on earth did he know about the cellar already? Bemused, she wondered if she might have sleepwalked during her restless night, and accidentally sent him an email.

The answer was much simpler, it turned out.

"Giovanni told me. He called me as soon as he left."

"Really?" Now Olivia's surprise curdled into worry. If he had called Marcello immediately, he might well have called other people, too. She didn't want anyone to know about it, at least not until the collection was in a safe place and had been properly valued. They'd agreed on that last night.

"You look as if something is wrong," Marcello observed.

"I', worried. If word gets out it could cause trouble." Olivia fidgeted nervously with the buckle on her purse.

Marcello understood immediately. She saw his expression harden into concern.

"Absolutely. That could be a problem. Have you put a lock on the door?"

"Not yet," Olivia said, now feeling so anxious she wanted to run back home and stand guard over the cellar.

"Well, lock it as soon as you can."

"I will."

"I have not told anyone else," Marcello reassured her.

But, at that moment, there was a cheery, "Buongiorno," from the lobby. Nadia sashayed in, looking happy to see Olivia.

"What is this I hear? You are the owner of a very old, legendary wine collection?"

Marcello spun around and stared at Nadia, aghast. Then he turned back to Olivia.

"I said nothing," he insisted in a low voice.

Nadia rolled her eyes. "Of course you didn't. Everyone knows not to go to you for gossip. Luckily I have better connections. Lara, the wife of Signor Mazetti who owns one of the bakeries, called me last night and told me."

"Mazetti's wife?" Olivia spoke the words at exactly the same time as Marcello, and in the same incredulous tone.

"How did she know?" Marcello demanded.

"Her husband told her, of course." Nadia gave him a conspiratorial wink.

"How did he know? Did Giovanni tell him?"

"No. He heard from Tino, who is working in the hardware store. Tino said his boss told him."

Olivia's shoulders slumped. If the hardware store owner knew about her cellar, the whole town knew.

"Oh, dear. I guess you wanted to keep it a secret," Nadia sympathized, finally comprehending the seriousness of the situation.

Olivia nodded sadly. "We've contacted someone who's going to value it. Hopefully they can remove it soon, and then all the gossip will blow over."

"Do you want to leave at lunchtime today?" Marcello asked. "You need to sort this out as soon as you can. I know what long hours you worked while I was away. You are owed time off. Take it."

"Thank you. I'll do that," Olivia said gratefully.

She headed behind the tasting counter, waving to Jean-Pierre as he arrived, and hoping that he didn't know about it yet. There was nothing she could do now. Word was out and spreading like wildfire. She felt nervous about what might happen next. Human nature was never at its best when a mythical fortune was at stake.

"It is amazing how busy we are becoming now that spring is here," Jean-Pierre enthused, joining her behind the tasting counter. He stared at the lobby entrance in surprise. "Look. It is not even opening time, and already we have a customer."

Olivia wasn't so sure. Her instincts were prickling. The curly-haired man who sidled over to the counter with an ingratiating grin didn't look like a customer, so who was he?

"Buongiorno," the man said. He continued in English. "You are the Americano owner of the farm where the underground wine cellar has just been discovered, no?"

Beside her, she heard Jean-Pierre gasp in surprise.

Olivia tried to absorb this bombshell without her face showing it. The man laughed loudly.

"I can see you are shocked. And no wonder. What news it is! I decided to come and find you immediately. My name is Pablo Pusilli. My great-grandfather…" He thought for a moment and then tried again. "I mean, great-great grandfather worked that land. Definitely, my great-great-great grandfather was an employee on that very same farm where you now live. I remember clearly how he told me."

"You do?" Jean-Pierre asked in surprise. "How old were you?"

Olivia maintained a stony silence as the man continued.

"I was a young child, very young, as was my father when my great-great-great-great grandfather told us of working on that farm at the time when that secret underground cellar, with all its riches, was constructed. He described it in detail. I believe he even kept a journal which all the family knew well, although sadly it was destroyed in a fire last year. But luckily the words inside I have committed to memory."

"I thought he told you," Jean-Pierre said, sounding flummoxed by this strange conversation.

"The point is." Now Pablo leaned forward, speaking in a confidential tone. "The point is that my great-great grandfather stated clearly that some of his own personal wines were stocked in that cellar. Many of them, in fact. All the workers received a share of the wines as payment. My great-great-great grandfather was a very frugal man who thought carefully about the future. He did not accept money for his work."

"How did he live?" Jean-Pierre asked.

"Very frugally," Pablo emphasized, slapping his hand on the tasting counter. "His only wish was for his great-great-great grandchild to be provided for through wise investment. That would be me." He tapped his chest.

"Are you saying that some of the wines in the secret cellar are yours?" Jean-Pierre glanced at Olivia. The conversation had left her at a loss for words. She felt as if she'd slipped into a waking nightmare. The cellar had been uncovered only yesterday afternoon! And already this was happening.

"Yes, that is exactly what I am saying!" Pablo fixed Olivia with a winning smile but his eyes were like laser beams. "I have waited for this for so many years. Now I have come to make sure you know of my grandfather's story and his noble sacrifice."

"You mean your great-great-great grandfather," Jean-Pierre corrected him helpfully.

"Exactly!"

Olivia took a deep breath. She had to take control of this situation and get this man out of here. She didn't believe a word of his ridiculous story and knew that anything she said might be held against her by this opportunist.

"We will certainly look into it," Olivia said. "As the legal owner of the farm, I have called in experts to assess the find."

She felt nervous about saying anything else. Remaining silent was the best recourse.

"Thank you," she added.

Pablo looked disappointed. "I will come back tomorrow," he told her, and it sounded like more of a threat than a promise.

He turned and marched out.

"Wine cellar? What is this, Olivia?" Jean-Pierre asked curiously.

"I'm surprised you don't know already, seeing the whole village has already heard it was uncovered yesterday," Olivia said, trying for a joke even though she wasn't finding this funny at all and was now seriously worried.

"I went to bed early last night and turned my phone off. Is it buried on your farm?"

"Yes, it is."

"Then surely it belongs to you?"

Olivia let out a despairing sigh. "I don't know. It seems to be getting complicated." She tensed as another group entered the winery, hoping they were legitimate tourists and not locals hoping to lay an ancestry claim to the contents of her cellar.

"I need to make an urgent call. Can you help these people?" she asked. Grabbing her phone she darted through the door at the back of the counter and into the quiet, gloomy storage room. There, in the safety of its cool confines, she quickly called Danilo.

"We need to put a lock on the door immediately," she told him in a low voice as soon as he answered.

"Why have you changed your mind?" Danilo's voice was full of concern.

"Someone just came in the winery and tried to convince me that his great-great-great grandfather worked the land and owned part of the collection." Olivia could hear how frazzled she sounded.

"Mio Dio. This is serious. I will go and purchase a strong lock and chain immediately. Begni said he could come by at three p.m. I will call him and ask if he can make it any earlier."

"I have the afternoon off, so can be there any time. Thanks so much, Danilo."

Olivia felt grateful that her wonderful boyfriend was being such a tower of strength in these trying times. She felt exposed, as if everyone who knew about this was going to use their heritage and history in the area, and her complete lack of it, to lay claim to the cellar's contents.

She had the uneasy certainty that this was going to turn into a full-blown war.

CHAPTER TWELVE

Shortly before two p.m., Olivia hurried through her farm's gateway. Danilo had managed to move the appraisal forward, and she felt grateful that the expert would soon be arriving.

In fact, Begni might be there already. An unfamiliar car was parked behind her Fiat.

"Look, Erba," Olivia said, hope filling her as her goat headed for the shady area behind the barn where she loved to nestle in the afternoons.

Olivia rushed up to the farmhouse.

Her mother met her as she opened the front door. As usual, Mrs. Glass was impeccably coiffed and dressed in a stylish blue jacket.

"Ah, angel. I'm very glad I smartened myself up after lunch, as we have a surprise visitor."

"The assessor?" Olivia confirmed with a smile.

"No, no. He's arriving only at two-thirty, your very polite and likeable friend Daniel told me. This gentleman drove in half an hour ago and said he needed to speak to you urgently. I made him coffee, and he is in the kitchen now."

It couldn't be, Olivia thought. Not another one?

Warily, she paced through.

"Signorina!" The suave man with gelled-back hair who had been sitting at the kitchen table got up, brushing crumbs off his lapels.

Crumbs of the Torta Paradiso cake that she'd been saving for dessert tonight, Olivia noted, feeling stressed. She hoped there was enough of it left.

"Buongiorno," she said without enthusiasm. Then she switched to English. Whatever this man said, she felt it was better if her mother also heard. "How can I help you?"

"Signorina, signorina. I am Heberto Zacconi." Moving closer, the man clasped her left hand in both his cold, damp ones. "I traveled here to find you today for a very important reason."

"And that might be?" As politely as she could, Olivia extricated her fingers from his clingy grasp.

"What a story it is! A story that begins many generations ago. You see, at one time, this magnificent farm which you have tended so lovingly was between owners. It was an abandoned piece of land with nobody living on it."

"Really?" Mrs. Glass asked from behind him. The man jumped, as if he'd been so focused on Olivia that he'd forgotten she was there.

"Yes, really," he said, regaining his silken calmness. Resuming his hawk-like eye contact with Olivia, he continued.

"While it was abandoned, signorina, my family was in need of a safe place to store a very fine and valuable collection of wines. They could not keep them on their farm. You understand how things were then? The political situation in those years was too volatile, as I am sure you know."

"In which years?" Olivia asked, deciding to take a leaf out of the Jean-Pierre questioning manual.

"In those years," the man emphasized with a frown. "Unfortunately, after constructing the secret cellar, my family then experienced some difficulties and had to leave the area. They were not able to return to Tuscany, and in fact to our original home town of Collina, for decades. By then everyone had forgotten where these fine and ancient wines, our family's most precious heritage, were buried. And now, by a stroke of sheer good fortune, you have unearthed them! Signorina, I am forever in your debt. Figuratively speaking, of course. It is not only the value of the wines." His eyes gleamed as he spoke the words. "It is the historical significance they have for our family. The vast, life-changing amount of money which we will be very grateful to receive, is not as important as knowing that the circle is complete, and treasures that my ancestors were forced to abandon are returned to us again. Are you able to open the cellar so that I may take my first look at my family's heritage?"

He took a deep breath, looking satisfied with himself.

Olivia was seething inwardly at the audacity of this fake claim. Despite his elaborate story, his motives were rooted in shallow greed, she realized angrily.

"No, I'm not able to open it," she snapped, but Mrs. Glass held up a warning hand.

"Angel, don't be too hasty. You don't want to be rude to foreigners. Andrew drummed that into me before my flight. If this man made a special trip to speak to you, he clearly believes that his family does have a claim. Surely it would be the gracious thing to do, to let him take a look inside?"

Smiling winningly, Heberto turned to Mrs. Glass.

"Why thank you, signora. Can we unlock it straight away?"

"No!" Olivia cried in a panic. She didn't want this awful opportunist knowing exactly where the treasure was. But it was too late for that, she realized, as her mother spoke again.

"I already took him to the field and showed him the door and he recognized it was made from his family's wood. It was locked, though, so I couldn't let him inside. Do you have a key?"

His family's wood? Olivia clutched her forehead. Her temples were pounding.

At that moment, she heard voices outside and the front door rattled.

"Buongiorno! Olivia, are you home?"

It was Danilo's voice. Not a moment too soon, the cavalry had arrived.

She rushed to the hallway, and into Danilo's arms.

"There's a man in the kitchen trying to lay claim to the wines. My mother believed his story. Please help," she whispered in his ear as she hugged him.

Releasing her, Danilo marched through to the kitchen.

"Signor, I am afraid you must leave immediately. This farm is private property and we are now busy in a meeting."

"But I have come to claim my heritage!" the man protested, waving his arms angrily.

"Claim it some other time." With a firm hand on his shoulder, Danilo propelled him to the door. "Off you go. Ciao."

"Goodbye, Mr. Zacconi! It was lovely meeting you," Mrs. Glass called, obviously still trying her best to be polite to foreigners even when they'd been outed as opportunists and were being evicted.

Danilo headed outside, intent on making sure the damp-palmed fortune hunter really did leave, and Olivia greeted Begni, the antique wine expert.

She was thrilled to see the gray-haired man, looking dapper in his well-cut suit.

"It's wonderful to see you again, and so kind of you to assess this at such short notice."

"It is an exciting time for all of us," Begni agreed. "The sooner I can have a look and give you an approximate value, the better."

"This is my mother, Anthea Glass." Olivia made the introductions, hoping that Begni's charm would help her mother forget the recent unfortunate incident with Heberto.

"A pleasure to meet you." Bowing his head, Begni chivalrously clasped her mother's hand. Glancing at her pleased face, Olivia felt relieved.

Danilo stuck his head back in the door.

"Our guest has left. Shall we head to the field?" He dug in his pocket and produced a large, solid key.

As they walked, Danilo updated Olivia.

"I bought the strongest chain and lock I could find, but I still feel worried about security. I wish I could stand guard over the door overnight."

"I feel the same," Olivia confessed. "You can stay here, though. Would you stay over tonight? I'd feel so much safer. Plus, I'm missing you."

Danilo squeezed her hand. "Me too. What will your mother say, though?"

"She seems to like you, Daniel," Olivia giggled. "In any case, it's time she knows the truth. At least we've broken it to her gently and in stages."

"Well, then, I will be glad to stay over," Danilo said, sounding relieved.

Letting go of her hand, he jogged ahead to the almost-hidden door. A moment later, metal clanked and jangled as he removed the chain.

Olivia heard Begni exclaim in amazement as Danilo lifted the wooden door open.

"Mio Dio. Truly a hidden cellar," he observed.

"The stairs are steep but solid. Let me give you a hand," Danilo said, stepping onto the first stair and holding out his arm.

"I'll take your bag," Olivia offered.

"Thank you," Begni smiled.

Olivia was surprised at the heaviness of the bag when he handed it to her. She followed the two men into the cellar, guided by the beam of Danilo's flashlight, treading carefully on the wooden stairs.

"Ouch," she said, as she reached the bottom and stubbed her toe on a small rock. Where had that come from, she wondered. Perhaps they hadn't noticed it yesterday in all the excitement.

Begni unzipped his bag and removed the tools of his trade. Powerful halogen lights, chamois leather cloths, dusters, tongs, a camera, and even a magnifying glass were all nestled in the bag.

"What a place," the expert said in a hushed voice. "Most definitely, this is indeed the legendary cellar that has been rumored to exist. How extraordinary that it was here on your farm. Had you not figured out the clues to its whereabouts, it might never have been discovered at all."

Olivia shivered at the thought, feeling goosebumps tingle her spine.

She moved out of the way and stood next to Danilo near the big wine barrels, breathing in the musty air which she now realized carried a faint tinge of vintage wine. Begni worked carefully and methodically, humming to himself as he jotted his findings into a small notebook. Olivia saw he was doing a sketch of the cellar, and she guessed an approximate count of the bottles.

How many were there, she wondered. She estimated a few hundred. Were there any hidden gems? They looked to be very old and Olivia knew that in terms of age, that meant they would most likely not be drinkable. But perhaps some had historic value, she hoped. At any rate, she was sure Begni would be thrilled to see the intact bottle made from the same glass he'd identified a splinter of.

Working on different areas of the cellar, they watched in silence as Begni picked a bottle carefully up, dusted it off, read its label, photographed it, and then repeated the process again.

Well, almost in silence. Danilo sneezed loudly. A small chunk of concrete fell from the roof.

"Bless you," Olivia said.

"Sorry," Danilo murmured.

Begni was so focused on his task he seemed not to hear at all. He continued with the slow, absorbing process. Olivia watched, fascinated, as he moved to the next section and examined a bottle from low down on the shelves and then one from higher up. He then made his way across the room where he picked up and cleaned off two bottles on the opposite side.

Finally, he let out a sigh, dusted his hands off, and said, "We are done. I have seen enough to get a good idea of the total collection. Let's talk when we are in the open air again."

Olivia rushed over to help him pack up his tools. The cellar had seemed like a bright and cheery, if dusty, place thanks to the intense lights. As they were turned off, the shadows rushed back in and she blinked in the sudden darkness.

She grabbed the bag and headed up the ladder first, with Danilo assisting the expert up the rough wooden stairs.

"What do you think?" she asked eagerly, when they were back in the fresh air and bright daylight.

Begni sighed sorrowfully.

“I am afraid I have some bad news for you,” he said.

CHAPTER THIRTEEN

Olivia's heart plummeted. She exchanged an appalled glance with Danilo. All her hopes and dreams shattered around her. That was all it was. A cellar full of worthless junk. At least it wouldn't matter who ended up claiming it, she thought sadly.

"How do you mean, bad news?" Danilo asked Begni.

The expert stared at them, his face serious.

"The cellar is structurally unstable. That roof in particular is extremely dangerous. I am sure moving the boulders exacerbated the weaknesses. The whole building could cave in at any time and that places on you an extreme need for haste."

"Oh, goodness!" Olivia said.

"You need to move the entire content out as soon as you can."

"So it has value?" Olivia asked. Begni seemed to be implying that it did, if the wine was worth moving.

Now his face broke into a broad smile. "I was not able to assess every bottle. To do that will take a few days. But from examining a selection throughout the shelves, I can tell you confidently that your wine is worth a fortune. A fortune! Most of the bottles look to be from the eighteenth century, and will be highly sought-after by collectors. Good quality bottles from that era are extremely rare. A few are older than that, and others more recent, from the nineteenth century. The historic glass wine vessel is, of course, the most ancient treasure in the collection and the most valuable. That item alone could set a new record for wine at an auction, as it is still sealed and has most of its liquid inside. The sale of that bottle will make world headlines, I am certain. There are a few others from the same era which might be almost as unique and valuable. I will need to research them to be sure."

Olivia felt speechless as Begni continued. Beside her, Danilo gasped in amazement.

"A real fortune?" her mother asked curiously. "How much of a real fortune do you mean?"

Begni explained further. "All bottles that I examined are impeccably preserved which will contribute to their value. Similar historic bottles have sold successfully at auction at around the twenty-thousand dollar mark per item, but I noted numerous gems from famous wineries that will be worth far more."

Olivia couldn't believe what she was hearing. She had no idea that the wine was that ancient, or that valuable. Were collectors really prepared to pay such vast sums to acquire a piece of winemaking history? It seemed they were.

She felt dizzy with excitement, and with anxiety, because from what Begni was implying, the entire cellar could collapse at any moment. Then her valuable wine would be nothing more than a heap of broken glass.

"I will move it first thing tomorrow," Olivia resolved.

"I will give you the name of a company who can help. If you want, I will be in attendance also, to record every item that is removed. We are living through winemaking history with this find," he smiled. "When I get back to my office, I will do some research and see what I can find about the farm's original owners. What happened to them after they collected, and then hid, such a remarkable selection of wines? It is fascinating, no?"

"It is," Olivia agreed. "I can't thank you enough for doing this assessment. And yes, please, will you oversee their removal and the full valuation?"

Begni shook her hand.

"Congratulations, Signora Glass," he told her formally. "Thanks to this find, your life is about to change."

Although Olivia was sure he meant nothing but good by the words, she couldn't help feeling a chill of apprehension as he spoke them.

*

Walking through the doors of the up-market and expensive Trattoria del Lucco, Olivia gazed in admiration at the colorful expressionism art displayed on the walls. In the hushed, white-tablecloth environment, she picked up on the muted voices and laughter of the well-dressed patrons.

The rich, sumptuous aroma of fine food wafted to meet them.

"I've wanted to come here for ages," Olivia whispered to Danilo as the maître-d rushed to greet them.

"It's lucky we got a booking," Danilo whispered back. "They said there was a last-minute cancelation, otherwise we wouldn't have been able to get a table for months."

“Well, we deserve to celebrate,” Charlotte added.

Olivia was pleased to see her mother gazing around the restaurant admiringly as they were shown to their table.

“A specialist seafood restaurant?” her mother then asked with a questioning note in her voice.

“It’s one of the best in Italy,” Olivia said quickly, before she could make any ill-advised comments on whether seafood was safe to eat in this part of the world. She sensed that a question like this was literally burning on her mother’s tongue!

Fortunately, in the bustle of being seated, the opportunity passed.

“I already know what I’m going to have. The crab cakes and the lobster tail.” Olivia said. “A while ago, people were raving about those dishes at the winery.”

“I need to peruse the menu,” Mrs. Glass said, as the waiter poured them a fragrant sauvignon blanc.

Since Olivia had a seat facing the room, she took a moment to look around the restaurant. How beautiful it was. The artworks on the wall opposite were magnificent. She adored expressionism, and stared in awe at the large, quirky collage of playing cards and padlocks that drew her eye. But as she admired it, something else snagged her attention. The people at the table nearby were pointing at her and whispering. They stopped as soon as they saw her staring.

“Buongiorno,” one of them said, sounding embarrassed.

“Can I switch seats with you?” Olivia murmured to Charlotte, deciding it would be better to sit with her back to the room.

“Sure. Why?”

Olivia bit her lip. She didn’t want to spoil the party, but she did want to get herself out of view of any other patrons. Even though she feared it was already too late.

Around the entire restaurant, people were staring, and then quickly dropping their gaze when she looked their way. Word had traveled like wildfire.

“I want to look at the art on the other wall,” Olivia said, hoping this would sound plausible. It didn’t. Charlotte gave her a deeply cynical look, as if she was hoping Olivia would blurt out the truth.

“Well, I’ll watch all the people who are looking at you, the new local celebrity” she said meaningfully, and Olivia sighed. No detail escaped her eagle-eyed bestie.

"How lovely to treat ourselves to this fancy meal. It's very expensive here! Exactly how much would you say these wines you found are worth?" Mrs. Glass said in her customary piercing tone.

With her face flaming, Olivia glanced around to see several people staring at her, listening eagerly for the answer.

"Not very much," she said loudly.

Danilo, sitting beside her, was staring at her as if she was mad.

"People are listening," Olivia whispered, and saw understanding dawn. Danilo swiveled around and glared.

Everyone hurriedly turned their attention back to their food.

The waiter arrived with bread and dips, and they placed their orders. Olivia tore off a chunk of the complimentary ciabatta and dunked it in a bowl of olive oil and balsamic vinegar. She bit into it, enjoying the mellow, pungent vinegar tang and the rich, almost sweet oil. How delicious!

"Are you keen to do any sightseeing tomorrow?" Charlotte asked her mother. "I'm seeing Artoro for breakfast. His shift starts at noon and he'll be working till late. So I'm getting quality time in with him at the start of the day, but then I'm free."

"We can discuss it tomorrow. I hope you're enjoying your vacation romance," Mrs. Glass smiled. "I can't help thinking that Olivia should get together with Daniel here. I might be speaking out of turn, but I think he really seems to like you, angel. You treat him very coldly."

Olivia felt stunned that her strategy had worked! Thanks to him being introduced as 'a friend,' her mother was foaming at the mouth to micromanage her romantic life. She could tell Danilo was delighted with this curveball, and was battling to hold back an astounded laugh. Even Charlotte's eyes were popping out of her head as she tried to control her guffaws.

"Actually, I'm growing very fond of Danilo," Olivia admitted.

"Oh, how wonderful you've come to your senses – in that area at least!" Mrs. Glass enthused.

Luckily, at that moment, the food arrived. Olivia was relieved, because she knew her mother would have gone on to discuss returning to the States. Quite how that was supposed to fit in with having a romance with someone she'd been 'treating coldly,' she wasn't sure. Logic was not always her mother's strong point when trying to control Olivia's behavior.

"This is delicious. What a triumph." Charlotte dug her fork into the rich, steamy, seafood risotto she'd ordered.

"I can see why this restaurant has such a great reputation," Olivia agreed appreciatively.

Only her mother remained unconvinced. "I'm not sure why Italian chefs have to put so much garlic into the food," she complained.

Despite her criticism, Olivia noted that she ate the dish with relish. If only she'd loosen up, enjoy her vacation, and abandon her mission, she wished.

The lobster tail was perfectly cooked and rich with garlic butter. Enjoying every scrumptious mouthful, Olivia couldn't help a sneaky thought that if everything went well with the secret cellar stash, she'd be able to dine here more often, instead of treating it as a once in a lifetime experience.

Just as she'd swallowed the last delicious morsel, she felt a tap on her shoulder.

She turned, surprised, and found herself staring into the wide, earnest eyes of one of the diners who'd been sitting two tables away.

"Signora, buona sera and good evening," he greeted her. "Perhaps you recognize me."

"From when we walked in?" Olivia asked, surprised. She certainly didn't remember the round-faced man, who looked to be in his forties, from anywhere else.

"No, no." The man laughed heartily. "I was hoping you might have noticed the family resemblance. I am Raul Porzio, the nephew of Gina, who originally sold you the farm."

"Oh, yes," Olivia said warily. There was absolutely no family resemblance whatsoever between that colorful elderly lady and this shifty, hopeful-looking man. Her heart plummeted as she realized why he was here. He was another fortune hunter. There was nowhere they were immune, not even in a top class restaurant.

This confrontation was going to cause a public scene, Olivia realized, her heart sinking. There would be absolutely no way to avoid it.

CHAPTER FOURTEEN

Raul continued blithely with his story, seemingly unconcerned about confronting Olivia in public. Or maybe he was doing it purposely, and it was part of his plan, she wondered suddenly, as he spoke.

"My family has a long history with your farm. Very long!" He gestured dramatically. "For decades, we loved and nurtured it. I myself remember many happy childhood days there."

Olivia sensed that smoke was coming out of Raul's ears as he battled to embellish his fake story and dress it up with untrue facts.

"Yes, indeed, I remember walking among the fields and eating many meals in the kitchen. Perhaps I even saw the cellar myself while playing hide-and-seek on weekends. It is a distant memory, but I feel it is a clear one, although as an innocent child I did not know what it meant."

Drawing in a sharp breath, Olivia interrupted his made-up musings.

"Signor Porzio, we are having dinner. What do you want?"

She braced herself for the unpleasantness that she knew would follow when he finally got to the point.

"As the previous owners, who cared for the property for so many years, you will naturally understand that our family will be entitled to a share of your treasure, signora?" Raul's eyes gleamed. "Many in Tuscany and in fact, a few in this very restaurant, know for how many years the property thrived in our hands. The loving care that we bestowed on it over many generations cannot be ignored. We kept the cellar safe."

Olivia heard a murmur of surprise from the listening guests. Anger surged inside her. This was the last straw! She couldn't take another word of his public lies.

"Your story is totally false!" she exclaimed.

"What?" Raul asked, sounding affronted.

There were gasps from behind her as the nearby diners heard the words. To make sure they didn't miss any, Olivia raised her voice.

"Your aunt told me, in person, that she hardly ever visited the farm and had inherited it from a distant cousin that she barely knew, who bought it from a friend," she snapped. "The place was an absolute dump when I took it over. The barn was full of rubble, everything was overgrown, the bathroom walls were peeling, and we must have removed a hundred spiders from inside. A hundred! And some of them were enormous! The place was covered in webs." Olivia shuddered at the memory.

She was aware that the restaurant had fallen silent and knew that all eyes were on her as the other patrons took in this gossip-worthy confrontation.

Raul blinked rapidly and took a step back, clearly thrown by the fact she wasn't a pushover. He opened and closed his mouth, but she guessed he was at a loss for words after her angry rebuttal of his claim and her eyewitness account of the farm's neglect.

Danilo sprang to his feet, clearly even angrier.

"How can you interrupt our private dinner with a nonexistent claim to the wines? Is this what greed does? Is this how it corrupts? I have had enough of this! Let us leave."

Olivia got up.

"I agree. Let's go." She felt distraught that their fancy outing had ended so badly. There was nowhere they could be anonymous anymore. Perhaps her mother was right, and she'd never be accepted in the community. Especially not now, with everyone trying to muscle in and say that the farm, or the wine, was theirs.

Charlotte relinquished the dessert menu with some reluctance.

"The tiramisu cheesecake looks delicious. We can always come back, I guess," she said.

Olivia detoured to the front desk and quickly paid, seething over the fact that a dinner which was meant to be such a wonderful treat, had ended this way. Then she joined the others in the car.

*

When they arrived home, Olivia felt her heart sink even further. There was another car waiting! Bright headlights blinded them. Beyond them, she could dimly see two figures.

She felt overwhelmed with dread. Her farm, her home, had become public property in the space of a day.

"Who could this be?" she asked apprehensively.

"Vai all'inferno!" Danilo groaned. "Another claimant? We are going to get no peace until these wines are sold."

"What a strange town you live in," Mrs. Glass observed. "People are very rude here. They have no sense of personal decorum. So unlike New York!"

With a sigh, Olivia climbed out of the car. Danilo walked shoulder to shoulder with her as she approached the waiting vehicle. Her stomach was doing flip-flops. She felt very glad of her boyfriend's protective presence beside her.

As they neared the car, her dread changed to astonishment.

These were police. The car was equipped with blue lights, even though they were turned off, and the two constables were smartly dressed in uniform.

"Buona sera. Has something happened?" Olivia asked the officers, feeling taut with nerves. Had she somehow gotten into trouble with the law?

The taller of the two stepped forward as a walkie-talkie crackled from within the car.

"Are you Signora Olivia Glass?" he asked.

Olivia swallowed hard. "Yes, I am," she said.

"We have received an official claim to certain contents of your farm, from a Signor Heberto Zacconi."

"He was here earlier today!" Olivia exclaimed in outrage. This was the smarmy man who Danilo had chased out of her kitchen.

"Yes. He says that the contents of the cellar on your land belong to his family. Furthermore, he states that you knew about the cellar already before buying the farm, and that was your reason for buying it. He declares that you simply waited for some time to pass before excavating the site."

"I did no such thing!" Olivia declared angrily.

"Why did you buy the farm, signora?" the other police officer asked.

"I was staying nearby on vacation. I went for a walk and saw it was for sale and liked it. I decided it would allow me to follow my dream and become a wine farmer."

Olivia realized her reason sounded flimsy, but she had bought it on a whim. It wasn't her fault she'd fallen in love with it.

"Is that so?" The policeman didn't seem convinced. Olivia couldn't blame him.

Danilo stepped forward, his voice quivering with outrage. "Surely you can see this is a false claim? These are opportunists, who hear about a fortune and try to take it for themselves. Olivia is being hounded by them!"

The taller policeman nodded. "Yes, I agree the gentleman's story seems to be without real merit."

"Can you please tell him so?" Olivia begged. Surely the police were busy and couldn't afford to pursue this frivolous waste of time?

"Signora, the problem is that this claimant has lodged a case with the courts," the tall officer told her in sorrowful tones.

"He's done what?" Olivia felt stunned by the latest horrific development. This was a disaster.

"He has lodged an official case. Unfortunately, even if it is without merit, he has the right for it to be heard, and our legal system must do its work."

"But that could take months!" Olivia gasped. "I'm the innocent party here. Why can't you protect me?"

"Signora, we are protecting you. The gentleman wanted us to break the lock and give him immediate access to the cellar so that he could view the contents and begin evaluating them. We refused to do that and have stated that he may not enter your property until the court case is finalized. Hopefully, if you can prove your side, the judge will believe your account and rule in your favor."

"What if he appeals?" Olivia asked faintly. This could take longer than months. It might take years. It could drag on indefinitely. Suddenly, returning to New York seemed like an attractive prospect compared to the lake of piranhas that Tuscany had become.

The police exchanged a glance.

"It is not likely, signora. We hope this matter will be resolved soon. In the meantime, nobody may access the cellar," the policeman said firmly. "We will deliver the court papers in due course."

They climbed back into the car and drove off. Olivia looked at Danilo and saw her own desperation reflected in his eyes.

"We were going to move the wines tomorrow," she lamented, wishing that she'd taken the bottles out immediately.

"It is massively unfair," Danilo agreed through gritted teeth.

What if this is just the start, and other people go ahead with lawsuits?" Olivia asked. "It might take months and months for everything to be concluded. And what if the judge rules against me for some crazy reason?"

“What if the cellar collapses?” Danilo asked in soft, worried tones and Olivia’s stomach did a sickening flip-flop as she remembered about its structural instability.

Until that moment, she hadn’t thought of the most dreadful scenario of all. How could she redeem this terrible situation, and save her wine before the entire stash was destroyed?

CHAPTER FIFTEEN

"At least you got my mother's official seal of approval," Olivia whispered to Danilo. They lay side by side in her darkened bedroom. Olivia had never felt more wide awake in her life. If only she could see a way out of this crazy mess. Since there wasn't, finding refuge in humor seemed the next best thing.

"She seemed pleased that Daniel was sleeping over at last," Danilo agreed. "I see now why you introduced me as a friend. She is a strong-willed woman, much like you! And given that she has doubts about you staying here, it's better she thought it was her idea that we start to date."

Olivia felt surprised that Danilo picked up a family resemblance in their personalities. "I'm sorry she keeps getting your name wrong," she said.

"I am so used to it now that it seems like my real name. I feel confused when people call me Danilo," he joked. "The more time that passes, the more awkward it becomes to correct her," he added ruefully.

"I did try at the start but she wasn't listening." Olivia sighed, feeling overwhelmed by her predicament again. "What are we going to do? Do you know a good lawyer?"

"I have not had need of one myself in recent years. But I know of excellent lawyers that my clients have used. We can make some calls tomorrow," Danilo murmured.

Olivia frowned angrily. It was ridiculous that she was being forced to defend herself when she had been the legitimate owner of the property for close to a year. And excellent lawyers would be expensive. Where would the money come from?

"What's that noise?" she asked, hearing a faint but distinctive rat-a-tat sound from outside.

Danilo sat up in bed, listening. Attuned to her favorite human, so did Pirate, who'd been snoozing at his feet. Danilo climbed out of bed and peered through the window. The cat followed, leaping curiously onto the sill.

"It's your goat," he whispered. "She is charging around. I can hear her squealing, and her hooves on the cobbles."

"She never charges around at night. Let's go and check everything's okay."

Feeling tense at what the commotion might mean, Olivia jumped out of bed and they both dressed in a few seconds. They had been expecting something to happen, she thought. Both of them had left their clothes right beside the bed.

Danilo grabbed a flashlight and they hurried downstairs. He wrenched open the front door and sprang outside, shining the flashlight in the direction of the noise. There was Erba, cantering energetically along.

Olivia let out a shocked cry as she saw Erba veer away to follow a black-clad figure that was running down her driveway at top speed, heading for the gate.

An intruder had been on her property, roaming around in the darkness. She couldn't believe this was happening.

"Stop!" Danilo yelled. Of course, the man didn't stop and only ran faster.

"The cellar!" Danilo sounded panicked. "He must have been there. I'm going to check it!" He sprinted away in the direction of the field.

Olivia turned to follow him, and then decided against it. Whoever this criminal was, they shouldn't get away scot-free.

"I'm going after you," Olivia declared, pointing to the fleeing intruder. She began running as fast as she could in pursuit.

Pounding down her cobbled pathway toward the gate, Olivia knew this was a crazy move. But with adrenaline surging inside her it felt like the most sensible option. Someone was trespassing on her farm, and their actions deserved consequences.

The figure glanced around. In the dim moonlight, Olivia could see it was a man, with short, dark hair. She couldn't make out more than that. Then he veered onto the grass and took off again at a redoubled pace, charging straight through one of her vine plantations.

"Wait!" she shouted, sprinting after him and floundering in the soft, damp soil, but it was too late. He'd vaulted the fence and was on the sand road, pounding down the hill at top speed. As she watched, he darted sideways and disappeared into one of the neighboring fields.

She'd never catch him now. Slowing to a jog, Olivia felt crushed that she'd missed her chance. If only she'd heard him sooner, or run faster, she might have caught up. Then her nerves jangled all over again as she remembered about Danilo.

This man could have been part of a group. Her boyfriend could be in danger. She needed to get to the cellar, as fast as she could.

"Come, Erba," Olivia called breathlessly to her goat.

Wishing she had more speed in her legs, Olivia powered back past the farmhouse. Stumbling in the dark, she followed the cobbled path and then veered off it into the grass, heading for the cellar.

She nearly jumped out of her skin as her goat whizzed past, leaping into the air as she ran.

Following Erba through the darkened field, Olivia approached the cellar. Gasping for air, she slowed as she reached it.

"Danilo?" she called softly. "Are you okay?"

Where was he? She peered into the darkness. There was the cellar door ahead of her, a darker shape in the tussocks of grass. But it was open!

Olivia gasped in shock as she saw the lock, bent and twisted on the ground, and beyond, the silvery tangle of the broken chain. Fear surged inside her as she remembered that the cellar was unstable. What if Danilo had gone in and been crushed?

Moving closer, she was reassured that a gleam of light shone from inside. Olivia scrambled down the steep stairway, hoping to goodness that it was Danilo's flashlight.

There he was, standing with his back to the staircase. Olivia felt massive relief as she saw him, but in an instant her relief turned to dread.

His flashlight was trained on a slumped form at the back of the cellar. As Olivia watched in horrified silence, Danilo cautiously approached the prone man, knelt, and grasped his outflung wrist.

He held it for a minute before standing up again and taking a shaky step back. He turned to Olivia, and she saw his face was sheet-white.

"He's dead," Danilo whispered.

"Dead?" Feeling dizzy with shock, Olivia grabbed Danilo's hand. They stared down at the prone man and for a moment the only sound was their rapid breathing.

"I don't believe it," Danilo whispered. "From the time we first found this treasure, I have been dreading such a thing would occur."

"We'd better call the police," Olivia said, and thinking of that made her feel even worse. They had already had one visit from the law this evening. This was going to land them in terrible trouble.

"I will do so immediately," Danilo agreed in an unsteady voice. He put the flashlight on one of the shelves and took his phone out of his jacket pocket.

Something about the man looked familiar. Grasping the light, even though she felt gooseflesh prickle her limbs at the sight, Olivia trained the beam on his face.

She gasped as she recognized him. That rounded jaw, the slicked-back hair.

This was Heberto, the man who'd been having coffee with her mother when she had come back from work. This was the man who'd made the legal claim against her!

As she realized the implications, the flashlight wobbled in Olivia's unsteady hand. This was going to land her in a world of trouble.

Olivia remembered that her mother had shown Heberto where the cellar was. Then he'd come back again when it was dark and forced his way inside. Why had he done that?

He was half-lying on a flashlight which must have broken as he fell. Her eyes widened as she saw something in the crook of his other arm.

It was a bottle of wine, unbroken.

What had happened down here? Had he also thought the legal case wouldn't succeed, and come back to steal the wine?

Shivering, Olivia looked away from the macabre sight.

"I have called the police. Let's wait out in the open," Danilo said.

Olivia felt relieved to climb the uneven stairs into the open air. Being inside the cellar felt dangerous and threatening in more than one way.

Erba was peering anxiously down at them, and Olivia rubbed her goat's head as she climbed out.

Her probably-pregnant goat! Erba shouldn't be running around at night in her delicate condition. Even so, she'd bravely alerted them to this crime. Erba was a superstar. Olivia couldn't imagine how empty life would be without her friendly, security-conscious orange and white companion.

"Should we walk back to the farmhouse and meet them there?" Olivia suggested.

"I will stay here, just in case," Danilo decided. "You go that way. They should be arriving soon."

Olivia took the flashlight and tramped back the way she had come.

Her mind was whirling with confusion as she followed the pathway. The man who'd opened the legal case had been trying to steal wine. What did it mean and why had he done that?

As she neared the farmhouse, she could see headlights approaching. An unmarked police car and a coroner's van swung through her gateway and parked outside her house.

Through the kitchen window she saw Charlotte, wrapped in a gown, peering anxiously out.

"Is everything okay?" she called.

"No. I'll update you later. The police are here now," Olivia replied, feeing stressed.

Approaching the convoy, she took a deep, anxious breath as the driver's door of the first car opened.

She let the breath out again in a dismayed sigh as her nemesis, Detective Caputi, climbed out and glared at her.

CHAPTER SIXTEEN

Neatly dressed in dark pants and a tailored jacket, with her gleaming gray hair perfectly styled, Detective Caputi looked scarily efficient. Just as Olivia knew she was.

No, Olivia thought. *Why her?*

She stared at the stern police officer, feeling panic surge inside her, as well as a misplaced sense of guilt.

The detective would suspect her of having committed the crime! She already thought Olivia was solely responsible for the murder rate in the wider area.

As she approached Olivia, Caputi's face grew even more forbidding.

"Ever since I heard of the mysterious cellar found on your farm, I was waiting for this to occur," the detective said by way of greeting as her gaze raked Olivia. "Yet again, a serious crime has been committed and I find you on the scene. What is this? What *is* this?" she repeated, sounding exasperated.

"Buona sera, detective," Olivia replied in wobbly tones. At least one of them could maintain the proper formalities.

"It is nearly midnight. Not exactly evening," Caputi replied acidly.

Olivia didn't know how to respond to that, so said nothing. Was the detective ever in a good mood, she wondered. She guessed being dragged out of bed late in the night wasn't going to put anyone in the best frame of mind.

She was going to have to argue convincingly that there had actually been a fleeing man. If only she'd seen his face more clearly. The police believing in that man could make all the difference between Olivia spending the night in a prison cell, or in her own comfortable bed.

Finding the fleeing man would absolve her completely. Perhaps, by a miracle, the police would be able to track him down and arrest him.

The detective snapped out instructions to the two officers accompanying her, as the coroner and his assistant assembled the wheeled stretcher.

"Show us to the scene," she demanded.

Olivia headed back the way she had come, her spine prickling as she heard the tramp of footsteps and the ominous rattle of the stretcher's wheels on the cobblestones behind her.

Danilo walked over to join her. "Everything is quiet. I have seen nobody else," he whispered.

As the convoy of police and medics approached the cellar, she heard incredulous murmurs from behind her. Detective Caputi marched to the entrance and peered inside, shining her powerful flashlight down the stairs.

Even she let out a huff of surprise. Recovering fast, she barked out commands in Italian, so rapidly that Olivia heard some, but not all of them. She was ordering her team to go down slowly, to work carefully, to record and photograph all their findings as there was a legal case involved.

Clearly, the scary Caputi was fully up to speed with developments.

"Be careful. We've been told it's unstable and might collapse at any time," Olivia called, as Detective Caputi led the way down.

"Noted," the detective called, undeterred as she descended into the depths. There, she began barking out instructions in a loud and resounding voice as the crew followed her down. She heard more gasps as they descended into the otherworldly space.

Olivia hoped they would work carefully! What if they knocked over some of the bottles, or damaged the cellar so that it collapsed? She felt anxious about having so many strangers moving among the fragile and ancient wines.

Although she was the first one down the ladder, Detective Caputi didn't spend much time in the underground cellar. Once she'd briefed her team, she climbed up again and headed straight for Olivia.

Thrusting a tape recorder in Olivia's direction, she snapped, "I will interview you now. Explain your version of tonight's events."

Even by Caputi's standards, this was brusque. Olivia guessed she was short staffed, and shorter tempered, having been dragged out to rural Tuscany at such an inhospitable hour.

"Heberto Zacconi, the deceased, was one of three people who approached me today. Each one of them had a trumped-up, ridiculous story. He went a step further and actually embarked on a lawsuit. I was feeling upset and worried about the whole situation. Even though we'd locked the cellar, I couldn't sleep. Nor could my boyfriend Danilo. We were both lying awake."

As she spoke, a terrible possibility occurred to Olivia. It made her blood run cold and she almost choked on her words.

She'd run after the shadowy figure. Danilo had been the first to reach the cellar, and he'd arrived alone. The police might suspect him, if they found out exactly what had happened.

Olivia swallowed, feeling intensely nervous at the challenge that lay ahead. She couldn't risk Danilo being arrested now. She owed him!

"We went out and saw a figure running down the driveway, heading for the gate. Danilo shouted to him to stop, but of course he ignored him," Olivia explained. "All I could see was that it was a man, with short, dark hair. He ran fast, so someone who was reasonably fit."

"Go on?" The detective had a look in her eye that told Olivia she thought this random running man sounded very convenient. She hadn't even gotten to the riskiest part of her version and already she could sense she was being doubted.

With her stomach churning, Olivia proceeded with her nearly-true account.

"We headed for the cellar, to check it was still secure, but the lock was broken. Danilo and I went inside, where we discovered the body and realized to our shock that we knew him."

She sensed Danilo stare at her in surprise and hoped he understood why she was tweaking the timeline of events.

Detective Caputi paused. Would she accept this version? Olivia held her breath, waiting for her to reply.

"When did the deceased man, Signor Zacconi, approach you?" she questioned. "How did he know where the cellar was? It is rather remote, is it not? Difficult to find in the dark."

"I arrived back from work after lunch yesterday, and he was in the kitchen telling a story that the wine belonged to his family. My mother had given him coffee and had unfortunately shown him where the cellar was," Olivia explained. "She's very naive and doesn't understand how complex the situation is."

Detective Caputi gave her a piercing look, that clearly said she thought Olivia's mother wasn't the only one of the family who battled to grasp a situation properly.

Turning, she jabbed the tape recorder in Danilo's direction, ready to subject him to the same forceful questioning.

As they spoke, Olivia sidled over to the cellar and glanced down.

The team below were very busy. The cellar was lit up in a halogen blaze that reminded her of the happier time when Begni had arrived to value the contents. She could hear them speaking in low tones but wasn't sure what they were saying. Then, she jumped back as one of the team started climbing the steep stairway.

"Detective?" the young man called.

Caputi hurried over and Olivia shrank back out of the way.

"The deceased suffered a head injury. Undoubtedly it was caused by the jagged rock lying near him. There are traces of blood on the rock, which is approximately the same size as a large cantaloupe. He was hit with it, hard enough to pass away instantly," the officer confided his findings.

"Hit with a rock?" Detective Caputi repeated.

She swung around and stared at Olivia, who could tell what she was thinking, that she had been defending her own treasure.

"It wasn't me," Olivia said, feeling edgy. Oddly, she realized this was the exact way she felt when speaking to her mother. Who would have thought that Mrs. Glass and Caputi were twin souls!

"We have finished interviewing you both – for now," Caputi added, after just enough of a pause to make Olivia hope she might be off the hook. "You may not access the cellar until the investigation is concluded. It is a crime scene and will be treated accordingly."

"I understand," Olivia said humbly.

"We will need to speak to you again, probably tomorrow. Do not leave town. Remain contactable. And do not interfere with police business," Caputi warned her sternly.

At least she wasn't arresting her on the spot. Hopefully she had believed Olivia's true account of the running man. Feeling frazzled, Olivia walked over to Danilo and the two of them headed back to the farmhouse.

"I need to tell Charlotte what happened," Olivia whispered as they reached the front door.

"I will try and go back to sleep," Danilo said.

Charlotte was waiting anxiously in the kitchen. She'd made hot chocolate and had cut Olivia a slice of cake. How wonderful to have a bestie who understood the need for carbs and sugar at critical times, Olivia thought, sinking gratefully onto a chair and digging in.

"What happened? Did someone break into the cellar?"

"Yes. The man who was here earlier. He was lying inside, dead."

Charlotte gasped, shoveling more sugar into her hot chocolate.

"Olivia, that's terrible! Dead how?"

"Hit over the head with a rock."

Charlotte frowned. “I thought I heard someone run past the study window earlier. Then I wondered if I’d been wrong and just heard your goat. Now, I’m wondering, could that have been the killer? Did you see anything? I think you woke up as well.”

“Yes. I saw him escaping. I tried to run after him but he was too fast.” Olivia dug into her cake.

“Olivia! You could have been hurt! What if he’d hit you, too?” Charlotte spluttered.

“He was too busy getting away.”

Charlotte shook her head. “You were lucky. Next time, call the police straight away. If he killed once, he could easily have done so again.”

“I’m hoping there won’t be a next time,” Olivia said. “In any case, we may have lost our chance at this one. He got away in the dead of night and nobody has a clue who he is. It was too dark to make anything out. He could never be found, and a crime investigation might take even longer than a lawsuit.”

Olivia drained her chocolate, feeling jittery with nerves.

“The killer ran away, the police have told us not to interfere, and worst of all, the cellar could collapse at any time! Imagine if the wine is destroyed, just as a result of everyone’s greed?”

She saw her own horror reflected in her bestie’s eyes.

“Let’s see what tomorrow brings,” Charlotte soothed. “Perhaps we’ll wake up to find out that they caught the killer, or that he turned himself in.”

Olivia felt differently.

She worried that she would be woken by the blare of sirens as Detective Caputi arrived to arrest her – or, worse still, the earthquake-like rumble that signaled the cellar roof had caved in.

CHAPTER SEVENTEEN

The next morning, it was her mother's cheery voice that dragged Olivia out of her troubled slumber.

"Where are the two sleepyheads? Wake up, Olivia and Daniel! Coffee's brewing!"

She jumped upright. It was morning. The sun was shining far too cheerfully through her window, and the smell of coffee filled the house.

The events of the past few hours whirled through her mind and she closed her eyes briefly. What a disastrous night it had been. An intruder had been killed, the prime suspect had run away, and the police had sealed the cellar.

Olivia felt like scrambling back into bed and pulling the covers over her head. What fresh horrors would today bring? She didn't feel ready for it. She didn't even want to walk downstairs and face her mother, but that had to be done.

Danilo leaned over and gave Olivia a warm hug.

"Whatever happens, we will get through it," he said supportively.

Danilo went to have a shower and Olivia headed downstairs.

"Goodness, I slept well last night, despite being in a foreign country. I think Charlotte's still fast asleep, too. Did you rest well, angel?" Mrs. Glass said, pouring coffee.

Olivia took a closer look at her mother. Was she joking? Or had she seriously slept through the entire commotion?

She didn't seem to be joking.

"We had a disturbed night. Someone was killed last night after breaking into the cellar. It was Heberto, the person that you made coffee for."

Mrs. Glass spun around, looking aghast.

"Killed? You mean, killed as in he fell down the stairs? Or was he actually murdered?" she asked in a hushed voice.

"Murdered," Olivia replied in the same hushed tone, feeling shivers course through her as she remembered the chilling sight.

"Sweetheart, this is shocking!" Abandoning her coffee making, Mrs. Glass slumped onto a chair, closing her eyes briefly. "Never did I imagine my own daughter would be caught up in such violence after her rash decision to move to Italy. You could have been in serious danger. Thank goodness you are unhurt. I'm not sure how I'll break this to Andrew. He'll want me to return home at once." Opening her eyes, and sounding more practical, she continued, "Why didn't you wake me, angel? I'm sure I could have been helpful."

Olivia wasn't so sure. Her mother sleeping through was the only thing that had gone right last night. She decided on a diplomatic answer.

"We were at the cellar when we found out what had happened."

"So someone killed him in the cellar, and then ran away?"

"Yes. I chased the killer, but didn't catch him." Olivia stirred sugar into her coffee, feeling a sense of unreality at doing such a normal action after the craziness of the night.

"Good heavens," her mother said faintly. "Chasing after a murderer in the middle of the night? Honey, I know I seem to be repeating myself, but this wouldn't happen back in New York!"

"I was never in any danger," Olivia replied, feeling defensive.

"Why was he in the cellar if he had staked a legal claim to it?" her mother wondered aloud. "I am beginning to think that the claim might not have been totally legitimate."

"I'm certain it was fraudulent," Olivia agreed.

As she sipped the coffee, Olivia couldn't help thinking about her mother's question. It was a good one. Why had Heberto decided to break into the cellar?

Olivia's best guess was that he'd wanted to familiarize himself with the contents so that he could back up his claim with mentions of the exact wines that had been supposedly owned by his family. Perhaps that was also why he'd stolen a bottle. So that he could claim it had been 'in his possession' all along?

But a missing bottle from the wine cellar would raise alarms. If he claimed that the bottle was his, it would only point more strongly to theft. It was a mystery.

Perhaps he hadn't been thinking clearly. It seemed that the contents of the cellar were making a lot of people lose their minds.

Olivia was mulling over that fact as Danilo came downstairs.

"Good morning, Mrs. G.," he greeted her mom solemnly.

"Oh, Daniel! Olivia's just told me what a terrible time you had last night, with a break-in and a murder. Are you going to be around today? Charlotte and I will need protection. I feel very unsafe in this strange country, after this terrible incident."

"Yes, I will stay here today," Danilo promised.

"What about your work?" Olivia asked, anxious about Danilo getting behind on his orders. His stunning handmade furnishings were becoming more and more popular.

"The set of tables I am working on now are still in the planning stages. I can perfect the designs online and price the wood and fixtures," he reassured her.

Olivia felt a surge of gratitude toward him. He was being a pillar of strength.

"I'm going to get ready for work. I shouldn't be back too late," she promised.

She headed upstairs, showered and changed, and then set off for the winery, with Erba following obediently behind. Her goat seemed tired after the exciting events of last night, Olivia thought, and then wondered with a clench of her stomach whether she was tired due to her pregnancy progressing.

She didn't look *that* fat, Olivia thought.

But she did look fat.

As she walked, she started planning her day at the winery. First, she'd have to tell Marcello what had happened. He'd know how to handle the situation.

She felt like the pariah of La Leggenda, with trouble following at every turn.

Power-walking down the driveway, Olivia felt impatient to get this uncomfortable tete-a-tete over with. Heading straight into the tasting room, she made a beeline for Marcello's office, relieved to see that he was already hard at work, his dark head bent over his leather-bound diary.

"Buongiorno," she greeted him.

"Buongiorno, Olivia." She could see concern in his eyes. Most probably, despite all her efforts to appear calm, she looked as upset and rattled as she felt.

"I've got some shocking news," she said, gathering her courage to spill it out.

To her surprise, Marcello gestured to the chair opposite.

"Sit down. The news, I know already. I was phoned very early this morning by a friend. Three friends, in fact."

At that moment, his cellphone started ringing. He glanced at the screen, sighed, and declined the call.

"Make that four friends," he said, sounding resigned. Pushing a lock of hair away from his face, he stared at Olivia with deep concern.

She sat down. Her mouth felt dry.

"What did the friends say?" she asked.

"They said that there was a break-in at the cellar on your farm, and that the man who attempted to steal the contents of the cellar was found dead inside."

Olivia pressed her lips together. As far as rumors went, those were pretty accurate. The village grapevine had done its work.

"Yes, that's true," she said. Then hope flared inside her. Perhaps the village grapevine might provide a helpful tidbit of information.

"Did your friends say anything about the other man? The one who ran away? Does anyone know who he was?"

Marcello's dark brows drew into a frown.

"Other man?" he asked.

Olivia sighed. Clearly, local gossip had its limits and couldn't provide the critical information she needed.

"We were woken by him. He set off Erba. I tried to chase him but couldn't keep up. It was definitely a man, of average height, fairly fit, with short, dark hair."

Marcello looked surprised.

"Nobody said anything about him. The news that each one of them gave me is that you killed the intruder using a large rock."

"What?" Incensed, Olivia half-rose from her chair. "Me? How can people think that?"

"I do not think that. Not for a moment," Marcello said in a firm voice.

Slowly, Olivia sat back down, still fuming.

Marcello spoke in a soothing tone. "People will always jump to the easiest conclusion. In this case, it is that you found him and you killed him. Now I have the true version, I can correct them, and say that the thief was overpowered by another man."

The truth did sound shaky, Olivia realized. Last night, her farm had been as busy as Grand Central Terminal with people coming and going and tracking each other down. What were the chances that two separate criminals had arrived at exactly the same time hoping to rob her cellar, one had killed the other, and then run away?

Not very likely, she admitted to herself. It didn't sound plausible at all.

There must be more to it. There were definitely a few puzzle pieces missing from the picture. How could they be found, she wondered, and how would it change things when they were slotted into place?

Would the police be up to it? Anxiety simmered inside her as she remembered that she couldn't afford to be a suspect, and definitely couldn't afford for this case to drag on for weeks or months. Not when her wine was in a structurally unstable cellar!

"Do not let this worry you," Marcello consoled her. "Let us get to work. We must trust that the investigation is in capable hands."

But even he didn't sound convinced.

Heavy-hearted, Olivia trailed back to the tasting room, to find Jean-Pierre had arrived. He put down the tasting sheets he was busy arranging, and stared at her in awe.

"I hear you overpowered an intruder last night. Are you all right?"

Olivia sighed. If the gossip had already reached Jean-Pierre, a relative newcomer to the village, it meant everyone knew. Everyone!

"I didn't overpower him. Someone else was there. They killed him and ran away. I chased after them, but lost them when they ran into a neighboring field."

Jean-Pierre clapped a hand over his mouth and stared at her, with relief and shock mingling in his eyes.

"I was certain you had done it. My friend said you showed ninja skills."

Olivia's eyes widened. Ninja skills? With not a single eyewitness to the crime, this elaborately detailed and entirely fictitious version had clearly captured the locals' imagination.

She sensed that a difficult day lay ahead.

Hearing footsteps approach the lobby, Olivia tensed. Would it be yet another opportunist laying claim?

No. The arrival was Antonio, the youngest of the Vescovis. He'd clearly been hard at work in the vineyards, because he stamped the mud off his work shoes before entering. Whistling to himself, he paced across the lobby toward Marcello's office. He glanced at the tasting counter and his whistling stopped abruptly. He stared at Olivia in surprise.

"Ciao Olivia," he said.

"Ciao," she replied.

Antonio paused. "You are well, and not hurt after your struggle last night?"

"There was no struggle." Olivia snapped, feeling her tolerance for the situation evaporate. Small towns? Seriously, who needed them! The anonymity of a big city suddenly seemed like a massive selling point.

"You were too quick for him and attacked him instantly?" Antonio nodded as if he'd solved a problem bothering him. Then he marched down the corridor to Marcello's office.

Turning to Jean-Pierre, Olivia could see exactly what he was thinking.

"No, I did not lose my memory and forget I'd done it. I was there and know what happened. The rest of the village was not!"

"Absolutely. Absolutely." Jean-Pierre spread his hands placatingly but Olivia didn't fail to notice how he stepped backward, keeping a safe distance away from any ninja skills she might suddenly display.

Seething with annoyance, she stomped to the storage room to fetch more bottles of the Sangiovese. It was certain to be a big seller today, because it was the start of Collina Wine Week. Finally, the event she'd been looking forward to and preparing for had arrived.

But, to Olivia's surprise, the tasting room was unusually quiet. Not a single car had pulled up outside.

She checked her watch. Half an hour after opening time. Marcello had said there were queues waiting by the doors last year.

Heading anxiously to the lobby, she peered out.

Not a soul in sight.

Olivia started getting a sick feeling in her stomach as she put two and two together, realizing why the local population was staying away.

They were keeping a distance from Olivia, just like Jean-Pierre was doing. Everyone was too scared to come near her, after what they heard had happened.

Olivia sensed someone behind her. Turning, she saw Marcello, and her stomach did a flip flop as he, too, stared out over the empty parking lot.

"It's me," she said in a small voice. "They're staying away because of me, Marcello. I'm so sorry. Collina Wine Week is such an important event for us."

The worst week of the year to put off the locals, and she'd managed to do it.

Marcello shook his head. "People," he said in an expressive voice as if he, too, was regretting living in a small town.

"I don't know what to do," Olivia said.

"For now, go home. You need to get some rest. I am sure that within a day or two this matter will be behind us," he soothed, rubbing her shoulders comfortingly.

Even though it was sensible advice, Olivia felt as if she was heading into exile as she fetched her purse from the back room, said goodbye to Jean-Pierre, and trudged out of the winery, bypassing the goat dairy so that Erba could join her.

Feeling crushed, as if she was a complete liability to the winery, Olivia trailed down the service road. How could she be letting her wonderful employer down so badly, she lamented. Worse still, how could she have aspirations for running her own winery one day when she kept getting caught up in these situations? Perhaps it really was time to abandon this pipe dream.

But, as she walked, she couldn't help feeling energized by the cool, fresh air and brilliant spring sunshine. With each step, her despair seemed to abate and in its place, resolve began to build.

This was her community. Her neighborhood. And somewhere in it, a killer was hiding. It was unacceptable. Why was she the one feeling miserable and anxious? The running man should be doing that.

Olivia wasn't going to go home to rest. She didn't even feel tired anymore. Instead, she felt determined. She would use her connections in the community and, if necessary, the threat of her legendary ninja skills.

She was going to find out who the killer was, solve the case, and save her wine before the cellar roof collapsed. Her farm and her future depended on it.

CHAPTER EIGHTEEN

When Olivia arrived home, Danilo rushed out to greet her. He looked anxious.

"Are you alright? Why are you back so early?" he asked, concerned.

"Nobody's coming to the winery because everyone thinks I did it," Olivia said. "The timing couldn't be worse, with Collina Wine Week under way. I've been so excited about making it a success, and now I've ruined it."

Danilo sighed in frustration. "The people in this village can be stupid," he agreed. "How can I help you make things right?"

"I've decided to investigate it myself," Olivia told him, hoping he would take this well and not think she was putting herself in danger.

Danilo considered her words for a few moments. Then he nodded reluctantly.

"I think that is the only solution. By believing you did it, the locals are shielding the real criminal. It is hugely unfair. And we are under pressure of time for this to be solved, because the wine is at risk. Can I help you?"

Olivia nodded gratefully.

"I'd appreciate help," she said. "I thought we could start by going and relooking at the scene where it happened. Perhaps there's some evidence to guide us. I know the police told us not to go down there but if we're fast, it won't matter."

"It cannot hurt to take a quick look," he agreed.

"Is my mom okay?" Olivia added, remembering that even though she was spending the day investigating, she also had to make sure her mother was looked after. Talk about time management challenges, she fretted.

"She is well. Currently, she is reading in the lounge."

Relieved that he was supportive of her plans, Olivia marched past the farmhouse and headed to the field.

Despite her brave attitude, she couldn't help feeling a chill of dread as she approached the cellar door. As she reached it, her heart sank.

The police had not just sealed the door with crime tape, as Olivia had expected. Instead, the door was shut with a giant steel bolt, fastened by a solid and seemingly unbreakable padlock.

The very first step in their investigation had resulted in a dead end.

Peering down, Danilo uttered a heartfelt curse in Italian. Olivia agreed with every syllable!

They stared at each other in frustration. Then they turned, and paced back toward the farmhouse. Olivia's mind was racing. She wasn't going to let Detective Caputi block her. There were other ways of moving ahead. By the time they reached the cobbled path, she had a new plan.

"I'm going to interview the crew who did the digging," Olivia said. "Detective Caputi made a very good point last night when she said that the cellar was hidden away. It's a door in the ground, in the middle of a dark field on a twenty-acre farm. Not easy to find unless you knew where it was. The crew might have created a stir when they spread the news. Perhaps someone they spoke to asked for the exact location? They could even have had a call requesting the information. That will give us a starting point."

Danilo nodded. "Yes. That sounds promising."

"I'll go alone. It shouldn't be risky. They are Marcello's friends," Olivia said, remembering that Danilo had promised to stay home with her mother today.

"Perhaps your mother would like to go out? It would be more interesting for her than staying here. Pisa is close by. I can take her to see the leaning tower," Danilo offered.

Olivia felt overwhelmed by gratitude.

"I'll ask her about the outing. Could you find out where the crew is working?"

"Give me ten minutes. I will make a few phone calls," Danilo said.

Olivia headed upstairs. She'd dressed cheerfully for work, in a spring-themed pink blouse and a bright blue jacket. Investigation required more conservative attire. She selected a black top and a light gray jacket in case the wind picked up. Smart low-heeled sandals completed her look. It was spring, and the warmest day this year, after all.

Suitably dressed, she went downstairs again and peeked into the lounge to check on her mother.

"Oh, Olivia, you're back. I didn't expect you until later."

Mrs. Glass was relaxing on a couch, engrossed in one of Olivia's books on Italian art. She closed it quickly and slid it behind her as if she hadn't wanted Olivia to see what she was reading.

"I'm going out again. I have to attend a meeting. But Danilo has said he'd love to take you on a tour. Pisa is close by. Would you like to see the leaning tower? He can take photos for you," she added, feeling this was a stroke of genius.

"Andrew was talking about the tower yesterday. He was asking when it was going to fall over," her mother observed.

"It might do so at any minute. Perhaps even when you're there," Olivia said casually.

"All right. I'd love to go. How kind of Daniel."

Feeling thrilled that her mother would be heading out somewhere she might actually enjoy, Olivia went outside. Danilo was pacing up and down, speaking on his phone in urgent tones. He disconnected a minute later and she saw his face was alight with triumph.

"I have found out where the crew is working today. I spoke to Giovanni himself. They are all at Casa del Vino winery, preparing a site for a new tasting room to be built."

Olivia grinned in relief. "I know exactly where that is. I'll go there straight away. And the Pisa trip is on. My mother seemed very keen to see the tower and hopeful that it might fall over while she was there."

"I will try not to disappoint her," Danilo said, keeping his expression deadpan.

Laughing, Olivia ran to her car, feeling hopeful that this journey might give her a foothold into the investigation.

Casa del Vino was a short drive away, on the other side of Collina, and Olivia used the journey to gather her thoughts and plan her questions. A lot would depend on the attitude of Giovanni and his crew. That might be positive, or negative.

If it was negative it would throw up another major stumbling block and she resolved to use all her charm in this meeting.

As soon as she drove through the winery's white-pillared gateway, she saw the distinctive yellow forms of the excavators, working to the right.

A paved roadway led part of the way, but then it petered out into a rather muddy track. If she drove any further the Fiat might get stuck.

Sighing with regret that she hadn't chosen boots, Olivia climbed out and squelched her way down the uneven path. The mud oozed over the top of her sandals and in between her toes.

She recognized Giovanni and waved hopefully, taking another few steps through the deepening mud. "Ciao!" she called.

The excavator swept past, and at the last minute he saw her. He stopped the machine, looking surprised.

"You?" he said. Surprise turned to suspicion as Olivia watched him mentally replay what he'd been told happened in the cellar.

"What are you doing here?" he shouted.

How did everyone think she possessed ninja skills, she wondered, feeling suddenly frazzled.

"I've come to ask you something," she yelled in slow, careful Italian.

"This is a construction site! We are busy, signora, and working to a strict deadline." He revved the excavator's motor loudly, illustrating the pressure of time.

"It won't take long," Olivia persisted. An excavator couldn't go that fast. She resolved to follow him around the site until he gave in.

"Is it important?" Giovanni sounded unsure, as if he'd realized she wasn't just going to go away.

"Extremely!"

She squelched determinedly forward, lifting each leg high out of the mire. Now the mud was all the way over her sandals and creeping up her pants legs. Her feet were coated in it. This was embarrassing. Why on earth had they chosen to build a tasting room on this site, when it was clearly more suitable for a rice paddy?

"I am sorry," Giovanni had clearly noticed her inconvenience and spoke in a more understanding tone. "A water pipe burst yesterday and flooded the area. We fixed it this morning,"

"That's good," Olivia said, with a bright, forced smile.

"How can I help?"

At least watching her ankle-deep in mud had convinced him of her human side, as he no longer sounded suspicious but instead, rather amused.

"I wanted to ask you a question. Did you speak to anyone about the cellar we found on my farm? Or mention exactly where it was located?" she said, carefully wording her question so that he didn't feel to blame. She wished her Italian was better.

"Oh, no, signora. I notified Marcello what we had found, and told nobody else."

"Did you have any calls or messages from anyone last night, asking where the cellar was?" Olivia asked.

"No, signora. No messages. Last night, I was at the village bistro, and would not have heard my phone ring. In any case the cellar is on private property. To give out any details could cost me my good name."

Olivia didn't know if she believed him. She hoped that any friend of Marcello's was trustworthy and reliable, but resolved to confirm his story in a way that didn't involve questioning him in an unfamiliar language.

"What about your crew?" Olivia asked.

Giovanni activated his walkie-talkie and had a rapid conversation. As he spoke she saw the two other vehicles, working at the other side of the site, rumble to a standstill.

"My foreman told one person only, his girlfriend, while at the bistro," he said, sounding satisfied. "He did not tell her where the cellar was, and in fact did not even know it himself, as his phone's GPS is not working. I can confirm that is true, signora. For a week now, he has had to follow me to sites."

"And the other driver?" Olivia asked, feeling confused.

"He, too, understood the need to keep the details private. He shared the news with only one person, his hairstylist. Straight after working the field, he went to get a haircut."

"Thank you," Olivia said. She was beginning to see how word had spread. There was nothing else she could think of to ask, so she turned and squelched out of the mire.

"There is a hose pipe to your right," Giovanni called after her. "So you can wash your feet!"

Gratefully, Olivia headed to dry ground and hosed her feet, sandals, and muddied pant legs with the icy, but clean, water. As she shivered in the spray, wiggling her toes to try and dislodge the sticky mud, she thought about what she'd learned.

A secret was still a secret if you shared with just one person, it seemed. Everybody who'd heard the juicy news had done their civic duty by telling only one other person and no more, but it seemed nobody had queried exactly where the cellar was.

That brought her no closer to knowing how the second man had arrived on site in the same place and at the same time as Heberto.

She had to find out who that man was!

Olivia decided to head to the salon and confirm the other driver's story. Perhaps he'd lied to Giovanni, and had described in detail exactly where the cellar was hidden away. Then the trail would be fresh again and she could resume her hunt.

Even if he hadn't, salons were hotbeds of gossip. Someone must know who the running man was. They might have shared his identity with just one person while having their hair done.

CHAPTER NINETEEN

The small, but luxuriously equipped hair salon in Collina was doing a brisk morning trade. Two hairdressers were hard at work and, staring through the glassed shop front, Olivia was thrilled to recognize one of them.

Francesca, Danilo's niece, was completing her practical hours toward her hairdressing qualification. She'd told Olivia that she was working locally, and today, here she was.

The pretty, slim young woman was putting on the artful finishing touches to a shiny bobbed hairdo. The middle-aged owner of it was staring into the ornately framed mirror looking satisfied.

Francesca smiled in delight as Olivia walked in.

"Ciao, Olivia! Are you happy with your hair?"

"I'm loving it," Olivia replied. "I've come to buy more shampoo."

"One minute, and I will assist."

After hair-spraying the bob, Francesca removed the woman's cape. "We are all done, signora," she said politely in Italian.

Then, switching to English, she sidled closer to Olivia.

"I was shocked to hear what happened last night. Clients have been speaking of nothing else. I called Danilo immediately to check you were not hurt in the struggle."

Olivia sighed. "Village gossip got it wrong. I wasn't involved in any struggle. But someone else was. A man ran away from the scene, and I need to find out who he was. Clearly, he was the actual killer."

As she spoke, Olivia realized something with a nasty twist of her stomach. There was in fact one other suspect that she had not considered until now.

Danilo could have committed the crime himself. After all, she'd found him alone with the deceased. Had he wielded the rock in a moment of protective rage, wanting to keep Olivia safe?

She was sure he couldn't have done such a thing, and in fact wished she'd never thought of it. Especially at that moment, while face to face with his favorite niece who was now staring oddly at her.

Her thoughts must be showing on her face. Pulling herself together and doing her best to banish this disturbing and clearly wrong idea, Olivia continued.

"I know one of the excavation crew who uncovered my cellar had his hair cut after working the site. He said he spoke to his hairdresser about his day. I would like to know how much detail he went into."

Francesca nodded, and Olivia could see that she understood.

"I remember when he came in. He was very excited. While Tomaso did his hair he was talking nonstop about the site that he'd excavated," she said in a low voice, glancing around to check nobody was listening.

Hope rekindled inside Olivia as Francesca selected a shampoo for her from the well-stocked shelves. Questions formed in her mind, important ones, which would hopefully pave the way to the identity of the mysterious running man.

"What exactly did he say?" she asked.

"He said how amazing it was that a large cellar full of wine could have been constructed in the middle of a small field, and then covered with boulders, so many years ago. He and Tomaso spoke about it for a while. They had quite a detailed discussion, working out exactly where the field is. Tomaso knows the area well as he has clients across the road from your farm."

Olivia was growing more and more excited. This was sounding promising.

"Was there anyone else in the salon at the time?"

Francesca thought, tapping her fingers on the counter.

"Yes. While they were speaking, there was a customer waiting for Tomaso. Also, I was doing Signora Patrizia's hair, but she's very deaf and wouldn't have overheard."

"How can I find out who the other customer was, and where he lives?" Olivia asked, on tenterhooks that Francesca would be able to help.

Francesca lowered her voice.

"I can look on the salon computer. It will take about ten minutes, as it is running an update. Can you come back just now? I will write down the name of the customer, and the address also if it is there. But please don't tell anyone I did this for you."

"I won't say a word," Olivia breathed, feeling grateful for the family connection with Danilo, and his loyal, clever niece.

A thought occurred to her. Could Tomaso himself have been the mysterious stranger she'd glimpsed?

Glancing at him, and comparing his build and appearance to her memory of the running man, Olivia decided against it. Tomaso was short, sturdy, and had bleach-blond hair. He was definitely off the suspect list.

Olivia paid for the shampoo and left. She'd had a brainwave about how to spend the time while Francesca was looking up the client. The local bistro was a block away, and this would allow her to confirm the crew's alibis and see if they'd been there the whole evening, as Giovanni had claimed.

At ten-thirty a.m. the bistro was bustling, with coffees and breakfasts being served. Olivia was pleased to see a group of eight tourists sitting at an outside table. It always made her feel happy to see visitors enjoying the ambiance of this village, which she happened to think was one of the most quaint and scenic places in Tuscany.

She headed inside, where the waiter on duty gave her a suspicious look. With a jolt, Olivia remembered the whole town thought she was a murderess with ninja skills. Well, she was going to play up to that role. Lifting her chin, she stared him down, feeling pleased when he looked away first.

Capitalizing on this advantage, Olivia quickly shimmied behind the counter and headed to the back rooms where she knew from experience that the owner, Ugo, would be working if he wasn't out front.

The genial, gray-haired man was in his miniscule office, singing along to the opera music blaring from his phone as he jotted notes in his day planner.

He looked up when he saw Olivia and surprise turned to consternation.

"Signora Olivia! How can I help you?"

He jumped to his feet, knocking over his coffee cup in his confusion. Luckily it was empty.

"Ugo, as a loyal customer, I need to ask you a favor," Olivia said in a low voice. She really was a loyal customer, because this bistro was one of Danilo's favorite local hangouts. As his girlfriend, she'd quickly become known by name.

"Of course. What?" He looked nervous, but cooperative.

"You know Giovanni and his crew?" she asked.

He nodded decisively. "Yes, very well. All are regular customers here."

"Were any of them here last night?"

Another nod. "They were all here."

“All?” Olivia was surprised.

Ugo smiled. “Cedro, the foreman, arrived first, for a drink with his girlfriend. Then Giovanni and Abramo arrived later, at about eight p.m. It was our weekly quiz night, you see. A very successful new venture I started this year. Giovanni and his team are very competitive and often win. Last night, though, they were beaten by a couple of points.”

“What time did the quiz end?”

“The winners were announced at around quarter to midnight,” Ugo said.

“And everyone was still there?”

“Yes. People began leaving as soon as the prize giving was done.”

That didn’t allow for any of the crew to have gotten back to her farm in time. All of them were off the list.

“Thank you,” she said.

“Why are you asking?” Ugo said curiously.

Olivia decided to spill the beans.

“I’m trying to help the police find out who committed the crime last night. It wasn’t me. But people think it was.”

Ugo nodded sadly.

“I never believed it was you,” he said, which Olivia considered a small white lie. “However, having worked in this village for many years, I would battle to suspect any of my local brothers and sisters of committing the crime. Everyone who visits my bistro becomes a personal friend. It is difficult for me to think of anyone who might have done this.” He spread his hands sorrowfully.

“I understand,” Olivia sympathized.

“I guess you never know. Perhaps, when the murderer is arrested, we will all have a terrible shock. But I certainly hope it is not one of my customers,” he told her, frowning sadly.

Thanking him, Olivia left, feeling thoughtful as she headed out of the bistro. Clearly, the crew had a confirmed alibi. But the town’s community was a tight-knit one and she would have to watch out for exactly the scenario that Ugo had described. People might look to protect their friends, and might even be prepared to lie if they believed that nobody in this town was capable of such a crime.

Gloomily wondering what would happen if the case ended up going cold, Olivia plodded back to the hair salon.

There, Francesca was peering out of the door excitedly.

“Olivia, I have a name for you!”

"You do?" Encouraged, she took the slip of paper that Francesca discreetly handed her. Whirling away, she disappeared into the salon, leaving Olivia to unfold the page.

She stared down at it, her heart accelerating.

This was more than a clue. This could be the big break that led to the case being solved.

The man who'd sat in the hair salon eavesdropping on the cellar's location, was none other than Pablo Pusilli, who'd arrived at La Leggenda the next morning to stake his fictitious claim on behalf of his great-great-great grandfather. And now, thanks to Francesca, she knew where he lived.

CHAPTER TWENTY

"Ninja skills," Olivia muttered to herself as she accelerated out of the village. She was going to fake them if she needed to. She would do everything in her power to pin down this prime suspect. He'd overheard the men gossiping about the cellar, and had then been the first to fabricate a claim. When she'd not accepted his story, knowing the cellar's whereabouts, he must have tried to steal the contents.

Pablo lived on the outskirts of Collina, so close that Olivia could have run there if she'd been feeling fitter. She zoomed up to the scenic cluster of cottages and screeched to a stop outside number three.

Olivia barely paused to admire the quaint stucco pillars on either side of the front door, and the pretty creeper climbing the wall which was just starting to bloom. She marched up to the door, lifted the brass knocker, and brought it down with an authoritative bang.

She tensed, feeling like a cat about to pounce as she heard footsteps approach. A moment later, the door opened and there he was.

His innocently unsuspecting expression turned to raw terror. Clearly, her reputation had paved the way. Looking panicked, he tried to slam the front door, but just in time Olivia got her foot inside. The door bounced off her sandal's rubber sole, and hit him on the nose.

"Ow," he groaned, recoiling back into the tiled hallway. "Ow, ow, ow."

He cupped his face in his hands, massaging his nose, which Olivia was glad to see didn't look seriously injured. She didn't want anything distracting him from her questioning. On the plus side, a suspect with a sore nose was less likely to suddenly turn violent. She was aware that if he was guilty, he might act out of desperation, but right now she was also desperate!

While Pablo was getting over the surprise of having been hit by his own front door, Olivia closed it behind her.

"Buongiorno," she said. "I'd like to ask you a few questions."

"Signora, there is nothing to discuss," he mumbled apologetically.

"I think there is," Olivia said, glaring at him.

He stared back, looking apprehensive. As he did so, Olivia noted that he was of a similar height and weight to the running man. And he had dark hair, too.

"I was joking." Pablo tried for a smile. "It was a small tease, nothing more. I do not really have a claim. Obviously I did not intentionally lie," he added hastily. "In my excitement at your good fortune, I was just mistaken. My grandfather did not get paid in wine. I misremembered the journal."

"Your great-great-great grandfather," Olivia corrected him in a stern voice.

He hung his head. "I am sorry, signora. A madness overcame me."

She felt encouraged by this admission.

"Where were you last night?" she asked, wanting to get the question in quickly while he was off balance. Hopefully, he would now confess to more.

"Last night?"

"Yes. Were you home alone or were you, perhaps… out somewhere?" she asked meaningfully.

"Ah." Pablo looked even more downcast and triumph surged inside her. Clearly, he didn't have an alibi, and couldn't think of one at short notice. No wonder he was looking discouraged and beaten.

But then, to her surprise, he spoke.

"I had to visit my mother in Florence," he said sadly. "It was my sister's birthday and we had a family dinner together, and attended a music concert in the town hall. You can see the ticket stubs are on the hall table there, next to my car keys," he pointed. "I then had to drop my niece at home, so only arrived back after midnight," he concluded in tones awash with sorrow.

Olivia stared at him, suspicion warring with disappointment. This sounded like a rock solid alibi, but why on earth would Pablo be so depressed about a fun outing? Did he not like his mother, or what?

Suppressing the thought that, given her conflicted relationship with her own mother, she wasn't justified in pointing a finger, Olivia asked, "Why is that a problem? You sound as if it's a problem?"

"It was a big problem." Looking as if his world had ended, Pablo massaged his nose again. "For the first time ever, my team won the pub quiz! Without me there! It is the first quiz I have missed since it started and the only reason was the family commitments. We may never win again, as Giovanni's team is very strong, especially on the sport questions," he admitted, practically stifling a sob as he confessed the sad news.

Olivia now felt as miserable as he did. Her very best suspect had fizzled out. She'd been certain that the case was solved.

"I'm sure you will win again," she encouraged him.

"I hope so."

"Well, thank you for your time." Olivia opened the door.

"Apologies again for having confronted you at the winery," Pablo said. "When I got the news my team had won, I could not help but think it was life punishing me for having tried to claim your wine. Even though it was done in a spirit of jest."

He said the last words weakly as if he knew she wouldn't believe them, but Olivia decided to be gracious and accept them at face value.

"Hopefully, you're all square with life now," she consoled.

"By the way, how did you find out my address?" he asked.

Olivia held up a conspiratorial finger.

"Ninja skills," she whispered, feeling pleased to see him look horrified by the words.

She turned and went back to her car, feeling frustrated and not knowing what way to turn next. Every minute that this case dragged on put more strain on the cellar roof.

As she climbed into her car, her phone rang. It was Charlotte calling.

"Here I am, sitting at the local bistro, and I suddenly thought I need company for lunch. Where are you?" Charlotte asked.

"I'm heading there. Give me two minutes," Olivia said.

As she drove back into the village, she felt grateful for the impromptu get-together with her bestie. Investigation was hungry work, and Charlotte always had good ideas. Hopefully, she'd be able to suggest a new angle to explore.

She squeezed into the same parking bay she'd vacated a short while ago, before hurrying back to the bistro, guessing Ugo would be surprised to see her again so soon.

There was Charlotte! She hugged her before sitting opposite.

"Have you found the killer yet? I suppose not, or you would have called," Charlotte said.

Ugo materialized with a jug of sangria topped with chopped fruit and ice.

"Welcome, welcome! What can I get you to eat?" He winked at Olivia as he set it down, clearly deciding that her previous visit must remain confidential.

"I'll have the insalata verde, please," she said. It was a tasty dish, spring-themed and packed with delicious greens, spring onions, croutons, olives and mozzarella cubes. Even though it sounded healthy and slimming, Olivia happened to know that in this bistro they included a thick slice of home baked ciabatta bread, and a generous pat of butter. Plus, the dressing was rich with olive oil, balsamic and herbs.

"Make that two," Charlotte decided wisely.

Olivia resumed her conversation as soon as Ugo had left.

"I have just interviewed a brilliant suspect. Unfortunately he wasn't the killer and had a rock-solid alibi."

"Oh, dear." Charlotte sounded troubled. "Who was he?"

"He was the first person who tried to claim the wine. The one who arrived at the winery."

"Well, you can see why he has a motive. But there were three claimants, weren't there? What happened to that lowlife who interrupted our restaurant dinner and robbed me of my tiramisu cheesecake? What was his name? Raul Porzio, I think."

Grumpily, she poured their sangria.

"That's a good point," Olivia said. "Raul also has a strong motive. And given that his distant family actually owned the land, he might have felt entitled to arrive at night and snoop around. Perhaps he bumped into Heberto. I still don't know how two people ended up there."

"It's very puzzling. But I think that you should check out all the claimants and see where they were last night. After all, if somebody was motivated enough to approach you in public with a fake story, they would be motivated enough to try and steal the wine. And even if they didn't plan to kill anyone, it might have happened in the heat of the moment," she added thoughtfully.

"I would have to find out where he lives," Olivia said, wondering how she would do that. She'd been lucky that Francesca had Pablo's details at her fingertips.

"Well, why not look in the phone directory?" Charlotte asked.

"The what?" Olivia stared at her friend in surprise.

"The phone directory. Remember, those old fashioned paper books with everyone's number in? They still have them here in the post office, and a few other places. And also, there's an online version which Artoro uses to track down witnesses and suspects. He says it's a wealth of information and that the simplest way is usually the best way."

"Well!" Olivia said. She felt embarrassed that the simplest solution had escaped her, even if temporarily. Perhaps she would have thought of it later.

The waiter brought them their salads.

"These are so scrumptious. And proof that it's impossible to diet in Italy," Charlotte said happily.

"Look at that butter, and the amount of cheese. And they've put my favorite black olives in." Feeling hungrily content, Olivia dug in. She felt thrilled that this impromptu break had not only provided her with highly nutritious calories, but also clear guidance on the next step to take.

As soon as she'd finished every bite of this scrumptious meal, she was going to pin down Raul Porzio, and subject him to harsh and unrelenting questioning about his whereabouts last night.

But as she attacked the delicious salad, Olivia suddenly realized that the conversation at the restaurant had fallen silent. Glancing up, she startled so violently that a rocket leaf fluttered off her fork and landed in her sangria glass.

Detective Caputi was standing at the bistro door. Her arms were folded and there was a grim expression in her eyes.

"Olivia Glass," she said. Her voice was not loud, but it carried all the way across the room. "I need to have a word with you. Come here."

CHAPTER TWENTY ONE

Her fork clattered down onto the plate as Olivia scrambled up and hurried nervously across the room. Detective Caputi was not alone, but with another plainclothes investigator, a tall man, who looked just as stern.

What did they want? Dread flooded her as she wondered if she was about to be arrested. They might have heard she'd been asking questions after being told to stay out of the investigation. Or perhaps they'd found evidence to incriminate her. If they locked her up now, it would mean the end of everything, starting with the cellar roof.

"I have a question for you," Detective Caputi said. She spoke slowly, as if savoring the words.

"Yes? I'll do my best to help." Olivia's mouth felt dry.

"We have picked up an inconsistency in your version of events," the policewoman said, her voice harsh.

Olivia felt her heart accelerate to warp speed. The outcome she'd dreaded most had happened. Her small glossing over of the sequence of events had become glaringly obvious to the police – somehow.

"What did you notice?" she said as innocently as possible.

"You said that you saw an intruder running past the farmhouse in the dark and that you and your boyfriend then headed straight to the cellar. We have evidence to the contrary."

Evidence? How had Caputi obtained it? Olivia felt overwhelmed with panic.

Breathing deeply, she fought to keep her nerve. Most probably, she told herself, the evidence was inconclusive and Detective Caputi was seeking confirmation. Perhaps she was hoping Olivia would confess to the facts, blurting them out in her fear. She needed to keep her cool and not play into the detective's hands.

"It was a very tense and scary time. I'm sorry if I might have gotten a minor detail wrong. But as far as I can recall, that is what happened. I don't recollect anything else."

"My sergeant was re-examining the footprints, based on your account of the evening," Caputi continued relentlessly. "He noticed something interesting."

“What’s that?” Olivia asked faintly. Deep breathing wasn’t working as well as she’d hoped. Running away seemed like a far better option. Using all her fortitude, she forced herself to stand her ground.

“When following the direction you pointed, he found clear footprints that crossed the edge of your vine plantation, some way from the house. The soil was soft there, and the prints could be clearly seen. They were from a worn men’s running shoe, European size 43. But he also picked up on another set of prints, in a size 39, most probably from a ladies’ loafer. You were wearing loafers at the scene; I took note of your attire. You will recall from previous investigations that we used your shoes to take a sole print. I went and checked up, and that’s your size.”

Caputi’s gaze pierced Olivia. Her salad was curdling inside her.

“I’m not sure what you mean,” she said, giving a confused, innocent frown.

“You could not have proceeded directly to the cellar if you, and you alone, chased after the running man. Only one set of footprints is in pursuit – yours. That casts doubt on the timeline of events. Did you arrive at the cellar as the same time as Danilo? Or did you arrive later?”

Olivia knew she was on dangerous ground. She was going to have to stick to her version, even if it meant that she wasn’t being truthful with Caputi. This could get her into trouble and she hated doing it, but she had to try and protect Danilo.

“I can’t recall running in that direction that night,” she said firmly, using poor memory as a convenient excuse. “However, I chase my goat out of the vineyard all the time. She tries to play there while I’m working. Surely the prints could have been from earlier in the day?”

Detective Caputi looked annoyed. Her eyes narrowed determinedly and Olivia knew she had done no more than buy herself a few moments of time.

But then, the police walkie-talkie crackled. Clearly, it was an even more urgent matter than her pressing need to arrest Olivia, because she grimaced in disappointment.

“No, we haven’t yet notified the victim’s next-of-kin,” she spoke briefly into the mouthpiece. “We are having difficulty tracing them. I will come back now and meet with you.” Then she turned back to Olivia, looking more cheerful again. “You will make yourself available at your farmhouse at four p.m., together with the shoes you were wearing that night. And Signor Danilo must also be there. I will re-interview you both, in light of this new evidence. It may well happen that the case will then be closed," she said in satisfied tones.

Olivia turned away and headed back to the table, feeling numb with anxiety. This was a far more serious predicament than she'd imagined. She was at risk of implicating Danilo if she changed her story and agreed with the police version. The only alternative was to implicate herself.

No wonder Caputi had looked so confident at the prospect of an arrest.

"What did she want?" Charlotte asked curiously.

Olivia sat back down and stuffed salad into her mouth. She wasn't hungry but she was stressed, and the food was soothing her.

"She wants to arrest one of us, and she's trying really hard," Olivia muttered. "Danilo and I have to be at the farmhouse at four p.m. for an interview with her. I guess that's so she can decide which of us to put in the back of the van."

Charlotte's eyes widened in concern. "It's already half past twelve."

"I know. That gives us only three and a half hours."

"But if the next hour goes well, you might have a new suspect to present to her."

"I hope so." Olivia put down her fork and stuffed the last of the bread into her mouth.

"The sooner you can do it, the better," Charlotte encouraged.

While Olivia was chewing, she rummaged in her purse and put down money to pay for the meal. Then she grabbed her jacket and headed out of the restaurant at a run.

Every moment that passed now was critical.

This was her final chance to find the killer. Otherwise, at four p.m., Detective Caputi would use Olivia's own innocent white lie to accuse her of the crime – or worse still, accuse Danilo.

Would her next suspect be the killer, and could Olivia make him confess in time?

*

Fifteen minutes after leaving the bistro, Olivia strode determinedly up the paved pathway that led to the spacious villa where Raul Porzio lived, according to the local phone directory at least. With the minutes ticking by, she hoped that her quick research was accurate and that he was still living here.

This wasn't a small house, Olivia observed, feeling bemused by people's greed. Clearly Raul was not wanting for money. It was a big, fancy house set in tracts of a prettily maintained garden, a few miles from the village and bordering picturesque farmland. The garage door was open and the gardener was taking out a large, ride-on mower. The shiny black SUV parked inside was another sign that actually, Gina's nephew was doing very well for himself without needing to claim a wine collection that wasn't his.

Well, seeing he'd been eating at the area's most expensive restaurant, it was clear at the time they'd first met that he was loaded.

The ornate electric gate was closed. Olivia rang the buzzer and waited for it to open.

It didn't. Instead, the intercom crackled.

"Who is that, please?"

It was a woman's voice. Olivia had no idea if it was a housekeeper, or one of Raul's family.

"Is that the home of Raul Porzio?" she asked, replying in careful Italian.

"Yes, it is," the woman confirmed.

"My name's Olivia Glass," she said, feeling encouraged. "I'd like to have a word with Raul, if he's in."

"Sure, he is in. Hold on."

Expectantly, Olivia braced herself for the moment when the gate would swing open and she could power her way up the long driveway and make a start with this important interview.

A minute passed by and then another. Olivia began shifting from foot to foot, wondering if the woman had got sidetracked. Perhaps she should ring the bell again.

Then the intercom crackled once more.

"I am sorry. He is not available," she said regretfully.

Olivia let out a frustrated sigh. "Not available? How do you mean? Must I come back later? What time can I see him?"

There was another short silence, and Olivia got the strong impression that a muttered conversation was taking place in the house.

"I do not know. I must go now," the woman said regretfully and the intercom cut off.

"Dammit," Olivia seethed. She'd been an idiot to say her real name, but using a false one wouldn't have got things off to a good start if he had allowed her in. There hadn't been a way to win this, she realized sadly. Raul was now secluded in his house and she was outside. Clearly, he didn't want to see her.

Olivia nodded to herself as she realized this was a definite sign of guilt. An innocent man would have had no problem answering a few simple questions. If he wouldn't speak to her inside, she was going to have to lure him out. But how?

Staring longingly at the post box, she wished she could open it and search through the mail. That would give her a clue about where to start. Unfortunately, though, her conscience wouldn't allow her to do that. It felt like going a step too far to read through someone's personal correspondence. She reluctantly abandoned the idea, knowing that Charlotte would have done it in a flash.

Having abandoned the 'What Would Charlotte Do' prognosis, Olivia then thought of what Erba would do.

There was a trash can near the gate, waiting for emptying. Erba would have nosed the lid off, and been inside, in a split-second. But Olivia didn't want to go through people's trash looking for a way to get through to them. It seemed wrong.

Although, she had to admit, the pressure of the four p.m. deadline was rapidly causing her to rethink her definition of 'wrong.'

As she prowled around the trash can, trying to work herself up into Erba's impish frame of mind, she noticed that next to the can was a clear bag that had been set out for recycling.

It contained a number of empty wine bottles, and she recognized a few from good local estates. Clearly, as well as being a lover of pricey restaurants, Raul was an appreciator of fine wine.

At that moment, Olivia had a brilliant idea. She had a way to lure him out successfully, and it needed the help of only one trusted person.

But would that person be willing to help out in this make-or-break scenario?

With nerves churning inside her, Olivia climbed in her car and sped off to ask him.

CHAPTER TWENTY TWO

Olivia hurried down La Leggenda's tiled corridor, feeling tense and expectant. So many things could go wrong with the plan she'd just dreamed up. But, if it went right, then her suspect could be trapped into a confession.

Marcello looked up inquiringly as she tapped on his office door.

"Olivia. You are back. Has there been any news?"

If only, she thought. She knew exactly what news he was hoping for.

"Not yet. But I have a strong suspect. He's related to the previous owner of the farm, and he confronted us with a fake claim to the wine while we were at a restaurant, a few hours before the murder. His name's Raul Porzio."

"How are you going to find out if he is guilty?" Marcello asked. His eyes were alight with interest.

"He refused to come out of his house when I went there to question him, so I thought, what if we – or rather, you – issue him a surprise invitation to Collina Wine Week. Over a tasting you'd have the chance to talk to him, and with some wine inside him, he might open up about what he did."

Marcello considered the idea. Olivia knew her level-headed boss would never agree to anything that would put her in danger, or compromise his beloved winery.

"I could hide out of the way and just listen in," she added.

Finally, Marcello nodded in agreement.

"If you think this person is a strong suspect then we must do whatever it takes," he emphasized. "I will call and invite him now. Since this is clearly urgent, I will say that the first few people to accept the invitation will receive a free case of wine."

"Marcello, thank you so much. This might save the day! I'm sure he'll jump at the offer of free wine," Olivia said gratefully.

She hoped that Raul would accept the invitation immediately, because the deadline was closing in. It was nearly half past one.

While Marcello made the call, Olivia headed back down the corridor to chat to Jean-Pierre.

"How's Wine Week been going? Busier since I left?" The tasting room was quiet at the moment but from the papers and used glasses he was tidying away, she could see it had been busy.

"Yes. People are starting to arrive. A lot of locals have made bookings for this afternoon," he said.

Neither of them mentioned that it had probably taken a while for word to filter out that Olivia was not in attendance.

"I'm only here for a short time. We may have to close the tasting room briefly. We're hoping that if the right person arrives, we can conclude the investigation soon," Olivia said meaningfully, glancing at Marcello's office.

Jean-Pierre's eyes widened.

"I can ask Gabriella if we can relocate Collina Wine Week to the restaurant for an hour," he suggested.

Marcello's office door swung wide and he hurried out.

"We have a special guest arriving for a private tasting. Perhaps everyone else can use the restaurant for the next little while," he said, clearly on exactly the same page as Jean-Pierre.

"Of course!" Looking thrilled to be playing his part in this pivotal event, Jean-Pierre rushed through to the restaurant.

"He is arriving in ten minutes," Marcello murmured. "He did not mention your name and is not familiar with the winery, so he should not suspect you will be here."

"It's sounding positive," Olivia breathed. She felt taut with nerves.

"You must hide. Behind the counter, perhaps? I will lead the questioning. It will probably be best if I pretend innocence, and he presents his version?"

"I agree. That sounds the best route."

Remembering that Raul had been lured with the promise of a free case of wine, Olivia took one of La Leggenda's smart, white-and-gold, branded boxes and hustled into the storage room, filling it with six of the nicest bottles she could find. Based on what she'd seen in the recycling bag, Raul had a particular love for reds, so she included five red wines, and the La Leggenda Metodo Classico sparkling wine.

It gave her a breathless feeling to think that if this went the way she hoped, Raul would be leaving without his wine, and perhaps even in the back of a police van. She placed the box on the tasting room counter, and then jumped as, from outside, she heard the growl of a powerful SUV engine.

“Good luck!” she whispered to Marcello, who nodded solemnly in her direction before composing himself into a demeanor of casual innocence. Olivia dived under the counter, nestling against the fridges as she heard the tramp of incoming feet.

“Buongiorno,” Marcello welcomed the arrival warmly.

“Marcello Vescovi? I am Raul Porzio. You invited me to a free tasting and mentioned a complimentary case of wine?” he said eagerly.

“So I did! You are the first guest to take us up on this special offer. It will be my pleasure to introduce you to our wines. Have you experienced them before?”

“Never. I did not know your winery was of a standard I would consider acceptable,” Raul said. “I only drink very high quality wines and am used to a more expensive price point, although I do see you have some high-end products at the top of your list.”

Bundled up behind the counter, Olivia seethed at this display of wine snobbery. She’d rather have her mother adding lemonade, she thought angrily. At least her mother was being honest and not ridiculously pretentious.

And why was it that these wealthy people who bragged about their money were always the first in line for free stuff, Olivia wondered, glaring at the lemonade bottle that happened to be at eye-level in the fridge under the counter.

Marcello poured the first wine. From the glugging and splashing, she guessed a very generous amount was being dispensed to encourage conversation.

“This is our award-winning vermentino. It is blended with a portion of sauvignon blanc and Semillon for a well-rounded finish that is bursting with fruit nuances while still maintaining a refreshingly dry character.”

“You have succeeded admirably in its balance,” Raul praised.

“Go on, have some more. With a white wine like this you really need a second and third taste to fully appreciate the wine’s vibrancy,” Marcello encouraged.

The sound of a clearly empty wineglass being put down soon followed.

“Now, our rose. When I say this is an easy drinking wine, you will soon see what I mean. It is fragrant, refreshing, and all about summer. I see this tasting bottle is half empty. We might as well finish it! I will join you in the appreciation of this very fine blend.”

The sounds of appreciative swallowing followed.

"I did not realize I was so thirsty today," Raul observed.

"The rose is a wine that truly quenches the thirst. Now, I am excited to offer you the third wine – our famous Miracolo red. This is the wine that brings most of the tourists to La Leggenda. Being such high quality, I often wonder how well it would last if it was laid down in a cellar for a hundred years or more," Marcello said.

Olivia pricked her ears, recognizing that her boss was now guiding the conversation to the critical issue.

"You must have heard about that cellar which was found on the land my family used to own?" Raul asked.

"I was away on a mentorship and have only just returned, so I do not yet know all the details. I understand that there was an incident last night. Most troubling," Marcello said.

"An incident? There was an actual killing, I believe. My family's historic wines could have been at risk," Raul corrected him.

"Really? I wonder what could have played out for that to occur. You say they are your family's wines?"

Raul hiccupped, causing Olivia's heart to leap. Clearly he'd reached a stage where he might abandon his reserve.

"This Miracolo is delightful. Can I have another glass? They are not legally ours, but I am convinced they should be returned to us. Clearly, our family buried those wines sometime in the past, to hide them. As many have been saying, the current owner, who is an extremely rude blond with no anger management skills, obviously got word of this and decided to buy the land and dig them up."

"You think?" Marcello sounded as anxious as Olivia now felt. That hadn't been how it played out at all, but if it was becoming common knowledge, others might try to interfere with pointless lawsuits.

Worse still, he seemed to be indulging in gossip, rather than confessing to the murder. For the first time Olivia felt a flicker of doubt. Had he done it?

"You must have thought about simply seizing the wine," Marcello said. Olivia let out a sigh of relief. Her boss was getting things back on track.

"I did. Being such an unfair situation, it occurred to me that I should simply take what I was owed."

Olivia's eyes bulged with anger. How dare he feel he was owed her wines? Horrible, entitled man. She heard Marcello give an irate snort, which he hastily turned into a cough before continuing his questioning.

"And did you explore that idea further?"

Olivia heard the unmistakable swallowing sound of Raul downing a glass of Miracolo.

"Yes. Yes, as it happens, I did. After finishing my dessert and coffee at the restaurant, I decided I was going to go and remove the wines from her property."

Clutching at the fridge to stop from toppling backward in astonishment, Olivia felt the situation was on a knife-edge. One more word, just one more word, and he would confess. She was sure of it.

"Then what happened?" Marcello struck exactly the right note with his casually curious tone.

"I went there at about ten-thirty p.m. I parked my SUV on the road. Then I walked through to the field whose whereabouts had been clearly described in the village gossip. It took me a while to find the door. Er, because so much time had passed since my childhood, when I played daily in that field," he added hastily. "Luckily, I had a flashlight in my trunk which I brought along with me."

"That was clever," Marcello praised.

"Basic logic. Not difficult for someone who attended one of the area's best and most expensive schools," Raul sneered.

"Even so, that must have been frightening! Did you carry anything with you for protection?"

How clever was Marcello, Olivia marveled, using the moment to inquire if he'd had a weapon, or picked anything up along the way.

Raul sighed. "Unfortunately not. Which as it turned out was a big mistake. When I found the cellar, I realized that this evil money-grabbing woman had locked it up. I couldn't get in and had brought no tools with me. So I decided I would go back home and collect the right equipment."

Olivia glowered at the lemonade. How dare Raul say such rude things about her?

"And did you do that?" Marcello asked. The edge to his voice told her he was simmering with anger at the insulting words.

Raul sounded regretful.

"It took me a while to find everything I needed and I had to call my neighbor to borrow a bolt cutter. He was not pleased to be phoned at quarter to midnight and started shouting at me. He even sent me a rude message back. Look!"

A short silence followed. Olivia hoped Marcello was taking note of the time the message was sent.

"Harsh words. Probably because it was so late at night," Marcello said. Olivia could hear that he agreed with every one of the words.

She felt a thud of disappointment that Raul seemed to have a concrete alibi. Meanwhile, he was continuing with his story.

"I decided I would use a crowbar instead, but the search had wasted a lot of time," Raul continued. "When I arrived back at the farm, I discovered the place was crawling with police! I hurried away again, sensing there had been a disaster, and I was right. There had been a murder. If I'd timed things differently, I might even have been caught up in it myself. It angered me to think that her selfishness could have put my own life in danger, had I not been lucky with the timing."

Olivia couldn't stand to hear another minute of this! Who did he think he was?

Before she could stop herself, or think better of it, she scrambled to her feet.

As her head popped up over the tasting counter, Raul gave an outraged cry.

He didn't get the chance to utter another word for some time. Opening her mouth, Olivia let him have it.

"I can't believe the ludicrousness of what I'm hearing. You were trespassing on my farm that night, looking to plunder a stash of wine which I rightfully own. And then when you nearly got caught up in a murder scene, you have the audacity to say that it was because I'm selfish? Me?"

She leaned over the counter. In her wrath she must have appeared terrifying, because Raul stumbled to his feet, tried to take a step back, and almost fell over his stool. Luckily Marcello grabbed his arm, dexterously retrieving the wineglass.

"You know what makes people have anger management problems? Having strangers butt into their life and start claiming their property. How would you feel if I walked into your fancy house and said your overpriced SUV belonged to me? Or that ride-on mower? I could use a ride-on, and yours looks like the one that used to belong to my mother, so it's clearly my family's property. I'll come around later to collect it! That's exactly what you're doing. It's raw greed and let me tell you, it's disgusting!"

Olivia was starting to feel dizzy after her outburst. She stopped to draw breath.

In the sudden silence that followed, Raul turned to Marcello. He wrenched his arm away.

"Signor Vescovi, I am horrified that you have clearly lured me here under false pretenses, just so that this dislikable woman can abuse me. I am deeply offended. I will certainly not be recommending your winery, or your wines, to anyone in the future. I will leave, now."

He turned and marched toward the door.

"Signor! Your complimentary parcel," Marcello called after him.

Raul hesitated and Olivia watched with interest as his greedy desire for free wine warred with his need to make a grand gesture by marching away empty handed.

The wine won.

He spun around, stomped back to the counter, grabbed the box, and headed for the door again. Olivia could almost see the trailing shreds of his dignity following him out.

"I'm sorry," she apologized to her boss. "I couldn't stop from saying something. I hope it doesn't reflect badly on the winery's name."

Marcello nodded sympathetically.

"I do not blame you. From the neighbor's message, it seems Raul is not well liked in the community, so his opinion should not be overly damaging. But sadly, despite trespassing with intent to steal, it is clear he was not the killer. He has an alibi, and was searching for equipment at the time."

"What a shame," Olivia sighed.

"I must get back to work now, but let me know if you need my help again." Marcello gave her an impish grin. "That was fun!"

He headed back to his office at speed. Olivia waved at Jean-Pierre, who waved back through the glass-paned restaurant door. With the suspect gone, Collina Wine Week could now resume in the tasting room and that meant she needed to hotfoot it off the property again.

As she headed out to the parking lot, her phone rang. It was Danilo.

He must be calling to update her on her mother's visit to Pisa. She hoped it had gone well. Smiling in expectation, she answered.

Her adrenaline spiked when she heard the panic in his voice.

"Quick! There has been a disaster. You need to come back home, as soon as you can!"

CHAPTER TWENTY THREE

What had gone wrong? Frantic with anxiety, Olivia sprinted for her car and zoomed out of La Leggenda.

Scenarios boiled in her imagination. It was already a quarter past two. Had the police arrived early? Were they about to arrest her loyal boyfriend? Visions filled her mind of Danilo at her farmhouse, surrounded by officers, being handcuffed and pushed unceremoniously into the back of a van. She had to get back as fast as she could, and tell the police to arrest her instead.

Danilo was innocent! After all he'd been through, she couldn't allow him to be locked up. It would be cruel and unfair.

"Just wait for me to get there. Please, wait," Olivia begged aloud, hoping her frantic thoughts had the power to reach Detective Caputi.

She skidded into the sand road and tore up the hill, swerving through the farmhouse gateway so fast that she came within inches of scraping the Fiat.

Trembling with nerves, she jumped out, but as she did, confusion filled her.

There were no police cars here. Only Danilo's pickup, which looked polished and pristine.

What was going on?

As she headed for the front door, it burst open. Danilo rushed out, his face taut with anxiety. He hurried over to her.

"I am glad you got back so quick. We have a terrible situation!"

"What is it? What?" Olivia gasped. With no police in sight, her imagination started running wild. Had the wine stash been stolen? Had the cellar collapsed?

"Your mother!" Danilo announced.

"What's happened to her?" Could this become a bigger nightmare? Olivia's mind reeled at the possibilities.

"She's leaving!" Danilo tugged at his hair, which looked spiky and disheveled. He seemed on the point of tears.

"Leaving?" Olivia took an actual step back. "Um – how do you mean? How can she be leaving?"

She tugged at her own hair. It seemed her mother's behavior was causing an epidemic of this!

"She is." Danilo sounded frantic. "It wasn't my doing, I swear. We had fun in Pisa. She seemed happy. She ate an ice cream and I took many photos of the tower for her. We got back about an hour ago and suddenly, now, she asked me to help her bring her bags downstairs, because she's changed her flight and is heading home!"

Olivia hugged her wonderful boyfriend as tightly as she could.

"Of course it wasn't you. It's her. She must have gotten upset for some minor reason. She can be like that. Perhaps I can sort it out."

Gathering her courage, Olivia stepped into the farmhouse.

There stood Mrs. Glass, in the hallway, with her two valises, which Olivia knew would be methodically packed down to the last undergarment and plastic-wrapped pair of shoes.

"Ah, Olivia," she said. "You're back. I didn't think you would be home today. I was going to leave a note for you. Isn't that funny? Leaving a note for my own daughter, who I traveled here to be with."

With her mind racing, Olivia thought she was getting the gist of why her mother was so unhappy.

"You're leaving because I wasn't here this morning? But I thought you went on an outing and had a lovely time."

"Pisa was very pleasant. Angel, it's a combination of things." Her mother let out a deep, dramatic sigh. "Firstly, I cannot get my head around the fact you're just a bartender."

Olivia opened her mouth to snap out an angry retort, but before she could, Mrs. Glass steamrollered on.

"Just a bartender in a little Italian village. Then I find you've been caught up in a murder and the whole of the village has started treating this farm, which I notice is inadequately fenced, as public property. Seeing you don't even bother closing the gate, I can't actually blame any of the simple local populace, with their poor command of English and basic understanding of life, for getting the wrong idea."

"But…" Olivia tried. It was all she had time to say.

"Thirdly, it's very obvious that you are ignoring me. I would have thought you'd have dropped everything to spend time with me. Although Daniel is a very pleasant man, I did come here to be with you."

"You didn't come here to visit with me at all. I know you better than that," Olivia retorted, glad that her mother had at last paused to take a breath. "You came to convince me to come back to the States!"

"Well, it seems that my efforts to save you from a meaningless existence, frittering your talents away in a remote village that nobody cares about, have been futile," her mother retorted.

"If you really wanted to save me, you could help me clear my name, since I've been caught up in a murder investigation," Olivia pleaded. "I haven't been ignoring you. I've just had a lot on my plate."

"Sweetheart, I know nothing about murders. The only way I can help is to convince you to leave this dangerous country, and come back home where it's safe."

Wrath surged inside Olivia as she put her hands on her hips and faced her mother down. Surprisingly, even though she was fuming, she found she was able to speak the harsh words in a level, calm voice.

"Mom, the problem is that you have never, ever, since I came here, taken my new life seriously. You've never tried to understand it properly even though I've done my best to explain. Rather than embracing, you've belittled everything about this wonderful place where I live. Which has an incredible history, and has been home to some of the greatest thinkers, artists and poets the world has ever known. It's a tourist mecca, attracting thousands and thousands of visitors from all over the world and filled with more wonderful sights than I'll ever have time to see!"

Then, gathering up her courage, Olivia addressed the point that stung the most.

"Winemaking is what I want to do and this is where I want to do it. This is where I feel alive, and that what I'm doing in life really matters. Compared to here, my marketing job in Chicago felt meaningless. This place and my new career have meaning! And I should probably tell you now, even though it's a bit late, that I am actually in a serious relationship with Danilo and have known him for nearly a year."

"What? Why didn't you tell me earlier?" Mrs. Glass sounded outraged.

Of all the points she'd made, Olivia was bemused that this one seemed to have offended her mother the most. Struggling to keep a calm tone, she continued.

"I didn't tell you because I was afraid you might give him a hard time if you thought he was one of the reasons keeping me here. Because that's exactly the sort of thing you do. I wanted to protect him, Mom. This is the kind of complication your behavior has caused. I'm done with tiptoeing around you now, so there won't be any more incidents like that. You need to accept that this is my life and this is who I am. Because I'm not changing my life and I'm not coming back!"

Despite herself, she couldn't help shouting out the last few words.

There was a resounding silence. The only noise was Olivia's rapid breathing.

"I think you've made yourself very clear," her mother responded.

"Please accept it. Because there is no other option," Olivia insisted.

And then, from outside the partly-open front door, she heard the putter of a Fiat's engine.

"I believe my cab has arrived," Mrs. Glass said icily. "Goodbye, sweetheart. Perhaps we'll see each other again one day."

Olivia's mouth fell open. She felt robbed of speech. Her mother was going? After she'd tried so hard to get everything out into the open, she was leaving with all their issues unresolved?

Danilo rushed into the hallway.

"What shall I tell the driver?" he asked, sounding as panicked as Olivia now felt.

"Nothing. No need to tell him anything. Perhaps you would be so kind as to carry out my bags?" Mrs. Glass asked him in clipped, formal tones.

Looking as if he'd seen a ghost, Danilo picked up the valises and hustled outside.

Olivia stared in shock as Mrs. Glass paced out of the front door without a backward glance. She felt frozen in place and couldn't even walk to the door. She stayed inside, running her hands over the polished wooden hall table that Danilo had made for her, and a moment later she heard the cab accelerate away.

Her mother was gone. She'd messed up any chance at mending things. Even though she'd tried not to shout and scream, her harsh words had broken their relationship in a way that couldn't be fixed.

With the murder investigation dragging on, the locals suspecting her, and the cellar unstable, her future here was in jeopardy. She might never succeed in the new life she'd defended so angrily.

Olivia felt as trapped as she'd ever been.

Was there a way out of this mess, she thought despairingly.

And then, from outside, she heard the distinctive buzz of a Fiat's engine, this time, incoming.

Had her mother reconsidered? Perhaps this would be a turning point in her life, and she could make everything right.

With wild hope surging inside her, she rushed to the door.

CHAPTER TWENTY FOUR

Bursting out of the front door, Olivia stared at the incoming car. Then her shoulders slumped. She'd never thought she would be disappointed to see Charlotte arriving home, but she'd been so hoping it would be her mother. Was she not having agonizing second thoughts about what had played out between them, just the same way Olivia was?

"Olivia's mother has left for the airport!" Danilo, still sounding upset, was updating Charlotte as she walked to the front door.

"But why?" Charlotte asked him, sounding confused. Then, seeing Olivia, she asked her the same question. "What happened with your mom? Why'd she go? We were discussing this morning that we should go clothes shopping in Florence tomorrow. We were even chatting about organizing you a surprise birthday dinner this coming weekend."

Olivia sighed, still feeling crushed by what had played out.

"She couldn't accept that I wanted to stay here for good. I think she lost her temper. She has a terrible temper."

"Well, to be fair, so do you," Charlotte retorted.

"Me?" Olivia stared at Charlotte, confused.

"Luckily you're not angry often but when you are, everyone runs and hides. Don't they?" She glanced at Danilo.

"I can confirm that," Danilo said.

"So there you go. Two fiery personalities. No wonder you rub each other the wrong way."

Olivia thought Charlotte must be mistaken. She was as gentle as a lamb. Wasn't she?

"What should I do? I'm feeling shattered by all of this. Should I go to the airport and find her?" Olivia pleaded.

"You can if you like, but it'll take two hours there and back, with the road works they're busy doing. Do you have two hours to spare?" Charlotte asked, twisting her fingers together anxiously.

"I don't! It's already quarter to three!" Turning to Danilo, Olivia delivered the bombshell. "Detective Caputi wants to re-interview us at four p.m., and I am certain she wants to arrest one of us. She found out that I chased after the suspect and you arrived at the cellar on your own."

"That is terribly unfair. Neither of us should have to take the fall for a guilty man," Danilo said firmly.

Olivia thought it was weird, but for a split-second that word 'fall' made her think of something. A connection flashed into her mind, but it was so brief and tenuous that she couldn't hold onto it and it slipped away.

"I don't want to risk it, Danilo. I know what that detective's like and she's draconian. We need to present her with a better suspect and I'm all out of leads. All the promising prospects have alibis. I have no idea, absolutely no clue, which direction to look in now. I don't mind admitting, I'm panicking majorly now," Olivia shared.

Charlotte sighed in frustration.

"What haven't we thought of? There must be something we haven't touched on yet. Let's sit down over coffee in the kitchen, and brainstorm this together.

Olivia led the way into the kitchen and started up the coffee machine. While it brewed, she joined Charlotte and Danilo at the table. She could see her own worry reflected in their eyes.

"Maybe they were working together," Charlotte hazarded.

"How do you mean?" Danilo asked.

"The two men. Perhaps they were a team, or partners in crime, and they had a falling out. One killed the other and then ran away."

Danilo jumped up and poured the coffee. He set the cups down on the table looking thoughtful.

"If so, why was nothing stolen? If one killed the other, he would surely have continued with his plan? He did not have to simply run away."

"That's the problem with that theory. But maybe he panicked." Olivia sipped her coffee – hot, strong, and with the perfect amount of cream. She hoped it got her brain working!

"The victim was the one trying to steal wine. He was the one with the bottle beside him," Danilo observed.

"That could have been planted there," Charlotte argued.

"I want to know why the bottle didn't break. Surely if he had been struck on the head hard enough to kill him, he would have fallen hard enough for it to smash," Danilo agreed.

"Maybe it was the way he fell?" Charlotte asked.

"He seemed to have almost collapsed while cradling it," Danilo agreed.

Olivia found herself watching one and then the other, as if she was a spectator at a tennis match. But thanks to the animated discussion, she had an idea. She knew what their next move should be.

"We need to investigate Heberto in more detail," she decided.

"How do you mean? He's the deceased," Charlotte said. "Investigate him how?"

"To see who he's connected to. He seems to be a mystery man, but he can't be. Isn't that the double-edged sword of living in a small village? Everyone knows your business? I have visited the homes of the other two claimants. But not his. Who's he connected to? What are they hiding? How does this mesh with what we know so far?"

"Yes, that's a very good idea," Charlotte said. "Let's start by looking in the phone book. It worked for Raul, right?"

"Shall we go into Collina and ask around? People will know him, or know of him. My first stop will be the hardware store," Danilo said.

"Those are good suggestions. Let's do them both," Olivia said.

Although both Charlotte and Danilo seemed quietly optimistic, she felt less so. There was something strange about the fact Detective Caputi was battling to contact his next-of-kin. If everyone in the village knew each other, why was there a problem with that?

And nobody was talking about him, Olivia realized. Why had no irate locals confronted her to say, "You murdered my friend!" Or perhaps, "You used your ninja skills to annihilate my next-door neighbor!" Or even, "Who am I going to buy my gnocchi from now?"

But there had been none of that. None at all. She instinctively felt Heberto had been lurking below the radar.

Draining his coffee, Danilo stood up. "We must hurry. We don't have much time before being arrested, apparently. Shall we all go in my car? We can stay in touch by phone and meet up along the way. Is everyone's phone charged?"

"Yes," Olivia and Charlotte said in unison.

They trooped out of the door. Danilo looked excited to be leading the way. And Charlotte looked ecstatic to be participating in an actual murder investigation.

"Wait till Artoro hears!" she whispered to Olivia as they climbed inside. "Not that I'm going to tell him. I wouldn't want him to worry, even though he'd have some great pointers for us. But they're very busy this afternoon after a diamond robbery in the city center. The criminals were wearing Disney masks, which makes tracking down the suspects difficult. I can't burden him with this."

She raised her chin courageously as Danilo sprayed gravel accelerating out of the farmhouse.

"We must split up in the village," Danilo said as he navigated the short route in record-breaking speed. "Charlotte, you will start with the phone directory at the post office. I will go to the hardware store. Olivia?"

"I'll go to the hair salon," she said. Hopefully they wouldn't think she was starting to lurk around the place. Since she was well supplied with shampoo now, she might need to justify her visit by buying a conditioner.

*

In the village, Danilo shoehorned his pickup into a parking space and they all bailed out. Olivia sprinted for the salon, hoping Francesca would still be there.

She was. She was accepting payment, and what looked like a generous tip, from a young woman with simply gorgeous platinum and pink locks. Olivia goggled in admiration as the beautiful client sashayed out. Then she quickly slunk in.

"Ah, Olivia! You are back? How can I help?" Francesca gave a conspiratorial wink as she spoke, to indicate that she knew the subtext of the scene that was playing out.

"Francesca, I would like to buy some conditioner," Olivia said loudly. Then, in a softer voice, she added, "I was wondering if you'd ever cut the hair of a local person called Heberto Zacconi."

Francesca frowned.

"Heberto who?"

"Zacconi."

"How long is his hair?"

Olivia thought back with a shiver to that unpleasant encounter and what followed. "Quite short. Neatly trimmed. Definitely not more than a month since the last cut."

Francesca casually sauntered over to the product shelves and picked out a conditioner. As she took it, she glanced behind her and called out to the barber.

"Was Heberto Zacconi ever our client?"

He listened, looking confused, and shook his head.

“Heberto who?”

“Zacconi.”

“Never!” he shouted.

Francesca turned back to Olivia. Moving to the till, she rang up the conditioner looking equally puzzled.

“As a hairdresser I have never heard of him. But as someone who has lived here all my life, I have also not heard of him. That family name is completely unfamiliar,” she said softly.

“Danilo wasn’t sure,” Olivia said. “He thought the hardware store manager would know.”

Francesca nodded wisely. “Remember, Danilo was away from the village for many years while working on the ships, and only returned a couple of years ago. He, like you, still feels that in a way he is a stranger here. Perhaps I should not tell you that, as it is personal. But I know it is true.”

Surprised, Olivia took in that news. How bizarre that Danilo still felt so far removed from the local community. Knowing that made her feel closer to him. But Francesca was continuing so she dragged her attention back.

“I have never left, apart from vacations to Europe. I know everyone in this town. And never, ever have I heard of this person.”

Olivia narrowed her eyes as she digested this golden nugget of information.

“He said his family was originally from here. They had to leave, probably decades ago, but then returned.”

“The wider area, maybe, but not Collina.” Emphatically, Francesca shook her head.

“That’s weird,” Olivia said.

“It’s very weird,” Francesca agreed. “I wish I could help you more.”

Olivia had a brainwave as she put the conditioner in her purse.

“You’ve been very helpful. Thanks to what you’ve told me, I think I know what to do next.”

Walking away from the salon, Olivia quickly dialed her co-investigators.

“Meet me at the bistro,” she hissed. “I have important information.”

She rushed across the road to find Danilo arriving at the same time from the direction of the hardware store. Quickly, they sat down at the last available outside table. There was Charlotte, hurrying across from the post office. Olivia waved to her and saw her break into a run.

"A pitcher of lemonade, please," Danilo said to the waiter. Olivia thought that was an excellent idea. Her throat was dry.

"I'm glad you have information, because the telephone directory was useless," Charlotte grumbled breathlessly as she sat down. "Not a single Zacconi anywhere in the wider area. You'd think it was a discontinued last name."

Danilo nodded, looking frustrated. "The hardware store manager knew nothing of him or his family. That means that as far as the village goes, he does not exist."

"Francesca said the same thing. She's never heard of that name among the locals. But the fact remains he ended up on my farm," Olivia agreed.

"How did he get there?" Charlotte asked, puzzled.

Ugo himself arrived with the jug and set the glasses on the table with a flourish and a welcoming smile. He seemed to be taking pains to show that he believed in Olivia's innocence. Perhaps that was a small but hopeful sign that others might also change their mind.

Feeling reassured, she poured the lemonade. It was delightfully tart and icy cold with springs of mint.

"He had a car when he arrived at your farm earlier in the day to stake his claim to the treasure. It was a small Fiat that could have been a rental," Danilo remembered.

"Yes, he did. A small, white Fiat. That narrows it down to a few hundred in the village," Olivia sighed.

"I wish I had taken note of the number plate but there was so much else to think about at that time," Danilo said, sounding regretful.

"But when he was found dead, there was no abandoned car nearby. So he left by car in the afternoon, but didn't drive back when he returned at night."

Olivia drank more lemonade as she watched her boyfriend and bestie reach the same conclusion she had done. She could see their eyes light up as they had the same 'Aha' moment.

"He walked!" Charlotte exclaimed.

"So he was staying in the village," Danilo nodded.

"Could he have taken a cab from further away?" Charlotte hazarded.

"I don't recall the police saying he had a phone on him. He had a flashlight, but I saw no phone," Danilo said.

"So then, he was staying at one of the hotels or B&Bs, and we need to question them," Charlotte then said.

"There are also a few Airbnbs," Danilo said.

"Exactly."

Feeling purposeful and full of hope now that they had a new direction to explore, Olivia drained her lemonade while Danilo slid a ten-Euro note under the pepper grinder.

The mysterious Heberto might have eluded them so far, but the facts proved that he must have been residing somewhere locally.

"I will start at the bottom of the village," Olivia said. That was one of her favorite walks, leading past the ruined castle and the gorgeous boutique apartments nearby. If she'd had a second life to lead here, without a doubt she would have bought one of those compact but pricey homes. She knew Francesca felt the same way. If she purchased one and Olivia played her cards right, she might be able to visit for dinner one day.

"I will start from the top," Danilo said.

"Well, I'll go down the side street as far as the small hotel, and work back from there," Charlotte said.

They all stood up and hurried out. As she strode determinedly down the hill, Olivia felt filled with hope. This line of investigation had to lead somewhere. With any luck, their tireless legwork would uncover where this fortune seeker had been staying.

CHAPTER TWENTY FIVE

At the bottom of the village, Olivia paused for a moment to admire the ruined castle, which seemed to take on a different mood every hour of the day. Now, bathed in sunshine, its crumbling battlements did not look spooky or threatening, but rather ancient, wise, and mysterious. In fact, Olivia decided, the castle seemed like a beacon of hope.

The first hotel was a quaint inn located just after the apartments she loved the most. Walking past their cream-plastered walls, Olivia glanced at the delightful wrought-iron balconies, featuring plant pots filled with colorful geraniums.

Next-door, the small hotel was just as scenic. It was a compact, seven-room establishment that was always booked solidly with tourists.

The door was open and Olivia headed into the hallway which served as the reception area. The aroma of coffee filled the air. The hallway would have been gloomy, were it not for the beautiful stained-glass window set high in the back wall.

There, looking frantically busy, speaking on the phone while she checked in a guest, was the plump and cheerful Signora Pacci, who ran the place together with her husband.

Signora Pacci's brown eyes widened when she saw Olivia and she looked alarmed. The message was clear. She was wondering what a suspected killer might be doing in her small, cozy hotel.

Luckily, Signora Pacci worked at whirlwind speed. Concluding her call, she guided the guest down the short corridor. Olivia heard her enthusing as she unlocked the door.

"Here is your room, signor. It has a lovely view of Collina's castle. We hope you will be happy here! Remember, complimentary tea and coffee are always available in the lobby."

She rushed back to the reception desk.

"Signora Glass. How can I help?" Now she sounded more reserved, and in fact rather suspicious.

Olivia couldn't wait to clear her name so that people stopped treating her like a pariah.

"I'm investigating the suspicious death that occurred on my farm," she said.

Raising her other eyebrow, Signora Pacci waited for her to continue, tapping her fingers on the dark-polished reception desk that was crowded with tourism pamphlets, restaurant brochures, and other paraphernalia.

"The victim, Heberto Zacconi, was killed by an unknown assailant who fled the scene. But while searching for the assailant, I have discovered nobody knows who Heberto is. Therefore, he must have traveled here and possibly stayed in local accommodation," Olivia explained.

"Ah, you want to know if he checked in here?" Signora Pacci asked. She seemed friendlier now. All it had taken was a simple explanation to set her right, Olivia realized in relief.

"Yes, that's correct."

"Nobody by that name has booked in here within the past few days. We've had no guests unaccounted for either," Signora Pacci confirmed. "All our visitors at this time are international, none Italian. So I think we are in the clear, no?"

To Olivia's surprise she gave her a warm smile.

"It seems so," she agreed.

'I am glad you are investigating. I, too, believe in taking action if I feel there is unfairness. I hope that you are able to resolve this and correct the misinformation that seems to have spread." Signora Pacci nodded approvingly.

Olivia felt much better as she left the quaint, pretty hotel. Even though she hadn't yet identified the deceased she did feel she'd re-forged a friendly relationship with one of the village's nicest people.

The next establishment, a couple of doors along, was an Airbnb that she didn't know at all. Luckily there was a small notice outside with the owner's phone number. Olivia dialed it, and found herself speaking to a grumpy man.

"I am sorry, we are full," he snapped. "We have only one apartment and it is currently in the middle of a two-week booking with a family of regular guests."

"Oh, dear. Thank you," Olivia said. The short conversation had given her all the information she needed.

The next hotel on her list, the Collina Inn, was a two-minute walk up the steep hill. It was one of the larger, and more affordable, in the local village. It was a twelve-room hotel and Olivia had always thought it represented great value. Even though the rooms were small, they were well furnished, with thick stone walls, and full of character. And if you got a street-view room, you could peer out of your window and see the rival bakers engaging in their fake feud.

She headed inside, where the receptionist was on a step ladder, dusting the small chandelier in the hallway.

"Buongiorno, how can I help you?" she said, climbing quickly down.

"Buongiorno," Olivia said. This receptionist didn't seem to know who she was so she decided to adjust her story accordingly. "I was wondering if a certain guest might have checked into your hotel a day or two ago. I've been battling to locate him."

"Sure, I can look for you," the receptionist said. She put the step ladder away and scooted around the desk, tapping her computer keyboard. "What is his name?"

"Heberto Zacconi," Olivia said.

"And you say he checked in a day or two ago?"

She peered at the screen, shaking her head. "No, signora, we have had no such person booking in."

Olivia was about to thank her and leave when something that Signora Pacci had said began niggling at her mind. The efficient hotelier had said that there was nobody unaccounted for. What if Heberto had used another name, Olivia suddenly wondered. She decided this idea would be worth pursuing.

"I might have got the name wrong. Heberto is a nickname. He might have used his real name but I unfortunately don't know what that is."

Realizing this story was developing more holes than Swiss cheese, Olivia decided to press on quickly before the receptionist could think too hard about what she'd said. "Have you had any guests unaccounted for? Anyone who checked in and then disappeared, or been absent from the hotel?"

The receptionist frowned, clearly thinking hard.

"Actually, now you mention it, we were speaking this morning about one of our guests in room number ten. He booked in yesterday morning and the chambermaid mentioned that his bed had not been slept in last night." She shrugged. "These things happen. Sometimes, guests make other plans. Or arrive for different reasons." She smiled mysteriously.

Olivia felt all her instincts prickle. This had to be the same man.

"What did this gentleman look like?"

"He was average height. Short, slicked-back dark hair, and a charming demeanor."

It was the same one! Olivia felt excitement flare inside her. She was sure this helpful woman would agree to let her take a look inside the room. All she had to do was word the question in the right way.

Her brain fizzed as she decided what the right way would be.

As Olivia was about to utter the all-important request, the back-office door clicked open, and a stern-looking, silver-haired woman swept into the reception area.

Quickly, she shut her mouth again, processing the sudden intrusion of this bossy-looking signora who, from her commanding attitude, was clearly the owner.

"The party staying in rooms two and three have requested the extra-firm support pillows. Have you provided those yet?" she asked the receptionist sternly.

"I was about to," the receptionist said. She grabbed a spare room key from the row of hooks on the back wall. Looking guilty, she hurried off.

The woman turned to Olivia and her face changed.

"I know you!" she exclaimed. "You are the Americano who has caused all the problems. I understand you are wanted by the police! What are you doing here?"

Her face was like thunder. Olivia knew instantly that this authoritative female would be immune to any charm, or any story. Searching room ten was out of the question now. Her only course of action was to leave without inflaming her suspicions to the extent she called the police.

If she did, Olivia would be in a world of trouble.

"Signora, buongiorno," she said. "I am not wanted by the police and am simply here on behalf of my employer, La Leggenda. They wanted to make sure that everyone working in this hotel is aware of Collina Wine Week which began today. Every Collina resident is welcome to claim a free wine tasting and also a large discount on the first bottle purchased." She smiled winningly at the owner, noting that the mention of free wine had already caused the angry gleam to disappear from her eyes.

"I had heard of it, but was not aware it had started already, or that we received a free tasting. That is very kind of La Leggenda and we will certainly come along. We, as hardworking locals, often feel unappreciated by businesses catering for tourists so this is a wonderful initiative. Tell your bosses, though, that in view of current events, it might be better for them to send somebody else to notify us."

"I will do," Olivia said. Feeling as if she'd managed to avoid catastrophe by the skin of her teeth, she hurried out of the hotel.

Stepping into the street, Olivia realized she'd left a ticking bomb behind her. As soon as the receptionist had organized the extra-firm pillows, the hotel owner might check up on Olivia's story. She seemed to be that sort of woman. If the receptionist spilled the beans, the owner would call the police immediately.

Before any of this could play out, Olivia had to get inside room number ten.

She had only minutes to come up with a plan that would allow her to sneak back into the hotel and enter that room, without being caught.

CHAPTER TWENTY SIX

As soon as she was out of sight of the hotel, Olivia called Danilo.

"Have you had success?" He sounded hopeful.

"It's complicated," Olivia admitted. "Success is near, yet far. I need your help as I can't show my face in the hotel again."

"Where are you? I am on my way."

"The Collina Inn. Or rather, I'm not there. I'm outside the shoe store on the corner."

"I will be there in two minutes." Danilo sounded as if he was already starting to run.

Olivia watched for him. In mid-afternoon, the street was a bustling hive of activity. She was struck by the amount of color that had erupted now that spring had arrived. The window boxes were brighter, and the roadside trees festooned with blossoms. Everyone seemed to have put their black and navy attire away and was sporting pretty pastel hats and tops.

There was Danilo, striding down the road. Quickly she waved him over.

"Heberto was staying in room number ten, but he booked in under a different name. The receptionist described him and it's a perfect match. But then the owner arrived and realized who I was. I got out of there as fast as I could, and can't go back. If the receptionist tells her what I was asking, she'll call the police, so it's extremely urgent."

Danilo looked concerned.

"We must act immediately! Do you have any ideas? What should we do?"

"I noticed the room keys are all hanging on hooks on the wall behind the reception desk. There was a spare key there for room ten. If you could create some kind of distraction, I could grab the key and go and look in the room. There must be some personal information in there. Perhaps a phone, or proof of address in his bag?"

Danilo's eyebrows were just about hitting his hairline.

"That is very risky. It would land you directly in jail if you are found out."

“Can you think of another plan? Because if not, no matter how reckless, it’s our only hope.”

Danilo nodded slowly. She could see his thoughts racing.

“Let me try,” he said. “I will ask to view one of the rooms. If the owner shows it to me then you will have your chance.”

He strode inside. Speaking loudly, Olivia heard him say, “Buongiorno!” She tiptoed forward, as close to the entrance as she dared, straining her ears to hear what he was saying.

Danilo was talking in Italian, deliberately slow and clearly so that Olivia could hear. “I have a friend visiting soon. I have heard your rooms are small but comfortable, but would like to see the size and furnishings for myself.”

“Of course, signor,” the owner replied. “Room nine is open. They are all similar. Would you like to see that one?”

Room nine? Olivia swallowed hard. That was going to be next to room ten. She’d have to be very careful. Risky had just become downright crazy.

“Please show me,” Danilo said.

Olivia peered around the corner to see Danilo following the owner to the staircase, which meant room ten would also be on the second floor.

Quickly, she tiptoed into the reception area, lifted the desk flap, marched to the back wall, and removed spare key number ten just as if she worked there. Then, with her heart hammering in her throat, she raced up the spiral staircase, aware of how loud her footsteps sounded on the wooden boards.

Inside room number nine, she could hear Danilo talking loudly and nonstop, obviously trying to provide a noisy distraction.

“Is the toilet modern?” she heard him ask. “My friend does not like old facilities.”

Olivia was filled with admiration that he’d managed to get the owner safely into the bathroom while she passed.

She unlocked the door of room ten, flinching as the key rattled in the lock. Quickly she pocketed it, and stepped inside. Closing the door softly behind her, she let out a shaky breath. She was in! Step one of this ultra-risky scheme had succeeded.

The room was neat and tidy. Heberto had unpacked, but his clothes only filled one shelf and two hangers. He hadn’t intended to stay for long, that was for sure. His valise was tidily stowed at the bottom of the wardrobe. The bed had been made, the coverlet smooth.

How could she find out more about him? Had he left notes anywhere? Did he have a phone or laptop with him?

She sighed in frustration as she pulled open drawer after empty drawer, closing them as softly as she could in case they could pick up any thumping from next door.

There was only one place still to look, Olivia realized. That was the valise itself.

She unzipped the pockets. No notepad, no phone, no convenient mini laptop.

But here was something!

Letting her breath out in a sigh of relief, Olivia drew out a car key, a passport and driver's license from the inside pocket of the valise. Inside the passport was the paper from the car hire booking.

Staring at the passport in puzzlement, Olivia realized this wasn't Heberto. Well, it was. The photos showed the same man, even though his hair was slightly different. Without a doubt though she recognized that narrow nose, that wide mouth, those well-groomed eyebrows.

But this ID was in a completely different name. Henri Zappi.

What did it mean? She had no idea. He'd been using a false name, but which, if either, were real? He must have had the Heberto Zacconi ID on him at the time of his death, or some proof of the name, but if that name was false, it could be why the police had been unable to contact any of his relatives.

She didn't want to risk taking the ID away but she photographed the driver's license and passport carefully. Her mind was racing about the implications of this find. They must be serious. She felt excited, nervous and confused.

She heard Danilo's voice speaking from next door, and then a rattle that indicated he'd opened the room's window.

"A pleasant street view," he said loudly.

Perhaps this was a message to her that she should peek out too, so that they could communicate. With trembling hands, she undid the latch and raised the sash window, which opened smoothly. She stuck her head out and peered nervously to her left.

There was Danilo, peering to his right.

"Olivia!" he whispered. "Are you done?"

"I'm done," she nodded.

"I'll distract her so you can go," he hissed. Then in a normal tone and switching back to Italian, he continued. "I see the bakers are already throwing bread at each other. So early in the season? It must bode well for good tourist numbers this year."

He closed the window. Olivia closed hers, too, as quietly as she could, and put the latch back. Then she took a final glance around the room to make sure everything was as tidy as she'd found it.

She heard the door of number nine close. The key rattled in the lock and footsteps retreated. Danilo was asking the owner something else – she thought she heard him say the word 'breakfast room' and she guessed this would lead the owner away from reception and clear the way for her to leave.

Tiptoeing outside, she closed the door and rushed back down the corridor.

There was the receptionist! The wild card in the equation they'd all forgotten about. She was bustling down the corridor ahead of another guest.

Olivia shrank back into the stairwell. If the guest was going upstairs, it was game over for her. She held her breath, feeling helpless as she waited to see what would happen.

They passed by the staircase. Quivering with tension, she rushed down the corridor. She lifted the flap, replaced the key on the hook, and turned, letting out a sigh of relief.

Just as she hustled out of the main door, she met two tourists heading in. Thank goodness she hadn't been a moment later, she thought, sprinting down the street to put some distance between her and the hotel. They would have caught her behind the counter and then things could have gotten extremely awkward.

As it was, she'd discovered that the deceased man had a double identity. He must be some kind of fake, or con-man. But what did that mean for the case?

And, more urgently, with the clock ticking down, how was she going to find anyone connected to him, when all his known names and identities might be false? It was already half past three. She needed to get together with the others for a last, desperate pow-wow. Perhaps Charlotte or Danilo would have a brainwave on what to do next.

*

Olivia felt the pressure mount as she sidled into the small village library. She'd told the others to meet here as soon as possible for their recce. A moment later, Danilo walked in, and a few seconds afterward, Charlotte hurried through the door to join them.

There was nobody in the library except two bored-looking schoolboys sitting at the large, majestic wooden table and paging through homework books in an unmotivated way. The place was cool, calm and peaceful.

Olivia retreated all the way to the back of the library and they clustered together.

"He's got a different identity from his name," Olivia said, showing the photos she'd taken on her phone.

"A con-man for sure," Charlotte said.

"If he behaved that way, others might have been cheated by him, too. Perhaps he was not killed by a fortune hunter, but by someone with a more personal motive for revenge," Danilo suggested, his eyes shining.

"Brilliant idea! Brilliant!" Charlotte punched the air.

"We need to find where he really lives," Olivia suggested. "How do you think we can go about that?"

Glancing over Danilo's shoulder, she saw that both the schoolchildren had abandoned their homework and were listening to her with interest. Both must have been paying attention during their English studies to understand what was being said.

"Ask the neighbors?" the closest boy volunteered.

"Find his mother? Mothers know everything!" the second one suggested.

Olivia glanced at Danilo and Charlotte in consternation. She didn't want her investigation to be the talk of the town.

"Great ideas. Thanks, kids. We'll keep them in mind," she said.

Charlotte grabbed her arm and spoke in a stage whisper.

"Actually, I do have a way we can research this. Remember, I have police connections now and have picked up a few pointers. They sometimes use the public records, just like you and I would do. I'll just have to go into the computer room. You keep the kids distracted, otherwise they might follow me in," she grinned.

"I'll wait outside," Danilo murmured, heading for the door.

As the others disappeared, Olivia smiled at the children, not knowing how to start this important conversation.

"Are you enjoying your homework?" she tried.

"No. That's a silly question," the closer boy said, frowning at her critically.

"Are you a detective? I don't think you look like a good one," the second one added.

"Why's that?" she asked, feeling hurt.

"Because you're blonde. All the detective ladies in the story books I read have dark hair," the second child explained.

"Well, I'm going to tell my father about her," the first one emphasized.

Thinking fast, Olivia said, "Uh – we're just playing a game. It's a murder mystery day. We have to outwit four other teams if we're going to win the prize. They've had us running all around town!"

"What is the prize?" the first child asked.

"It's a free dinner at Trattoria del Lucco."

"Seafood," the first child said, making a face. "Yuk! If I were you I wouldn't try too hard to solve it."

"I hope you don't like seafood, because you won't win anyway," the second one added helpfully.

Luckily, Olivia was saved from having to reply by Charlotte's arrival. Her bestie hustled through looking excited.

"I have the answer," she said, mysteriously.

"Bye, kids," Olivia said, and hotfooted it outside behind her friend.

Outside, Danilo was waiting eagerly and they clustered together again.

"I looked up his property records. Apart from the address on the ID, he has several other properties listed in that second name, Henri Zappi," Charlotte announced excitedly. "The most recent of them, a large home in a very fancy area just outside Collina's village, was acquired just a month ago and it seems he obtained it after opening a legal case."

"So, are we going there?" Olivia asked, feeling hopeful.

"No. We're not going there. I did some further research and found out where the previous owner of that fancy home is living now. He's residing locally and I think he will be able to provide us with answers. Lots of them! In fact we might just have found the killer."

Olivia stared at her friend excitedly. "A previous victim of the conman would have a strong motive for murder," she agreed.

"How will we get him to confess, though?" Danilo asked, sounding worried.

The pressure of the imminent deadline gave Olivia the inspiration she needed. In a flash, a workable idea came to her.

"I have a plan," she said excitedly.

CHAPTER TWENTY SEVEN

Ten minutes later, having made some very hasty plans as they hurried along, Olivia strode up to the humble front door of a small, shabby apartment. It was nestled in between two smarter homes, in a side street behind one of the bakeries.

Danilo walked next to her. Charlotte was hovering a few yards behind, ready to step in as backup in case something went wrong.

With her heart in her mouth, Olivia hammered on the door. She waited, feeling breathless with anticipation, as she heard footsteps approach.

A moment later, the door opened. She stood face to face with a dark-haired, slim man who looked to be in his forties. His face was haggard, as if he'd recently lost some weight.

He stared at her suspiciously.

"Are you Signor Bardo Gagliardo?" Olivia asked in Italian.

"What do you want?" he asked in English, clearly pegging her as a tourist immediately thanks to her accent.

"You knew Henri Zappi, didn't you? Did you know him under that name? Since he obtained your property from you using that identity, I'm guessing so," she said firmly.

The man gasped. "What are you talking about?" he asked, his voice taut and panicked.

"I'm talking about the con-man. He took your property from you a month ago. Did he approach you with a false claim and launch a legal case?" Olivia said smoothly. "Perhaps it was an inheritance gone wrong? You were supposed to be the legal heir and then he muscled in with a story?"

Despite having a well-tanned face, Bardo was turning pale. He glanced from left to right, with a hunted expression that changed to panic as he saw Danilo standing next to her with his phone held casually in his hand.

Olivia hoped that the call Danilo had made as they rushed here, and which was still connected, was being listened to. It was all part of their last-minute plan.

"You're wrong. I sold that place a while ago, just after I inherited it from my grandmother. Downscaling," he stammered out.

"Downscaling? From a beautiful, five-bedroom villa on six acres, with a swimming pool and a peach orchard and three income-producing vacation cottages – to this?" Olivia repeated disbelievingly, staring at the tiny, shoddy apartment and feeling glad that Charlotte had researched the previous home so thoroughly.

"I live humbly," he tried, but Olivia shook her head. She stared at him intently, confirming what she'd suspected ever since she first saw him.

"I recognize you! I saw you running away that night. You were there, weren't you? You followed Heberto, or Henri, there with the intent to kill him out of revenge for what he did to you. And the police saw your shoe prints in my vineyard soil."

She glanced down at his worn trainers. They were just as Detective Caputi had described, and she was sure they'd be a match. And he couldn't continue to deny the facts. Not when the property records, and the footprints, told the true story. It was just a case of waiting for him to acknowledge the truth.

"All right, I was there! I was there!" he cried out.

Danilo drew in an excited gasp and Charlotte edged closer. Feeling triumphant, Olivia knew this was the start of the confession they needed. But it seemed there was more to come.

"I didn't kill him," Bardo protested. "I was tracking him down. I knew he was up to no good when I saw him back in town. He is a fraud and a criminal. He did take everything from me! After my grandmother passed away, I was the rightful heir, but he muscled in with a crazy claim that his family had been gifted the land, and launched a legal case which he won."

"He did?" Olivia felt horrified that such a thing could have succeeded.

"There was a small confusion over the inheritance, as the title deeds could not be found, and that gave him the opportunity to make the counter-claim. He seems – seemed, rather – to be a person who exploits weak points and capitalizes on them."

"Oh," Olivia said. He would have done exactly the same to her, she realized, using the double argument of his family's supposed history, and that she'd known about the wine and was nothing more than a fortune hunter herself.

"I was astounded to see him back here yesterday, just after your cellar was discovered," Bardo continued. "I was buying bread from the bakery in the late afternoon, and could not believe my eyes when I saw him walk in. He did not recognize me, and I quickly left, but I knew him instantly."

"Go on?" Olivia said. She was breathless with triumph, and also fascinated to hear how the criminal's modus operandi had worked.

"I put two and two together immediately. He was after your wine, of course. When he walked out, I followed him, and saw where he was staying. I then watched the hotel, hoping I would have an opportunity to catch him doing something illegal and that this might help me launch an appeal."

"And what happened?" Olivia asked, wanting him to explain in his words.

"He left the hotel after dark and headed straight to your farm on foot, clearly knowing the way. He held a flashlight, so I followed the bobbing light from a distance. He went into a deserted field and then stopped near the middle of it. He took a large rock and bashed something until it broke. I later realized that it was a lock which you must have put on the door."

The mention of the rock had Olivia's instincts prickling all over again. Had this same rock been used as the murder weapon, she wondered. It was highly likely. This information was an important part of the confession.

"Then what happened?" she asked.

"Then he opened the door and climbed inside."

"Go on?" Danilo encouraged, glancing down to check his phone.

"I followed him into the cellar and saw that he was searching the shelves, muttering the names of the wine to himself. He'd taken one bottle off the shelf and put it on the floor. He got a big fright when he saw me and yelled at me, asking what I was doing there."

"What did you say?" Olivia asked.

"I said I had come to stop him, and that I was going to call the property owner and would have him arrested. I told him I would not allow him to do again what he'd done to me."

"And then?" It was time for the confession. What had happened? Breathlessly Olivia waited for the eyewitness account of the crime.

"Then he recognized me. At first, he started laughing. He said I was a loser and a deadbeat and that since he'd just won a legal case against me there was no way the police would even listen to me. He said that if

I told anyone I'd been in the cellar he would get me arrested for theft. And that his intention was simply to take a bottle and plant it near your farmhouse so that he could accuse you of trying to steal the contents for yourself."

Olivia gasped. What dastardly motives! He would certainly have strengthened his case against her by doing that, she thought with a shiver.

"You must have been angry about that?" she asked. It was clear that this was the moment where Bardo had snapped. "Did you hit him with the rock?"

"Rock? What rock?" Bardo frowned, seeming confused. "Oh, you mean the rock I mentioned earlier. No, I don't know what happened to it after he used it to break the lock. It must still be outside the cellar somewhere. In any case I was not there to assault him, but simply to determine his motives."

"Well, then what did you do?" Olivia said, feeling puzzled that this account had veered away from its expected track.

"I told him I was going to find you immediately and warn you about what he was doing."

"Why didn't you?" Olivia asked, needing to drill down into the main inconsistency of the story to uncover the truth.

"I didn't get a chance. Suddenly, as I spoke those words, Henri lost his temper and began yelling and screaming at me to come closer, and that he wasn't finished with me, and that he would kill me and leave my body here."

"What?" Olivia asked, shocked by the drama that had played out in her cellar.

"He lunged at me and I realized he was deadly serious, even if deranged. I decided to run away to save myself. I was near the stairs and managed to scramble up. I fled through the field but in the dark I soon realized I'd gone in the wrong direction and was lost. Luckily, out of nowhere, a goat appeared and ran ahead of me, leading me to a cobbled pathway, which I followed."

Olivia glanced behind her, exchanging a knowing look with Charlotte. This was the moment when Charlotte had also heard the intruder flee.

Bardo closed his eyes as if reliving a terrible memory. "Even though I was running at full speed, I was surprised by how fast Henri was," he continued. "I reached a building and got my bearings again. Seeing the village lights in the distance, I headed for the road. But he was following! Behind me. I heard him yelling for me to stop. Turning, I saw a shadowy figure pursuing me in the darkness."

Olivia knew the voice he'd heard had been Danilo's and the figure had been herself. But it was clever how Bardo had woven them into his version to make it sound more plausible. She exchanged a worried glance with Danilo. If only he would confess!

"I redoubled my pace, veering into the next-door farm in the hope that I would shake him off. There, finally, I lost him. I ran back to the village as fast as I could. I did not sleep last night, remembering everything that had happened. I expected him to arrive at my front door this morning, with new trumped-up charges against me. Then, I heard the news that he'd been found dead. The local gossip was that you had killed him."

"I didn't!" Olivia snapped. This was ridiculous. The murderer himself was insinuating that local gossip was right?

He stared at Olivia pleadingly.

"He was a terrible man. Terrible! He would have destroyed you. However he was killed, you can be thankful that he is no longer trying to take what is yours."

Olivia frowned. This story had detoured from what had sounded like perfect truth, into the realms of fantasy and fiction. Bardo had seamlessly transitioned between the two and at the end, had hinted that since Olivia had benefited from his death, she must have been the killer.

At that moment, she heard Charlotte call, "They're here!"

The scream of a Fiat's engine filled the air. Arriving at speed, Detective Caputi braked sharply on the nearby road. A police van followed her, stopping behind.

The detective climbed out, looking satisfied.

"You can end the call now," she said to Danilo. "We have a clear record of this entire conversation."

Danilo disconnected his phone and pocketed it. Olivia felt weak with relief that their hastily cobbled-together plan had worked. Thank goodness Detective Caputi had answered Danilo's call when they were on their way to Bardo's house. She'd patched it through to headquarters and her team had listened in to the conversation that had played out between Olivia and Bardo. Meanwhile, Caputi had got onto the road with her arresting officers, and hustled here to join them.

Calm and composed, Detective Caputi marched up to Bardo, who was looking both astonished and afraid.

"Signor, you clearly confessed to following the victim to the cellar and confronting him inside. We are arresting you on suspicion of murder."

Bardo's jaw dropped.

"No, please! You do not understand. Henri has ruined my life already. Please, it is not fair that even in death he is causing more trouble for me. I was only trying to help. Signora, please do not do this. I am begging you. You have heard my story. Spare me, help me! Do something!" he entreated, as the officers marched him inside his house to process the arrest.

Olivia felt an overwhelming sense of relief as she saw the door close behind them. Finally, their ordeal was over and the police could start wrapping up the case.

She hoped they would soon allow her to unlock the cellar. And she wished that she didn't feel so sorry for Bardo. He hadn't struck her as a murderous type, but rather as a gentle and non-violent person. He must have been pushed to his limits to do what he did. She found to her surprise that she didn't even mind that he'd lied to her.

Life had certainly dealt him a short straw if he'd been the victim of Heberto, or Henri, whichever his real name was. Beyond that, his choices had been his own to make and she mustn't feel regret about their outcome.

Danilo sighed heavily. She guessed he also wished that this strange case could have had a happier conclusion. But there it was. It was over and they must move on.

They trailed back to where Charlotte was waiting.

"Home time?" she said, looking at their faces.

Olivia nodded. "It wasn't the best outcome. I feel sad for him. But at least it was an outcome."

"I guess that's the thing about investigations. They don't always go the way you expect. It's probably why that gray-haired detective is so grumpy. Imagine having to deal with this all day, every day. It must sour you. Artoro is certainly exceptional in that he's a very cheerful person, despite his job." Charlotte sighed happily.

"Well, I'm going to be cheerful, too," Olivia said determinedly. "I'm going to count my blessings and be glad I'm in the wine industry, which is all about making people happy."

"I'm glad I work in the imported goods industry. Everyone enjoys ordering online, and nobody ever kills each other if the Sardinian anchovies are out of stock. At least, not so far," Charlotte said.

“I am glad that I make furniture and work with wood. It is always positive to work with an organic substance and make customers items they love,” Danilo said.

“There you go. We all feel better, right? Shall we go home now?” Olivia said. She didn’t even sound convincing to herself.

“I’ll walk back later. I’m heading to the village deli first, to look at some new products that have just come in. I plan to buy samples, so we can assess them together. Stuffed olives, chocolate spread, and artichoke hearts,” Charlotte said cheerfully before rushing off.

“I have to drop off a table at a customer’s house. Can I give you a ride home first?” Danilo said.

“I’ll also walk. It’ll give me a chance to clear my head,” Olivia said.

“Well, then, I will see you later,” Danilo promised, giving her a fond kiss goodbye.

Olivia trailed dispiritedly out of the village. She was racking her brains for something nice to make for dinner. She didn’t feel like cooking, but also didn’t want to eat out because her budget for the month was blown. Blown! And it was her birthday in a few more days. How was she going to celebrate?

As she turned onto the quiet, winding back road that led to her farm, she found herself wishing she could have been born on the first of the month, after payday, instead of mid-month, when everyone was broke.

The uphill walk gave her a chance to reflect on the case. As she plodded along, she pondered over the weird truth that though a killer had been brought to justice, she still felt as if nothing was fully resolved.

When she neared her gateway, she was horrified to see an unfamiliar Fiat parked outside the farmhouse. Its engine was idling and it must have just arrived.

“No!” Olivia hissed. Surely not? She was all out of patience with uninvited guests on her land. Who was here now, and what did they want? Marching toward the Fiat, she wished that either Danilo or Charlotte was with her. Without backup, she’d have to handle this all on her own.

Then the Fiat’s door opened and Olivia goggled in astonishment as she saw the occupant.

This was now officially the weirdest day of her life, ever!

CHAPTER TWENTY EIGHT

"Hello again, angel," Mrs. Glass trilled, climbing out of the back of the cab and patting her already tidy hair.

"Mom. What happened?" Scenarios flooded Olivia's mind. "Did you not manage to change your flight? Was it delayed?"

She couldn't think of any other reason for her mother to be standing expectantly by the cab's trunk while the driver got out and unloaded her valises.

"Oh, no, sweetheart. None of the above."

Olivia saw that Erba was peeking curiously around the farmhouse. She looked pleased to see Mrs. Glass arrive back.

With a resigned expression, the driver picked up the heavier case and headed for the front door. Before her mother could make any ill-advised comments on her goat's advancing pregnancy, Olivia grabbed the lighter one and hustled along behind them, rummaging in her purse for a tip for him.

She unlocked the door, tipped the driver, and then followed her mother inside.

"Look at the time. It's almost five o'clock," Mrs. Glass commented, glancing at Olivia's kitchen clock. "It's lovely and warm in here, isn't it?" Removing her smart red jacket, she hung it on the back of the kitchen chair.

Olivia guessed her mother was going to suggest coffee, but yet again she defied predictions.

"I think we need a nice glass of wine!" she announced.

"Wine? Um, absolutely. There's a chenin blanc in the fridge."

Relieved that this was one of the fruitiest and least dry of her available stash, Olivia quickly poured them each a glass.

"Cheers!" Mrs. Glass announced, taking a large sip. "What an excellent wine!"

Olivia collapsed onto the chair opposite. Now her mother was saying nice things about a local wine? What was going on?

"You might be wondering why I came back," Mrs. Glass then said.

For a moment, Olivia felt like screaming in hysterical laughter, but she was worried that if she started, she might not be able to stop.

Fighting for control and a vaguely normal-sounding response, she said, "Yes, I have been wondering ever since I saw you."

"I started feeling as if I'd made a very bad decision after I left. It was quite a lengthy trip to the airport, as there were road works, so it gave me a long time to think. I started having second thoughts about what I'd said and done, and decided I should ask Andrew's advice before I actually boarded the plane. You know what a tower of strength your father is! I was sure he'd tell me I was being silly, and should go ahead and come home. When I got to the airport I called him, and to my surprise, he felt differently and had quite a lot to say."

Olivia was also surprised. Her father usually didn't have anything to say. She guessed he'd figured out years ago that silence was the safest response.

"I was shocked that he became critical of my decision to leave. He didn't support it at all, and in fact spoke against it! He said I'd made a huge mistake. I started feeling terrible about my hasty actions," Mrs. Glass said faintly.

"I see," Olivia said. She wasn't sure what else would be appropriate.

"Andrew said I needed to stop being emotional and think of things from your perspective. I told him I'd always done that but he said I was wrong and hadn't."

"My goodness," Olivia said. Those really were harsh words from her father.

"It made me rethink my behavior and angel, I had to face up to the truth. I have been acting through selfish motives. I've never been able to imagine you living in Italy, so far away. I guess my vision has always been for you to live in the very same neighborhood as your parents, or at least a short drive from us. I've always been sure that would happen, once you'd made your name in the advertising agency and built a reputation for yourself. It has been very difficult for me to come to terms with the fact you don't want that, and in fact what you want is to do something very different from what I ever imagined, in a place I'd never believed you would end up. No wonder I resisted the idea!"

Her mother sniffed, rummaging in her purse for a Kleenex. Was she crying? She certainly seemed overcome with emotion.

Olivia suddenly felt her eyes water as well. Her mother could be super-annoying, and irritatingly stubborn, but it had not been from any other motive than love for her daughter and an inability to let go.

"I've realized I must embrace your independence. My wonderful, strong-willed daughter! That's what Andrew said. He said between the two of us, we had enough stubbornness to break the planet apart, and one of us had to make a compromise because he didn't want to end up floating in outer space. He said it was unfair for you to have to do it, with your life and dreams ahead of you, and that I had to. Well, it was quite an epiphany."

It must have been. Her mother's glass was already more than half empty.

"I'm so glad you came back," Olivia said, trying her best to hold back a sudden sob. "I was devastated when you left."

"And I had such a lovely outing with your wonderful boyfriend. He explained to me that he allows people who know him well to call him by his nickname, Danilo, and invited me to do so. I think it was after seeing the Leaning Tower that I suddenly lost hope you would return to the States, and it made me angry and sad. But I'm happy now," she said, brightening.

"I'm so glad, Mom," Olivia said, squeezing her mother's hand.

"After all, Andrew mentioned that we haven't traveled nearly enough. And now we have a wonderful home base in Tuscany! He said he'd put some plans together for the next few years. So you'll be seeing a lot more of us, very soon. Tuscany will become our second home," Mrs. Glass said, seeming thrilled by the new life journey she'd be embarking on.

"That's wonderful, Mom." Olivia felt warmed by happiness. It would be fun having her parents here more often, especially if they weren't trying to get her to come back to the States. She guessed it would be a chance to re-forge her relationship with her mom.

"And now, angel, is there anything I can do to help you out of your predicament? After all, there's still a murder unsolved, isn't there? Or have I missed something?"

"I think it's all solved," Olivia said, even though as she spoke, she felt a twinge of guilty doubt. Then she thought about the tricky circumstances surrounding it.

"Actually, there is something you can do. Something very important. If you could write a testimonial explaining how and why I bought the farm, it would be hugely helpful and might just save the day, and my cellar!"

"I'll do that with pleasure, angel," Mrs. Glass enthused, draining her wine eagerly.

Olivia felt a sense of deep contentment that her mother was back home and that all the problems with her seemed to be resolved. Except for one! As she thought of it, Olivia decided to address this burning issue first thing tomorrow.

*

The next morning, Olivia headed to La Leggenda, feeling optimistic that the second day of Collina Wine Week would be a huge success. She got there twenty minutes early, but that wasn't so that she could spend extra time getting ready. Olivia had other plans.

She marched determinedly past the winery buildings and headed straight to the goat dairy. Erba skipped alongside, delighted that her adopted parent was walking her the whole way to her daycare center.

As she walked, Olivia realized that the upcoming conversation was likely to be difficult. She hadn't had many dealings with the dairy manager, who was responsible for maintaining the herd as well as the production of the top quality goat's cheese that La Leggenda manufactured.

She'd 'sort of' adopted Erba after the goat had taken a liking to her. She had told the dairy manager the first time Erba had followed her home. He'd simply laughed, said she was their naughtiest goat, and told Olivia to bring her back the next day.

Since then, Erba had stayed with Olivia every night. Without really asking permission, she'd taken over the part-time custody of a member of La Leggenda's carefully curated dairy herd.

Now she'd have to explain herself. Her stomach wrenched at the thought of saying goodbye to Erba, but if Erba was on her way to becoming a productive adult member of the herd, she would need to stay at the winery overnight.

Ahead was the high-roofed dairy building, with the herd of goats dotted artfully nearby. As Erba frolicked away to join her friends, Olivia paused at the dairy door and then headed inside.

Beyond a set of doors and up a short staircase was the cheese making facility where the goat milk was transformed into the tasty end product.

She swung open the door and stepped inside.

Wearing a protective overall and a plastic hat, the smiling manager hurried over.

"Olivia! Buongiorno. Would you like to taste our latest Capra cheese? We have just perfected a delicious new flavor, with capers and sundried tomatoes."

Olivia was relieved that he addressed her in English. Even though her Italian was progressing every day, she'd rather have this difficult conversation in a familiar language.

"I'd love to taste." Eagerly she accepted the cracker he handed her, topped with a heaped teaspoon of the fragrant cheese.

"It's sublime," she complimented him. "The cheese is deliciously creamy, and the capers provide such a piquant contrast. And the sundried tomatoes add a gorgeous layer of flavor."

"I am pleased you like it," he smiled, and then looked at her inquiringly as if guessing she had not come all the way to the dairy on the off-chance there would be a new cheese to try.

"I wanted to speak to you about Erba," Olivia began, and found herself reddening even as anxiety clenched her stomach.

"Our naughtiest youngster," he agreed with a rueful shake of her head.

"I – I – well, my mother noticed she was looking fatter than usual. And so, I came to ask if she should start staying overnight at the dairy now."

Her heart sank as she spoke the terrible truth. She waited, with her head bowed, for the hammer-blow of the manager's words to fall.

CHAPTER TWENTY NINE

To Olivia's surprise, the dairy manager frowned inquiringly, as if he didn't understand where this conversation was going. Taking another breath, she battled on, shamefaced over this difficult discussion and filled with dread over her goat's future.

"I mean, she'll need to be milked soon, as she is probably pregnant now," she concluded.

"Pregnant?" To Olivia's astonishment, the manager let out a hearty laugh. "No, no, no. Erba is not pregnant. She is too young, as yet, to be allowed to run with the bucks – but in any case, we only do that in the fall. The rest of the year the two bucks in our herd are kept separate, so we can control the breeding cycle."

"I see," Olivia said, relief washing over her.

"Puppy fat," the manager teased with a grin. "Your goat is just fat. We have already decided not to run her with the bucks in the future, though. She is likely to remain a very small animal, and her mother, who is also small, is a low milk yielder. So we do not want to breed her. She can remain your pet, yes? She plays a more important role by entertaining the tourists with her antics during the day."

"Oh, thank you!" Olivia felt giddy with relief at this amazing outcome.

Erba was just going through an adolescent puppy-fat stage, and better still, she hadn't been selected as a breeding animal. That meant she could be Olivia's goat forever!

Feeling as if she were floating on a happy cloud, Olivia left the goat dairy and hurried back to the winery.

Walking through the main entrance, she was pleased to see Marcello was in the tasting room. They'd brought extra tables in from the restaurant and clearly he was expecting a very busy day.

"Olivia. A suspect has been arrested, I hear? This is excellent news."

He strode over to her and hugged her hard.

"I'm so relieved. I feel sorry for the killer though. It's awful that somebody from our village did such a thing. I don't feel he was fairly treated by life," Olivia admitted.

Marcello nodded. "I heard that he was a previous victim of fraud at the conman's hands. Even so, a few of my friends who knew him well have said that they cannot believe such a gentle and restrained person would do such a thing."

"Really?" Olivia said. Thanks to those words, she was feeling even more conflicted about what had played out.

"I spoke to his mother, who said that they cannot even argue that he acted in self-defense, as the police said that from the wound, and the position the body fell, the conman was hit on the top of the head, and the killer must have been standing behind him. That would not indicate a defensive blow by someone about to run away."

"Oh, dear. That's a pity," Olivia said, wishing that Bardo had chosen another course of action, rather than snapping and attacking a man whose back was turned.

"His mother says despite the evidence, he is claiming innocence," Marcello continued.

"Bardo did say that Heberto, or rather Henri, was alive when he saw him, and sounded very convinced of it," Olivia admitted uneasily. There was no other solution, was there? There was literally nobody else in the village who could have done such a thing. Logic and evidence pointed toward this unfortunate man.

"If only we could warn people that their decisions will be unwise. Often, I have wished I could do so. But sometimes the only way is to learn for yourself, painful as it is." Marcello nodded, looking sad.

Olivia sighed. "It's not over yet. I still have to prove that I didn't know about the cellar when I bought the land. But at least it's on the right path now. Marcello, I'm so grateful for your help. I'll never forget how we interviewed the suspect together, right here in the tasting room!"

Marcello stared at Olivia with a warm expression in his eyes. "Olivia, there are many things that have occurred between us that I will never forget. You have always been extremely special to me, and always will be."

"And you likewise," Olivia mumbled, feeling her face burn crimson just as she'd known it would do.

Marcello let out a sudden laugh. "It was funny in the tasting room! When Raul began shouting and screaming his voice was so loud I thought plaster might fall from the ceiling. I fear that even though he will drink our free wine, he will never buy any from us in the future."

Olivia snorted. "You'll have to bring out a new label that doesn't say La Leggenda."

As she spoke, she felt the wheels start turning in her mind. Something Marcello had said had triggered a thought process, and the idea she'd almost been able to grasp the day before now flitted back into her mind, clearer and more tangible this time.

But at that moment, the first big group of locals arrived and Olivia pushed the thought aside, turning to welcome them with a warm smile.

*

At five p.m. Olivia closed up, feeling happy that she'd had such a productive day. Everyone who'd arrived for Collina Wine Week had been especially friendly to her, as if the locals had collectively resolved to apologize for suspecting her and for their behavior after the cellar was discovered. A few people had asked her if the wine was safe, but they'd done so in a concerned way. Walking up to the goat dairy, she felt hugely relieved that the storm had passed over and that life could now return to calmness – or close to it at any rate. She hoped the police would soon call to say that Bardo had confessed and the case was closed.

"Hello, Erba," she said, grinning with delight at her chunky, teenage goat who would be hers, forever. How lucky was she to have Erba's fun, entertaining presence in her life without any responsibilities to the goat dairy?

Olivia wasn't sure if she wanted a herd of goats in her winery. After all, Erba on her own was quite a responsibility. Perhaps it would be better to focus just on the wine, she decided. There were many other places making cheese, and she was sure they were doing it better than she ever could.

Then her thoughts returned to the idea she'd had earlier and she puzzled over it. As she walked along the familiar route home, the pieces clicked together in her mind.

The dust on the bottles. The stones that had cascaded down when they'd first walked into the cellar. The way the body had fallen and Marcello's joke about Raul shouting. Bardo's fervent protests that he was innocent.

Finally, she had a clear picture and realized what it meant.

She'd been wrong! They had all been wrong. Things had played out a different way down there in the cellar. Now she was convinced of it.

"Erba, quick!" Olivia broke into a run. "This new theory of mine could turn everything on its head, and it might just free an innocent man. I have to see if it's true – as fast as I can!"

Breathless and gasping for air, Olivia stumbled up the steep road to her farm. Why did she always have these great ideas when home was an uphill run away, she wondered. She needed to get as fit as Erba. Despite carrying a few extra pounds, her goat was gamboling along energetically while Olivia was spending the last strength in her legs on getting to the gate.

There was Charlotte's car. She didn't see Danilo's. Hopefully he would be here soon.

She jogged to the front door and quickly opened it.

"Charlotte! Mom!"

Charlotte arrived at the door.

"Hello. Your mother's gone shopping with Danilo. They wanted to buy your dad a local gift. And she's taking us out to dinner tonight, so we don't have to cook." She looked more closely at Olivia and then said, sounding concerned, "What's up? Something's happened, hasn't it?"

"I know what played out in the cellar," Olivia gasped.

"Yes," Charlotte said in a calm voice, giving her a strange look. "Heberto was there, stealing the wine, but Bardo climbed down and confronted him and obviously killed him. We spoke about all of this last night in detail. Has the stress caused a memory gap? I'm sure we can find a good supplement to help you get back to normal. Rosemary and lemon balm are great. They do a fabulous herbal tonic here which we're planning to distribute in the States."

"No, no!" Finally, Olivia had enough breath to speak in a clear sentence. "Charlotte, I think we've all been wrong. I'm convinced that something different happened. All the evidence points to it!"

"But what?" Charlotte paled. "Olivia, you're not telling me you think Danilo did it? I really don't think he'd be capable of such a thing!"

"No. I think something else entirely happened. And I'm going to prove it." Olivia raised her chin determinedly.

"You are? How?"

"By examining the scene."

"But it's locked up!"

"Nothing a shovel can't fix," Olivia insisted.

Charlotte goggled at her.

"You're going to get into trouble with the police. Wouldn't you rather come inside and have a glass of wine?"

"No," Olivia said firmly. "Right now, I need to go to the cellar with a shovel, break my way inside, and confirm whether my theory is true." She stared at her friend challengingly. "So the question is: are you going to help?"

CHAPTER THIRTY

Charlotte brightened at Olivia's forceful words. "Of course I'll help. I was just checking you were fully committed to the idea. Even if it is crazy enough to get you fully committed!" She laughed at her pun, louder than Olivia would have liked.

"Let's go," Olivia said.

They detoured to the lean-to at the back of the house where Olivia had stashed her gardening equipment. She picked out the biggest and sturdiest shovel she could find. This tool was going to have a tough job. The weak point would probably be her own strength, already sapped from her uphill run.

Then they marched to the cellar.

"I'm quite excited about this," Charlotte confided, as they left the paved path and struck out along the grassy track. "I hope that your theory is going to astound me when you disclose it. You don't want to give me a preview?"

"No. I want to wait until I'm standing where he fell," Olivia said.

There was the door ahead. Olivia bit her lip. The police lock was solid and firm. But the chain was less so.

"I'd go for the chain," Charlotte echoed her thoughts. "Pick one link and stamp down on it with the blade of the shovel as hard as you can. When you get tired, I'll take over. We will make it the weakest link!" she added confidently.

Olivia placed the shovel's blade on the gleaming chain. She stamped down hard.

Nothing whatsoever happened. She didn't even think she'd scratched the metal.

"It takes time," Charlotte encouraged. "Mighty rivers don't carve their way through rock in a day. It takes millennia."

"We don't have millennia!"

Charlotte grabbed the handle to steady it, and Olivia climbed onto the shovel, pushing with both feet, bouncing up and down, in an effort to make a dent in the chain.

"If the shovel breaks we might have to rethink," Charlotte offered, sounding doubtful.

"Just stand strong. I am going to snap this link."

Gaining confidence from Charlotte's support, Olivia grew bolder, treating the spade as a pogo stick as she stamped it down again and again on the chain.

The shovel was banging and smashing down, plus she was deafened by her own breathing. She was going to persist for as long as it took! Even if she broke a fingernail or sprained an ankle, nothing would stop her. Nothing!

Through the red mist of effort, Olivia became aware of Charlotte speaking loudly.

"You can stop now. You can stop. You've broken it."

Olivia climbed shakily off the blade.

"I have?"

"About two minutes ago. You kept on going. For a while I thought you were planning on hammering straight through the wooden door. I let you carry on because I thought it might be therapeutic. But enough's enough, right? We need to test your theory now."

Charlotte grabbed the handle with Olivia, and they hefted the door up and open.

Suddenly, fear flooded through Olivia as she stared at the darkness below.

"What if I'm wrong?" she whispered. "I'll be in such trouble."

"No, you won't." Charlotte spoke in firm and reassuring tones. "We'll say it was broken by some other fortune hunter. There have been enough of them for it not to be suspicious. I don't remember a thing about coming out here. I'm still in the kitchen, researching restaurants for your mother to treat us to dinner tonight, because she wants something that doesn't specialize in seafood and doesn't specialize in pizza, and offers a friendly mix of dishes that everyone will like."

Laughing made her feel better, Olivia discovered.

"Now get down there. If there's anything to find, let's find it."

Charlotte snapped on her phone's flashlight and handed it to Olivia.

Her brain was buzzing as she descended the stairs. She had to be right. Didn't she? In her mind's eye, she saw exactly how the scene had played out. Different from how anyone had imagined.

"You see, Heberto, or Henri, was in the cellar," she said, carefully stepping down. "He was surprised by Bardo. That was all true. What Bardo said was accurate. Heberto lost his temper. He began shouting and screaming. He lunged forward and tried to attack Bardo."

Olivia walked onto the cellar floor. It felt cold down here, she realized, shivering. Charlotte was following close behind.

"Then what?" her bestie asked.

"Then Bardo ran away, just like he said he did. But Heberto didn't follow him. He had more important things to do. He had a plan and needed to get on with it. So he turned back to his work, but as he did so, a rock hit him on the head. Not an intentional blow. It fell from the ceiling."

Olivia trained the flashlight beam on the exact place where Heberto's slumped form had lain. Then she shone the light upward, and took a look at the area above.

"Wow!" Charlotte gasped.

In that part of the cellar roof, the concrete had crumbled away completely. The jagged forms of rocks were clearly visible. They looked precariously rooted in the stony soil, as if they might come loose and tumble down at any moment. And, in fact, there was a dark gap among them where one already had.

"Hit by a falling rock. It makes so much sense. Especially after all the shouting and commotion," Charlotte whispered.

"Exactly. That's what made me think of it. Marcello made a joke about someone yelling so loudly that plaster fell from the ceiling, and I realized that's what must have played out. It's structurally unstable. Begni said so and we've seen it for ourselves. Small stones scatter down continually. It's no surprise at all that a large rock would eventually do the same."

"The cellar was defending you!" Charlotte breathed, her eyes wide. "So, what are you going to do now?"

"Call the police. They've got to see this for themselves and accept that this is what happened. If they do, it changes everything and they might be able to close the case immediately. If they don't, I'll be in a world of trouble and you'll be going to dinner without me. In fact, you'd better wait in the farmhouse. I'll handle this alone," Olivia said, feeling terrified about the ordeal that lay ahead.

*

As she watched the trio of police officers tramp along the path toward her, Olivia tried to stand tall and swallow down her nerves. It wasn't easy, especially when Detective Caputi's furious gaze locked onto her.

"You deliberately defied police orders and broke the chain? Do you realize that tampering with a crime scene is a serious offense for which you can be arrested?" Anger and triumph warred in the detective's voice as she spoke the words.

"My theory is that it's not a crime scene and never was." Olivia spoke the words firmly. "Signor Heberto was hit by a falling rock. It was dislodged from the ceiling, possibly as a result of the shouting and commotion during his confrontation with Bardo."

"Hit by a falling rock?" Caputi's voice sounded incredulous. Olivia could see a total lack of belief in the policewoman's eyes. But one of the officers behind her was nodding thoughtfully.

"It would explain the angle that the body fell. Remember we could not work out how someone could have approached from the back, and struck him on the head, with so little space behind him?"

Grumpily, Caputi glared at him.

"We will re-examine the scene." Olivia's heart leapt at the words. Then Caputi continued. "It may be necessary to get the forensic experts out here. They are in Florence today. If that is the case, we will take Signora Glass into custody overnight, to avoid any further tampering with the scene."

Olivia's heart dropped all the way to the cellar floor on hearing that. The detective didn't believe her, and there was no telling how this would play out.

"Please, not tonight! My mother's taking us to dinner, and she's only just started to like Italy."

Detective Caputi gave no sign of having heard her words. Instead, she led the way down the ladder, snapping on a powerful flashlight as she descended. Her team followed, and so did Olivia, tiptoeing down the rungs, feeling taut with anxiety.

By the time she got down, the three officers were clustered together, speaking in rapid Italian. One of them had an iPad out and was scrolling through photographs of the crime scene, while the other had a flashlight trained on the ceiling above.

Caputi and the officer holding the iPad were frowning disbelievingly. Only the third seemed to accept Olivia's theory.

Why couldn't the others see it immediately, she wondered, feeling despairing, as if all her efforts and thinking, not to mention her aerobic struggle with the shovel, had all been a complete waste of time. And, an even more serious question – what would happen to her now?

Detective Caputi was shaking her head emphatically. She began speaking loudly, in rapid Italian, clearly driving home her point as they all stared down at the iPad again.

And then, Olivia saw it. Perhaps triggered by the noisy words, a fine shower of dust from the ceiling was followed by an almost imperceptible tremble.

"Look out!" she cried in panic, knowing her warning would be heard too late. "Get away!"

CHAPTER THIRTY ONE

Acting instinctively, Olivia leaped forward. She grabbed Detective Caputi's wrist and pulled her out of the way, just as a large boulder dislodged from the ceiling and crashed down so hard that the floor shook with its impact.

Trembling all over, Olivia stared at the rock, and then up at the ceiling again. It seemed no more were ready to fall – for now at any rate. She'd dragged the detective away from probable death, and certain injury. That boulder was even bigger than the previous one!

Shocking as this rock fall was, it certainly couldn't have happened at a more opportune time.

For someone who'd narrowly missed having their head crushed, Detective Caputi remained remarkably calm. She turned to Olivia.

"Without a doubt, you have saved my life. I owe you thanks. And an apology," she said. Turning back again, she stared up. "It is clear that the ceiling is far more unstable than we thought. This does, indeed, put a different light on the matter, and confirms Signor Bardo's version. Let us leave this cellar before any further rocks dislodge."

She headed for the stairs. At the foot of the steps, she paused, and stared at Olivia with a strange look on her face. Was it kindness? Humor? At any rate, it was highly unexpected.

"You will not be taken into custody, Signora Glass. Go to dinner. We will notify you later this evening as soon as we have closed the murder case and ruled that the death was accidental. In fact, your input in this investigation has been most valuable to us. And I hope your mother learns to love our beautiful country," she said with a hint of a smile.

Olivia felt massively relieved as she watched the police leave. The case had been resolved, Caputi had praised her efforts, and best of all, the death had been confirmed as accidental.

That meant everyone in her wonderful village, who could be exasperating when they chose to, but who felt like family most of the time, would be in the clear. She was sure Charlotte would be especially thrilled that Olivia herself hadn't been arrested! But her conscience was still bothering her in one regard, she realized. There was something else she needed to do to make things right.

*

The next morning, Olivia and Danilo waited excitedly outside the small apartment where they had first confronted Bardo. Olivia held a big bunch of flowers together with a card, which contained a voucher for the local pizza restaurant. Danilo was carrying a mixed case of wine.

"He should be home, shouldn't he?" Olivia asked.

"Yes. The police confirmed he was released last night already," Danilo nodded.

Swallowing hard, Olivia stepped forward and knocked on the door. Apologizing was never easy but she resolved to do it right.

A few seconds went by. They felt like an eternity. Then the door opened. Bardo, dressed in an old but comfortable looking pair of jeans and a shabby shirt, looked out at them in surprise.

"Signor Bardo, I owe you a huge apology," Olivia said, stepping forward with the bouquet. "I jumped to the wrong conclusion and got you arrested yesterday. I know nothing can make up for that, but I brought you flowers and wine, and a restaurant voucher, to say sorry. I'd like to help you with anything else you need."

She felt embarrassed to ask if he might be in need of a grocery delivery or a rental check. Not knowing his situation, but suspecting times were tough, she hoped that he'd suggest what she could do.

"I appreciate the gifts," Bardo said, taking the flowers from her. "They are very welcome. And actually, my arrest yesterday resulted in a surprisingly positive outcome."

"Oh, really?" Olivia asked.

He nodded. "Being in need of a lawyer, and not wanting to use my previous one, I used a new one that a friend recommended. When he arrived, we had a long discussion and I was able to explain my previous issues."

"What did he say?" Danilo asked curiously.

"He was shocked that my other lawyer handled the previous case so badly as there were many options still available to us. He was lazy, gave up, and did not look into things thoroughly enough. After our meeting yesterday the new lawyer promised to act immediately, and open a case to reclaim the property in my name. He will use the relevant points of law that will mean the decision can be easily reversed, and of course, now that the information surrounding his other identities and misdemeanors has come to light, it will further strengthen the case."

"Bardo, that's incredible. Does he feel there's a good chance of success?" Olivia asked.

"Yes. He is confident that the courts will set aside the previous decision, and restore the house into my name. He says I could even claim damages from Henri's estate, but I will not do such a thing. I do not want to burden his relatives with that, especially since they are willing to testify against him after finding out what he did."

"That's wonderful!" Olivia felt thrilled that Bardo had not only had his name cleared, but would see justice done and his rightful inheritance restored. "I'll be very happy to testify myself, or provide anything you might need."

"It will hopefully be an open-and-shut case, but I thank you, and will contact you if I need anything," Bardo reassured her.

Olivia gave him a big hug goodbye. She felt elated as she left. Who would have thought that this dire predicament could have been resolved in such a positive way? She was thrilled that Bardo would soon be the rightful owner of that lovely home.

She glanced at Danilo, who looked as happy as she felt.

"And now, we go around the corner to the local magistrate's court," he said.

Yesterday, with Danilo's help, Olivia had hired a lawyer to contest the claim that the conman had made and to get his case dismissed.

As they walked, Olivia delved in her purse to find the documents she needed.

There was one final step she had to take to handle the court case that Henri or Heberto had opened, and prevent anyone else from trying the same tactic. The lawyer had explained that she must bring an affidavit to the police station. In it, she should state that she had bought the property without any knowledge of the wine cellar. In order to prevent future claims, the lawyer had advised that she should back up this affidavit with actual evidence.

Olivia had written a detailed account of how she'd stumbled across the farm, and had also included the steps that had led to the cellar being discovered. Danilo's detective work had only been done after the old wine bottle's label had been restored, and that had only happened after

Olivia had cleared all the junk out of her barn. She'd given the lawyer Begni's contact details to confirm the timeline of the other finds.

And, as for supporting evidence – well, luckily, she'd had that prepared already. Knowing that she would need proof, Olivia had asked her mother to provide a record of all the messages and emails that Olivia had sent her when she'd first gotten this 'crazy idea' into her head.

There was the magistrate's court ahead.

Olivia glanced at Danilo who gave her a supportive grin.

"Everything will be in order. I am sure they will accept what you have here," he said.

The dark-suited lawyer was waiting for them at the entrance to the police station, peering anxiously out. He smiled in relief when he saw Olivia and Danilo approach.

"Signora Olivia. Signor Danilo. I am Avvocato Passero. How wonderful to meet you in person after our long phone call yesterday. Do you have all the paperwork?"

"Yes, it's all here." Olivia handed over the manila envelope.

"Let me check it at the front desk. The case is being heard first thing this morning and we are obviously hoping for a swift verdict that includes a complete dismissal of the fraudulent claim and a ruling that the contents are yours.

"I'm so grateful you could take this on at such short notice," Olivia said.

The lawyer paged through the documents.

"Your affidavit. The timeline of the discoveries on the farm. The date of purchase of the property. Ah, and this is your supporting document?"

"From my mother," Olivia confirmed with a smile.

As he read through the printed page, Passero's eyebrows rose. This document pulled no punches! Mrs. Glass had vented a lot of her frustration with her daughter's impulsive ways. In fact, Olivia thought that she might well have none left after having faithfully recorded just how her daughter had come to own that farm.

"*Ever since she was young, Olivia has been regrettably impulsive. We can't imagine where she gets it from as it's from neither side of our families. Deciding to buy a farm is very typical of her irresponsible, rash, reckless and immature behavior. Bear in mind, Your Honor, this followed hot on the heels of losing her temper and quitting an excellent job which could have seen her rise to great heights in the prestigious world of advertising. I trust that the record of messages and emails will prove this was just another one of her silly decisions, made with no forethought or regard for the consequences whatsoever. If only she would learn!*"

Olivia thought the lawyer was trying to conceal a smile as he read through.

"Your mother has certainly brought her argument across strongly," he said.

"I think she needed to get a few things off her chest," Olivia agreed wryly.

"I will submit the documents to the judge. As soon as we have an outcome, I will call you," he said.

"Are you sure you don't need me to be there?" Olivia asked anxiously.

"No. With the claimant deceased and no legal representation from their side, this is now simply a matter of following procedure, and providing the documentation to conclude the case. Do not worry, Signora Glass."

The lawyer nodded confidently. Olivia wished she felt as certain. There had been so many nasty surprises during the rollercoaster ride of discovering her cellar. She couldn't quite believe that they were all over now, and no more lay in store.

"I know it's in the best hands, and thank you," she smiled, trying her best not to show that, through no fault of this excellent lawyer, she couldn't help but have trust issues.

She mulled over this during the short drive home, hoping that things would go smoothly. In fact, she was so wrapped up in her musings that she didn't even notice the strange car parked outside until Danilo remarked on it.

"Look, Olivia! Begni is here," he said.

"So he is! Did you know he was going to come by?" she asked Danilo in surprise.

He shook his head. "I had no idea."

Quickly, they scrambled out, with Olivia feeling worried all over again as she hurried over to greet the expert.

"Buongiorno," he called. "Olivia and Danilo, I have some answers for you on the history of your farm, and how the wine ended up in the underground cellar. It is a fascinating story. So full of intrigue that I thought I would come past and tell you in person."

CHAPTER THIRTY TWO

"The farm's history? You actually found out what happened? I can't wait to hear it," Olivia enthused to Begni. Remembering her manners, she added, "Would you like to come in for coffee?"

She led the way to the farmhouse and opened the door. Inhaling the smell of freshly brewed coffee and toast, she heard the murmur of voices from the kitchen that signaled her mother and Charlotte were both up and about and enjoying a late breakfast.

"We have a visitor," she called, as she made a beeline for the kitchen.

"Oh, it's Mr. Begni!" her mother exclaimed. "How wonderful you stopped by. Can I offer you some coffee, and a piece of toasted ciabatta bread with delicious chocolate spread? I'm enjoying these wonderful local dietary customs, I must say."

"How nice to see you again," Charlotte welcomed him.

They sat down, and her mother bustled about, organizing coffee for everyone. A plate in the center of the dining room was laden with toast, biscotti and sliced fruit.

Begni stirred cream into his coffee.

"My research into the history of your farm uncovered some fascinating facts," he told Olivia, smiling.

"What did you learn?" she asked, feeling eager to know more of the mysterious background.

"Centuries ago, your farm was used as a small vineyard and a retreat by a very wealthy family. The Sabinos owned hundreds of acres in the wider area and farmed wine in a number of different regions. They mass-produced wine in the low-lying, fertile regions and in the high-lying and hillier areas, they grew more exclusive vines and this is where their top quality wines came from."

"That makes sense," Charlotte agreed.

"As well as being wine farmers, the family were wine merchants and wine sellers. In the late 1800s, the oldest brother, Valentino, decided he was going to acquire the finest collection of wine in Italy. They already had a number of superb historic bottles from Tuscany. He went on a buying spree throughout Europe, obtaining some of the most famous wines that had been produced in the area in the past two centuries. His plan was to display the wines at his mansion, which was in southern Tuscany, on an enormous wine estate in that area. However, unfortunately, during his shopping spree, it seemed that wine was not the only thing he got his hands on."

"What else?" Olivia breathed. She caught Danilo's eye and he grinned, clearly as fascinated by the tale as she was. Her mother was staring at Begni, enraptured by the history.

"Valentino Sabino embarked on an affair with the wife of one of the biggest rival winemakers in the region. Of course, it was not a secret for very long. When he learned of this, her husband vowed that he would destroy Valentino, whatever it took, and that he would smash his collection to smithereens and render it worthless."

"Oh, my goodness!" Charlotte exclaimed.

"After a murder attempt almost succeeded, Valentino and his two brothers loaded up their collection in the middle of the night and fled. After that, history is hazy about their whereabouts for a while. What is certain is that they were going to hide out in one of their more remote properties, while they made plans to conceal the wine collection. But until now, nobody knew where they had gone.

"And they dug the whole cellar on this farm?" Olivia asked, wondering what it had taken for three men under pressure of time to have constructed it.

"No, that is the interesting thing. The cellar appears to have already existed. From other, separate research I did, it seems that there was an ancient medieval outpost on the land. It comprised a simple fort and an underground building which had either been used for storage, or perhaps as a dungeon. More likely, though, it was a large cold storage room. The fort was long gone, collapsed over time, but the underground building remained, and Valentino must have known about it. All that was necessary was to fit it with shelves, stack the wine inside, and then conceal the cellar. From having glanced at the roof, I feel sure they realized its instability and might have tried to patch it over also. Then they hid the door."

"So the stones were there already," Olivia said, as light dawned.

Begni nodded. "Many of the stones in that field would have been left over from the original fort and only needed to be piled over the door. I imagine that oxen, or plow horses, would have assisted with this task."

“Ah!” Danilo nodded. “I was wondering how they had transported the stones so far. But if they were the remains of a medieval fortress it makes sense that they would have been close by already.”

“And they hid the map,” Olivia marveled. “They cut the most important piece out, and stashed it somewhere it could be found again.”

“Exactly,” Begni agreed. “Then the brothers fled onward, leaving Italy and dispersing to other countries. I imagine they planned to lay low for a while before returning, but the two younger brothers perished soon after in a shipwreck. Valentino himself returned a few years later, and continued making wine, using that mysterious label among others. Obviously without the rest of the map, nobody could have had an idea what, or where, it referred to. Perhaps he did it to taunt his rival. Or maybe it was his promise to himself that the wines would see the light of day again.”

“I wonder which it was,” Olivia hazarded, feeling enthralled.

“Perhaps he intended to dig the cellar contents up when it was safe to do so, but he never got the chance. One spring morning, he was found dead on the side of the road with a cracked skull. They never knew whether he had fallen from his horse, or whether his enemy had caught up with him at last and made good on his threats.”

Olivia shivered. She felt entranced and appalled by the story. What a checkered history her wine collection had.

“That’s amazing, Begni,” she said.

“It’s a fascinating account,” Mrs. Glass agreed.

At that moment, Olivia’s phone rang. Her heart leaped into her mouth as she saw it was the lawyer. What had happened?

“I’d better take this. It’s urgent,” she said. Rushing outside, she answered.

“Signora Glass?” Passero sounded poised and professional. Unlike herself. Standing out in the courtyard, staring at Erba perched on top of her Wendy house, Olivia could hear how tense and breathless her voice was.

“Is everything okay? How did it go?”

There was a short pause, during which time Olivia felt her entire life flash before her eyes. Then the lawyer spoke again, sounding satisfied.

“Everything went according to plan. The judge accepted my argument and ruled in your favor. The case is now closed. She also noted that you had provided clear and compelling proof of having purchased the land without knowing about the cellar, which has satisfied the court, and will prevent any further claims from being made."

Olivia felt her knees buckle in relief.

"That is wonderful. Thank you so much. I can't believe it's all over at last."

"You are the legal and rightful owner of the cellar and its contents. Congratulations, signora," the lawyer said.

Feeling as if she were walking on a cloud, Olivia returned to the kitchen.

"The case is closed and the judge has made the ruling. The cellar is mine. Thanks so much, everyone, and especially you, Mom," she said in a shaky voice.

"Oh, that's amazing!" Jumping up, Charlotte hugged her. "This is cause for serious celebration. Maybe we can get another booking at that fancy restaurant, even if it's just for dessert."

"It is nothing less than you deserve," Danilo said, clasping her hand in his.

"Sweetheart, when are you going to remove the contents?" her ever-practical mother asked. "We'll need to research how to do it, won't we? How does one go about that, do you know?"

Begni nodded, his face serious.

"If I might make a suggestion?" he asked.

Olivia thought he was going to recommend a specialist removal company, but Begni sounded stressed as he spoke again.

"You cannot waste another moment. I cannot emphasize to you how fragile that cellar's structure is. I have been having nightmares, thinking of the wine inside, and how every minute's delay brings terrible risk."

Every minute? Olivia's eyes widened. Begni was implying that the cellar might collapse at any time.

"You need to remove the wine now. At once! You do not have a specialist company but I am here and will help. As soon as it is out of danger, we can then package it up properly for the next step of its journey. Please, signora, it must be done this instant. Already, it will be very dangerous, and might even be too late."

CHAPTER THIRTY THREE

Olivia stared at Danilo. This was going to be a highly risky endeavor. Should they do it at all? Her stomach churned as she thought of the tough decision that needed to be made.

Danilo nodded, looking determined. "Let's get down there immediately," he said. "Despite the perils, we need to try and save the wine."

"I'm ready to help. What equipment will we need? Perhaps we can bring along these two plastic buckets under the sink, so that we can pack multiple bottles inside," Olivia's mother said.

"I still have one of the halogen lights in my car," Begni remembered, rushing outside and heading for his vehicle.

"There's some nylon rope in the barn. I'll go and get it," Charlotte said.

No time to lose! Olivia led the charge out of the kitchen door, closely followed by Danilo. With adrenaline surging inside her, she sprinted down the pathway and headed for the field.

Danilo was hot on her heels as she skidded to a stop by the door. He helped her lift it, and they stared down into the depths.

"Let's use my phone flashlight for now. Not a moment to waste," he said breathlessly. Snapping it on, he climbed down and shone the beam for Olivia to follow.

As soon as she reached floor level, she realized Begni was right. The place smelled of fresh dust, and there were several stones strewn over the ground that she didn't remember from before.

"I think we clear the most dangerous area first," Danilo said breathlessly, heading over to the side of the cellar where the rock falls had occurred.

"You should wear headgear," Charlotte hissed from the top, sounding concerned. "Olivia, we can't let him work without some form of head protection!"

"I agree, but what? I don't have a miner's helmet," Olivia called back anxiously, keeping her voice down in case loud sound waves dislodged any rocks.

"Can I bring a saucepan? It would offer some protection. We could line it with dishcloths and tie it under your chin with string. At least it would be something. Danilo, do you think you would be a medium size pan?"

Olivia snorted with mirth at the thought of Danilo working with one of her steel pans on his head. This situation might be fraught with tension, but Charlotte always had a knack for bringing out the humor.

"Stop laughing. I'm not joking," Charlotte said, sounding miffed.

"I have a cycling helmet in my car's trunk," Danilo then thankfully remembered.

"I'm on it. Health and safety officer en route," Charlotte called, her voice receding as she hurried back to the farmhouse.

Meanwhile, Begni and her mother were organizing the halogen light. In another few moments, brightness flooded the cellar as her mother climbed carefully down the stairs with it.

"Shall I position it here, sweetheart?" Mrs. Glass stared, assess the row of bottles which Danilo had already taken from the furthermost shelves. "Climbing up and down with those will take a lot of time and will tire us out. I think it will work better if we organize a human chain and pass them from person to person."

Olivia considered. Her mother was right. It would be far more efficient.

"Here's your cycling helmet, Danilo!" Charlotte's voice came breathlessly from above.

"Thank you," Danilo called.

Olivia felt vastly relieved that her boyfriend had at least some protection between him and anything that might fall from the unstable ceiling. While he fastened the helmet, Olivia put a plan of action into place.

"We have two buckets that will safely hold about six bottles each at a time. Danilo and I can work on the cellar floor. He can fill the bucket and I'll carry it to the stairs. Charlotte, you can then lift it halfway up, and Mom, stand near the top of the stairs and hand it to Begni. He can hand you back the empty bucket while he takes the full one and unpacks the wine a safe distance away."

"That sounds like a great system. Clearly the Glass family has a natural grasp of logistics," Charlotte said admiringly.

They quickly got into their places and Charlotte passed the first bucket down.

From then on, it was a nonstop whirl of activity. Danilo filled the bucket, carefully packing the ancient, dusty bottles so that they would travel securely. He then passed it to Olivia who carried it across the cellar floor and lifted it to Charlotte, perched on the stairway. Charlotte then lifted it further to Mrs. Glass, and she in turn handed the bottle to Begni for unpacking, receiving an empty one in return which she quickly passed down. And the process began again.

Six bottles at a time weren't always possible. Some of the bottles were larger, or oddly shaped, and had to travel up in smaller batches. Olivia spent a precious moment admiring the gorgeous and unique shaft and globe bottle, which Danilo placed carefully into the bucket on its own. Its wide base almost filled the bottom of the bucket. She watched anxiously as it was lifted, and felt a huge sense of relief once this unique treasure was safely out in the open.

Knowing the history of the collection made removing it even more memorable, she thought, thinking back to what Begni had told her and wondering if the brothers had worked just as hard and intensely to place the wine inside. Most likely the work would have been done under cover of darkness, or perhaps nobody had been living on this remote farm at the time. Had they hoped they would be able to retrieve it, she wondered. Or, being wealthy and successful already, had they intended to leave it down there as a treasure for future generations to find?

"I've cleared the shelves in the rock fall area," Danilo announced breathlessly as Olivia hurried toward him with the empty bucket.

Just as well. At that moment, with a loud, thunderous rolling, three more large stones crashed down onto the floor. One landed so hard it actually knocked a wooden shelf off its hinges.

Grabbing Danilo's arm, Olivia leaped back.

"You okay there?" Charlotte called anxiously. "I hope the helmet is helping!"

From further up, Mrs. Glass called, "Sweetheart, you should come up now. I don't know how I'll explain to Andrew that you were crushed in a rock fall while clearing out your own cellar. I don't think he'll ever see Italy in a positive light if that happens."

Danilo stared up at the ceiling.

"Every stone that falls is weakening the support. We do not have long," he said. "Begni was right. It seems moments away from collapsing."

"Are you sure we should stay down here? It feels extremely dangerous at this point," Olivia asked nervously. She thought she could see hairline cracks developing the whole way across the ceiling. She had a feeling that the last warning shot, or boulder, had been fired. Next, annihilation would follow.

Olivia had always been terrified of being buried alive! Now the prospect was suddenly far too real.

Danilo nodded somberly. "It is dangerous. You should go up. I can work here alone."

"Not a chance. I'm staying down here until you leave," Olivia argued, grabbing the filled bucket and hustling over to Charlotte.

She scanned the shelves. Their bucket-line system was working well and the cellar was more than half cleared. It would only take another ten, perhaps fifteen minutes before all the wine was safely out. But did they have that time?

Olivia thought she could feel the actual earth vibrating. She rushed back across the floor with the empty bucket. All they could do was what they were doing, as fast as possible.

"You carry on." Danilo thrust the filled bucket into Olivia's hands.

"Me? Why?"

Looking around, she saw that Begni was throwing coils of nylon rope down the stairs. As Danilo hurried to the corner of the cellar, Olivia realized that they were going to try and save the barrels.

She'd given up hope of getting those big, noble barrels to safety and had thought they would be too heavy. But if they were half-rolled, half-dragged, it might just be possible to save them, too.

Olivia rushed over and cleared the items off the top of them. Those antique wine openers and glasses and corking tools. They were going to see the light of day and be proudly admired! She was not going to let them be buried in the dark.

She headed to the stairs with her precious bucket load and watched it get hoisted to safety. Meanwhile, with a bang and a scrape, Danilo had the first barrel ready to be hauled up. Mrs. Glass scrambled out of the way while Charlotte and Begni grabbed the rope from the top. Olivia got behind the barrel with Danilo and shoved as hard as she could from the bottom, feeling triumphant as the barrel rolled, jerkily but steadily, up the steep stairs.

She sent two more buckets of wine up while Danilo prepared the next barrel for its journey to the top. Then it was time for another backbreaking wrestle with the heavy wooden barrel as it, too, was hauled to safety.

Olivia managed three more bucket loads of wine while Danilo prepped the final barrel. The shelves were looking emptier now. There were only a few more loads to go. And thank goodness this was the last barrel! She was sweating now, gasping for breath thanks to this impromptu weightlifting exercise.

"I'm so glad we got the barrels out," she shared to Danilo as they headed back to fill the final bucket loads, working in the area closest to the stairs. If you worked fast enough, Olivia realized, it helped you stop thinking about the fact you might be moments away from getting crushed. And at least they hadn't had time to worry about spiders. That was a small plus in this crazy race against a deadly outcome.

"Just these last few." Reaching high, Danilo cleared the last bottles from the topmost shelf. Olivia spied a few in a far corner and reached for them, feeling the glass cool and grainy with dust. Her hands were black and smeared with dirt. She felt so grateful that she had such a trusted and hardworking team helping her. This was a group effort and Olivia knew already that one of the most fun parts of selling off this treasure was going to be giving many of the bottles away to people she loved.

A shower of gravel spattered down, landing on the place where the barrels had been. Charlotte literally threw the empty bucket down the stairs to Olivia.

"It's going!" she entreated. "Get up here, quick!"

Olivia grabbed the last of the bottles from the almost-hidden space behind the shelves and packed them in. She handed the bucket to Charlotte and then climbed the stairs, boosted by Danilo who practically flung her up the steep wooden runners.

Behind her she heard a terrible roaring, groaning sound.

Charlotte squealed in terror as she clambered to safety. Her mother grabbed her shoulders and pulled her out. Olivia turned and grasped Danilo's hand, helping him scramble to safety as the entire roof caved in.

"Get away from the entrance!" Begni shouted, and they all fled in the other direction. Turning, Olivia saw an astounding sight. The earth itself was caving in. Cracks appeared in the grass and with a groan and a roar, it subsided.

A freight-train of dust shot out of the cellar door. Volleys of earth sprayed and plumed, and then the door vanished as the ground folded in on itself with a crashing noise.

"Oh, my goodness! I don't believe it. You got everything out with seconds to spare." Charlotte said, her voice shrill and high with shock. "That was officially the scariest experience I've had, ever. I can't believe both of you are out and alive."

"Angel! This is something I can never tell Andrew about and must remain our little secret. It would affect his blood pressure which at the moment is problematic. Luckily, my blood pressure is perfect; it was tested a few weeks ago. And I'm so pleased to have played a small role in saving your wine," her mother said, giving her a huge, warm hug. Olivia hugged her back. Then she hugged Danilo, and Charlotte, and finally Begni. She couldn't stop laughing from relief and amazement and the sheer joy of having escaped a seriously dangerous situation. If any of them had known what would happen, and how soon it would collapse, she didn't think they would have set foot inside.

But now they had, and all her wine was safe. Begni had carried it well away from the danger zone and stacked it neatly on the ground. Rows and rows of bottles lay in the stony soil, cushioned by tussocks of grass.

Wanting to immortalize the moment, Olivia took a photo. Then she photographed the new sinkhole on her property where the cellar had collapsed. Perhaps one day these images might be shown in a museum, a small sliver of history, a puzzle piece that helped fill in this incredible story that stretched back centuries.

For now though, she had to organize safe transport for the stash of wine that was now seeing sunlight for the first time in hundreds of years. And she had to take a very thorough shower. And she had to do all of that before eleven a.m., which was when she had to be at work.

Just because she'd managed to escape death and save a fortune of wine from being crushed, didn't mean she could be late for the job she loved.

EPILOGUE

"Well, it's a wrap," Marcello said to Olivia. She smiled in tired satisfaction as the last local visitors left La Leggenda's tasting room, chattering and laughing and each carrying a case of wine. "I think Collina Wine Week was a huge success. There were many positive comments about our wines over the past seven days. This has taught me how important it is to have support from our local friends, right here in our home village," Jean-Pierre said. "I can't wait for next year!"

He bustled into the storage room to replenish the bottles in the fridge.

"Talking of next year, we need to speak for a moment," Marcello said in a low voice.

Olivia followed him to the office. There hadn't been time, in the craziness of the past week which had grown busier and busier, to properly discuss the implications of everything that had happened.

"Firstly, I must thank you for the incredible gifts. Twenty rare bottles of wine from your underground cellar collection? One of which is a La Leggenda original red, from the very first harvest the winery ever produced? It is an astonishing gift, but far too generous for us to accept."

"No, no, I absolutely insist," Olivia said. "Please keep the La Leggenda bottle. It's part of your heritage after all. And sell the others. They're very good, and very old. They will fetch an excellent price at auction."

"I speak on behalf of all my family when I say how grateful we are," Marcello said.

After the wine had been assessed, and the bottles cleaned and given an approximate value, Olivia had realized she couldn't possibly keep close to three hundred bottles for herself. So she'd given some away.

Twenty to La Leggenda, twenty to Charlotte, twenty to Danilo, and twenty to Begni, as a thank you for their incredible help at a time when she'd needed it most. Without them, there wouldn't be a pristine, historic wine collection waiting to be auctioned, which was already causing major waves in wine-selling circles.

There had been a few other historic bottles which were early vintages from local wineries that were still in business, and Olivia had donated these to the wineries themselves. After all, they deserved to keep their own history!

She'd given Bardo five bottles that, if he sold them, would pay for all his legal fees and leave a generous nest-egg over, and had set ten bottles aside to sell on her mother's behalf in what Mrs. Glass had dubbed the Tuscany Vacation Fund. Given their likely selling price, Olivia was happy that her parents would be vacationing in luxury as often as they wanted.

The wine would be going on auction very soon, and was likely to fetch an astonishing price. The bottles were all listed and on view online, and there was already healthy competition and rivalry among renowned collectors, museums, and leading international wineries. Selected wines from the collection were going to be on view – under tight security – in Collina's town hall in the coming week, and Olivia had heard that every place in town was already booked solid for this event.

The ancient glass shaft and globe bottle would be the major draw card of the auction and leading London bookmakers were laying odds on what it would sell for. Apparently the million dollar mark was the two-to-one hot favorite price that they were predicting, and there were a few others from the same era that were also of great historic significance and value.

A million dollars for that mysterious artifact? Olivia simply couldn't believe it, and hoped that the bottle itself would bring as much joy to whoever bought it, as the proceeds would bring to her, in allowing her to achieve her dreams.

Marcello's next words, echoing her own thoughts, brought her back to her current reality.

"I am so happy that the dream of running your own winery will soon become reality. But for how much longer will we have you here?" Marcello asked. "I have been worrying about that, and hoping we might be able to keep you at least a few more months."

Olivia felt thrilled, and complimented, by Marcello's kind words.

"I'm not going to be able to do much for a couple of years, as all my vines still need to grow. I'll be able to harvest my wild vines in the fall, and hopefully make another batch of ice wine if there's a frost, but that's all I can do until the others mature. So, please can I stay for at least another year full time, and even longer, part time? I'll make sure

Jean-Pierre is fully trained. And then, if I do leave, will you let me fill in for him when he goes on vacation?" she asked anxiously, realizing how much the relationship with Marcello and La Leggenda meant to her.

"Of course." Now Marcello grinned in relief. "And you will not be able to keep Nadia from your winery for long. She already has so many ideas about collaboration wines, and joint events, that we can both benefit from."

Olivia simply couldn't believe the generosity and support she was receiving from La Leggenda. It made her feel as if she truly was part of the local community.

"Have a good evening," Marcello wished her, turning back to his work with a smile. "I believe it is your birthday tomorrow? You can expect cake and Metodo Classico sparkling wine for lunch."

"Thank you!" Olivia felt delighted that Marcello had remembered her birthday and was going to provide cake.

Heading out into the balmy spring evening, Olivia jogged up the pathway to the service road, pleased to see Erba was waiting for her.

"We have a big evening tonight, Erba," she told her goat. "It's my official birthday party, as my mother's flying back home tomorrow morning, and we're going out to eat pizza at the local restaurant."

Olivia stopped speaking. She should probably not have confided in her goat about that. Erba was likely to follow them to the nearby restaurant and start stealing from customers' salad bowls. She'd done it before and had to be escorted home in shame.

Erba was intelligent enough to guess where they'd be going. She was the cleverest goat Olivia knew!

Instead of giving away any more damaging clues, Olivia enjoyed the rest of the short, peaceful walk in silence, taking in the view she loved so much. Today, the scenery was calm and peaceful, with the hills glowing in the late afternoon light, and barely a breath of wind stirring the vividly green cedar trees.

To her surprise, as she reached the farmhouse gate, she met her mother, dressed in jeans and walking shoes, heading out.

"Hello, angel. I'm going to go up to the top of the hill and capture the sunset over the fields. Since it's my last night, I want to show Andrew how pretty it all is. I can't believe I'll be heading home tomorrow. What an adventure it's been."

"Enjoy the walk. We will leave for the restaurant in about an hour's time," Olivia told her.

“That’ll be perfect.”

Olivia was pleased to see as her mother set off, videoing as she strolled along, that she’d clearly gotten over any fear of having her belongings snatched just because she was in Italy.

As she got into the house, she almost collided with Charlotte, rushing out.

“I’m going to meet Artoro in the village to choose a gift for you. We’re also going to look at an apartment for me that’s just come available. Olivia, you won’t believe it. It’s one of the ones by the castle!”

“Seriously?” Olivia gasped, joy and envy warring inside her. “That’s amazing!”

“It’s a two-story two-bedroom apartment, with a tiny walled garden so I can grow herbs and there’ll be a place for Bagheera to prowl. There’s the most magnificent view of the castle from all the back windows, they say. I can’t wait to see it! Just imagine if I’m here for good in a few weeks, along with my cat? Isn’t it the luckiest thing that work got so busy?”

“It’s the most brilliant thing ever,” Olivia said, feeling stoked that her bestie would be able to live in the apartment she herself had always longed for. If she did, there would be many wonderful dinners together there.

“I’ve decided to keep just one of the wine bottles you gave me, in memory of all of this. All the others I’ll send to auction. I’ll be able to buy a home here if I want, never mind rent one. This is so exciting!”

Charlotte rushed off and Olivia headed into the farmhouse, ready to tackle her list of chores. Feed Pirate, feed Erba, make sure that all her mother’s laundry was upstairs and ready to be packed – although given her mother’s efficiency, there didn’t seem much chance of that not being done already.

At that moment, the front door rattled and Danilo walked in. He was dressed for the evening in the smart, ice-blue dress shirt she’d given him. Olivia’s heart leaped when she saw her handsome beau. Abandoning her chores, she rushed to welcome him.

“Salve, gorgeous,” he greeted her, with a loving hug and kiss.

“It’s so good to see you! What fun tonight will be. It’s feeling like a real party. I’m so glad Francesca and her new boyfriend can join us.”

“It will be a wonderful occasion. By the way, I have decided what to do with the amazing wine you gave me. There is one bottle, the most local one, that I will keep in memory of this astonishing time. The others I will send to auction."

"That's exactly what Charlotte's doing," Olivia said, pleased that they'd decided on identical plans of action for their wine.

"I brought you a gift," Danilo said, his voice serious.

Olivia took the packet he gave her, from a leading jeweler on Ponte Vecchio. Inside was a small, royal blue, velvet box.

She glanced at Danilo, wondering what this meant, but he simply smiled mysteriously back. She felt as if her heart was in her mouth as she opened it. Then she gasped in amazement at the stunning ring inside – braided gold, set with gleaming sapphires, just like the bracelet he'd given her.

"Danilo! This is – this is…" She stared at him again, at a loss for words. What did this beautiful ring mean? Was she missing something here? It was too soon for a proposal! Wasn't it?

He grinned, enjoying her surprise.

"It's a promise ring. It is my promise to you that I love you, and I want to be with you, and I hope we will go forward into the future together."

"Oh, Danilo! It's absolutely beautiful and thank you. I feel the same!" Olivia felt tears prickle her eyes. What an amazing and timely gift, symbolizing the way her boyfriend felt. This was better than an engagement ring because it was the first step of an exciting journey. It was a commitment to sharing more, and growing together.

What a gift the past week had been, Olivia thought in bemusement. It had turned out more incredibly than she'd ever expected. Not just the dreams of her winery made real at last, her bestie moving to Italy, and a new harmonious friendship achieved with her mother, but the deepening relationship with her beloved Danilo, now confirmed by this exquisite piece of jewelry.

Gazing at the sparkling sapphires, Olivia knew one thing for sure.

No matter what challenges the future might hold, it truly was filled with promise.

A NEW SERIES!

NOW AVAILABLE

A VILLA IN SICILY: OLIVE OIL AND MURDER
(A Cats and Dogs Cozy Mystery—Book 1)

"Very entertaining. Highly recommended for the permanent library of any reader who appreciates a well-written mystery with twists and an intelligent plot. You will not be disappointed. Excellent way to spend a cold weekend!"
--Books and Movie Reviews (regarding *Murder in the Manor*)

A VILLA IN SICILY: OLIVE OIL AND MURDER is the debut novel in a charming new cozy mystery series by bestselling author Fiona Grace, author of *Murder in the Manor*, a #1 Bestseller with over 100 five-star reviews (and a free download)!

Audrey Smart, 34, is a brilliant vet—yet fed up by her demanding clients who think they know more than her and who don't care about their animals. Burnt-out with the endless hours, she wonders if the time has come for a new direction. And when her 15th year high school reunion (and her hopes for re-sparking on old flame) end in disaster, Audrey knows the time has come to make a change.

When Audrey sees an ad for a $1 home in Sicily, it captivates her. The only catch is that the house requires renovation, something she knows little about. She wonders if it could be real—and if she may really be crazy enough to go for it.

Can Audrey create a life and career—and the home of her dreams—in a beautiful Sicilian village? And perhaps even find love while she's there?

Or will an unexpected death—one that only she can solve—put an end to all of her plans?

Are some dreams too good to be true?

A laugh-out-loud cozy packed with mystery, intrigue, renovation, animals, food, wine—and of course, love—A VILLA IN SICILY will capture your heart and keep you glued to the very last page.

Books #2 and #3 in the series—FIGS AND A CADAVER and VINO AND DEATH—are now also available!

Fiona Grace

Fiona Grace is author of the LACEY DOYLE COZY MYSTERY series, comprising nine books; of the TUSCAN VINEYARD COZY MYSTERY series, comprising seven books; of the DUBIOUS WITCH COZY MYSTERY series, comprising three books; of the BEACHFRONT BAKERY COZY MYSTERY series, comprising six books; and of the CATS AND DOGS COZY MYSTERY series, comprising nine books.

Fiona would love to hear from you, so please visit www.fionagraceauthor.com to receive free ebooks, hear the latest news, and stay in touch.

BOOKS BY FIONA GRACE

LACEY DOYLE COZY MYSTERY

MURDER IN THE MANOR (Book#1)
DEATH AND A DOG (Book #2)
CRIME IN THE CAFE (Book #3)
VEXED ON A VISIT (Book #4)
KILLED WITH A KISS (Book #5)
PERISHED BY A PAINTING (Book #6)
SILENCED BY A SPELL (Book #7)
FRAMED BY A FORGERY (Book #8)
CATASTROPHE IN A CLOISTER (Book #9)

TUSCAN VINEYARD COZY MYSTERY

AGED FOR MURDER (Book #1)
AGED FOR DEATH (Book #2)
AGED FOR MAYHEM (Book #3)
AGED FOR SEDUCTION (Book #4)
AGED FOR VENGEANCE (Book #5)
AGED FOR ACRIMONY (Book #6)
AGED FOR MALICE (Book #7)

DUBIOUS WITCH COZY MYSTERY

SKEPTIC IN SALEM: AN EPISODE OF MURDER (Book #1)
SKEPTIC IN SALEM: AN EPISODE OF CRIME (Book #2)
SKEPTIC IN SALEM: AN EPISODE OF DEATH (Book #3)

BEACHFRONT BAKERY COZY MYSTERY

BEACHFRONT BAKERY: A KILLER CUPCAKE (Book #1)
BEACHFRONT BAKERY: A MURDEROUS MACARON (Book #2)
BEACHFRONT BAKERY: A PERILOUS CAKE POP (Book #3)
BEACHFRONT BAKERY: A DEADLY DANISH (Book #4)
BEACHFRONT BAKERY: A TREACHEROUS TART (Book #5)
BEACHFRONT BAKERY: A CALAMITOUS COOKIE (Book #6)

CATS AND DOGS COZY MYSTERY

A VILLA IN SICILY: OLIVE OIL AND MURDER (Book #1)
A VILLA IN SICILY: FIGS AND A CADAVER (Book #2)
A VILLA IN SICILY: VINO AND DEATH (Book #3)

A VILLA IN SICILY: CAPERS AND CALAMITY (Book #4)
A VILLA IN SICILY: ORANGE GROVES AND VENGEANCE (Book #5)
A VILLA IN SICILY: CANNOLI AND A CASUALTY (Book #6)
A VILLA IN SICILY: SPAGHETTI AND SUSPICION (Book #7)
A VILLA IN SICILY: LEMONS AND A PREDICAMENT (Book #8)
A VILLA IN SICILY: GELATO AND A VENDETTA (Book #9)

www.ingramcontent.com/pod-product-compliance
Lightning Source LLC
Chambersburg PA
CBHW030616310726
48979CB00003B/745
* 9 7 8 1 0 9 4 3 9 1 0 6 9 *